THE CHAUTAUQUA GIRLS AT HOME

THE CHAUTAUQUA
GIRLS AT HOME

ISABELLA ALDEN

LIVING BOOKS®
Tyndale House Publishers, Inc.
Wheaton, Illinois

Visit Tyndale's exciting Web site at www.tyndale.com

Tyndale House Publishers edition 1997

Living Books is a registered trademark of Tyndale House
Publishers, Inc.

ISBN 0-8423-3190-5

Printed in the United States of America

01 00 99 98 97
5   4   3   2   1

CONTENTS

WELCOME

◄━❉━►

by Grace Livingston Hill

As long ago as I can remember, there was always a radiant being who was next to my mother and father in my heart and who seemed to me to be a combination of fairy godmother, heroine, and saint. I thought her the most beautiful, wise, and wonderful person in my world, outside of my home. I treasured her smiles, copied her ways, and listened breathlessly to all she had to say, sitting at her feet worshipfully whenever she was near; ready to run any errand for her, no matter how far.

I measured other people by her principles and opinions, and always felt that her word was final. I am afraid I even corrected my beloved parents sometimes when they failed to state some principle or opinion as she had done.

When she came on a visit, the house seemed glorified because of her presence; while she remained, life was one long holiday; when she went away, it seemed as if a blight had fallen.

She was young, gracious, and very good to be with.

This radiant creature was known to me by the name of Auntie Belle, though my mother and my grandmother called her Isabella! Just like that! Even sharply sometimes when they disagreed with her: *"Isabella!"* I wondered that they dared.

Later, I found that others had still other names for her. To the congregation of which her husband was pastor she was known as Mrs. Alden. And there was another world in which she moved and had her being when she went away from us from time to time; or when at certain hours in the day she shut herself within a room that was sacredly known as a Study, and wrote for a long time, while we all tried to keep still; and in this other world of hers she was known as Pansy. It was a world that loved and honored her, a world that gave her homage and wrote her letters by the hundreds each week.

As I grew older and learned to read, I devoured her stories chapter by chapter, even sometimes page by page as they came hot from the typewriter; occasionally stealing in for an instant when she left the study to snatch the latest page and see what had happened next; or to accost her as her morning's work was done with: "Oh, have you finished another chapter?"

Often the whole family would crowd around when the word went around that the last chapter of something was finished and going to be read aloud. And now we listened, breathless, as she read and made her characters live before us.

The letters that poured in at every mail were overwhelming. Asking for her autograph and her photograph; begging for pieces of her best dress to sew into patchwork; begging for advice on how to become a great author; begging for advice on every possible subject. And she answered them all!

Sometimes I look back upon her long and busy life, and marvel at what she has accomplished. She was a marvelous housekeeper, knowing every dainty detail of her home to perfection. And a marvelous pastor's wife! The real old-fashioned kind, who made calls with her husband, knew every member intimately, cared for the sick, gathered the young people into her home, and loved them all as if they had been her brothers and sisters. She was beloved, almost adored, by all the members. And she was a tender, vigilant, wonderful mother, such a mother as few are privileged to have, giving without stint of her time, her strength, her love, and her companionship. She was a speaker and teacher, too.

All these things she did, and *yet wrote books!* Stories out of real life that struck home and showed us to ourselves as God saw us; and sent us to our knees to talk with him.

And so, in her name I greet you all, and commend this story to you.

Grace Livingston Hill

(This is a condensed version of the foreword Mrs. Hill wrote for her aunt's final book, *An Interrupted Night*.)

1

◆━◆◆◆━◆

TREADING ON NEW GROUND

THAT last Sabbath of August was a lovely day; it was the first Sabbath that our girls had spent at home since the revelation of Chautauqua. It seemed lovely to them. "The world looks as though it was made over new in the night," Eurie had said as she threw open her blinds and drew in whiffs of the sweet, soft air. And the church, whither these girls had so often betaken themselves on summer mornings just like this one— how *could* two or three weeks have changed it? They could not feel that it was the same building.

Hitherto it had been to them simply the First Church; grander, by several degrees, than any other church in the city, having the finest choir, the finest organ, and the most elegant carpets, and making the grandest floral display of all the temples, as became the First Church, of course; but today, this glowing, glorious August day, it was something infinitely above and beyond all this; it was the visible temple of the invisible God, *their* Savior, and they were going up to worship—aye, really and truly to *worship*. They, in their different ways, according to their very different natures, felt this and were thrilled with it as their feet trod the aisles. People can feel a great many things and not show them to the casual observer. Sitting in their respective pews, they looked in no sense different from the way they had looked on a hundred different Sabbaths before this.

Ruth Erskine, in the corner of her father's pew, attired, as she had often been before, in the most delicate and exquisite of summer silks with exactly the right shade of necktie, gloves, and sash, to set off the beauty of the dress with the soft and delicate laces about her white throat, for which she was especially noted, looked not one whit different from the lady who sat there three weeks before. You wouldn't have known that her heart was singing for joy.

Flossy Shipley, aglow with elegance, as she always was, looked the same airy butterfly that had flitted in and out of that church on many a summer day before; and Marion, in her corner of the gallery, was simply the grave, somewhat weary-looking schoolteacher at one of the wards—"a girl with infidel tendencies," that is all the great congregation knew about her—in fact, comparatively few of them knew even that.

Eurie Mitchell was the doctor's eldest daughter, and had in no sense improved as to her toilet—"a thing which could hardly be expected, since she had thrown away so much money on that wild scheme of living in the woods"; that was what some of the congregation thought about her.

Dr. Dennis saw all these girls and looked gloomy over them; he was in the mood to need sympathetic hearers, to long to be in accord with his audience and feel that they could sympathize with him in his reach after a higher type of religion. What could these four girls know about a higher type, when they had no religion at all and had been spending two lawless weeks in looking at the subject, till their hearts were either attuned to ridicule or disgusted, according to their several temperaments? That was what the faces of our four girls said to him. Yet how they listened to his sermon.

"I shall be satisfied when I awake with thy likeness." These were the words on which he spoke; and the burden of his thought was that satisfaction was not to be sought for here; nothing less than the absolute *likeness* should give absolute satisfaction; and this likeness was to be forever eagerly, earnestly, constantly sought for, striven after, until someday would come that blessed awakening, and the picture would be found to be complete!

Was it the best sermon that had ever been preached? Was it the *only* spiritual sermon that the First Church people had ever heard, or was it that four girls had been to Chautauqua, and there learned how to listen? Their cheeks glowed, and their eyes dilated over the wonderful thoughts that the subject presented, the endless possibility for climbing!

Marion Wilbur had been counted ambitious; she had longed for a chance to reach high; here was her chance; she felt it and gloried in it; she meant to try. Every nerve quivered with the determination and the satisfaction of realizing that she belonged to the great royal family. No more obscurity for her. She was a child of the King, and the kingdom was in view. A crown, aglow with jewels—nothing less must satisfy her now. The sermon over, the hymn sung, and amid the pealing of the organ, as it played the worshipers down the aisles, our four girls met.

They knew each other's determination. The next thing to do was to go to Sunday school. But I suppose you have no idea how strange they felt; how much it seemed to them as if they were children who had come to a party uninvited, and as if they must at this last minute hide their heads and run home. The very effort to go up to the Sunday school room seemed too much a cross to undertake.

There were so many to stare and look their amazement; there was no one to go with; nobody to think of such a thing as asking them to go. It would have been so much less awkward if they could have followed in the lead of one who had said, "Won't you come up and see our Sunday school?"

The superintendent passed them as they stood irresolute; he bowed courteously, and no more thought of asking them to join him than though they had been birds of brilliant plumage flying by. Dr. Dennis passed them; *he* said good morning, not gladly, not even graciously; he dreaded those girls and their undoubted influence. They had not the least idea how much mischief they had done him in the way of frittering away his influence heretofore. How should they know that he dreaded them? On the other hand, how was he to know that they absolutely longed for him to take them by the hand and say "Come"? They looked at him curiously as he passed, and Eurie said:

"Doesn't it make your heart beat to think of going to him in his study and having a private talk?"

"Dear me!" said Flossy, "I never shall think of such a thing. I couldn't do it any more than I could fly."

"There are harder things than that to do, I suspect; and it will come to a visit to his study if we are to unite with the church; don't you know that is what he always asks of those?"

And then these girls looked absolutely blank, for to two of them the thought of that duty had never occurred before; they did not understand it well enough to know that it was a privilege.

"Well," said Eurie, rallying first, of course, "are we to stand here gazing around us all day, because nobody knows enough to invite us to go upstairs? It is clear that we are not to be invited. They are all come—all the Sabbath-school people; and, hark! why, they are singing."

"Dear me!" said Flossy; "then it is commenced; I hate to go in when it is commenced. How very unfortunate this is!"

"Serves us right," said Marion. "We ought to be in a condition to invite others, instead of waiting here to be invited. I'll tell you what, girls, if we ever get to feel that we *do* belong, let's constitute ourselves a committee to see after timid strangers, like ourselves, and give them a *chance in,* at least."

"Well," said Ruth, speaking for the first time, "shall we go home and wait till next Sunday, and take a fair start. As Flossy says, it isn't pleasant to go in after the exercises have fairly opened?" As she said this, for the first time in her life Miss Ruth Erskine began to have a dim idea that possibly she might be a coward; this certainly sounded a little like it.

Each waited to get a bit of advice from the other. Both Marion and Eurie, it must be confessed, bold spirits that they were, so dreaded this ordeal, that each hoped the other would advise retreat as the wisest thing to be done next. It was Flossy who spoke:

"I am going up now; it won't be any easier next Sunday, and I want to begin."

"There!" said Eurie, "that is just what I needed to shame me into common sense. What a company of idiots we are! Marion, what would you think of a day scholar who would stand shivering outside your doors for this length of time? Now come on, all of you"; and she led the way upstairs.

How very awkward it was! It was during the opening prayer that they arrived, and they had to stand by the door and be peeped at by irreverent children; they had to invite themselves to a vacant seat near the door. The superintendent came that way presently and said:

"Good morning, young ladies; so you have come in to visit our school? Glad to see you; it is a pleasant place, I think you will find."

"That is extremely doubtful," Eurie said in undertones as he passed on. How the children did stare!

"They are certainly unused to visitors," Ruth said, growing uncomfortable under such prolonged gazing. "What is the use of all this, girls? We might better be at home."

"If we had grown up here," Eurie said bravely, "we should probably have our place by this time. It all comes of our graceful lives. But I must say they make it very easy for people to stay away. Why on earth don't they invite us to go into Bible classes? What right have they to take it for granted that we came out of pure curiosity?"

The business of the hour went on, and our girls were still left unmolested. As the newness wore somewhat away, the situation began to grow funny. They could see that the pastor and the superintendent were engaged in anxious conversation, to judge by the gravity of their faces; and as their eyes occasionally roved in that direction, it was natural to suppose they were discussing the unexpected visitors.

Could they have heard the anxious talk it would have been a solemn comment on their reputations.

"That Morris class is vacant again today," the superintendent was saying; "I don't know what we are to do with that class; no one is willing to undertake it."

The pastor looked toward his own large class waiting for him and said with a weary sigh:

"I believe I shall have to give up my class to someone and take that. I don't want to; it is a class which requires more nervous energy than I have at command at this hour of the day. But what is to be done with them today?"

"Would it do to ask one of the young ladies on the visitors' seat?"

And then the eyes of the two men turned toward the girls.

"They are afraid of us," whispered Eurie, her propensity to see the ludicrous side of things in no whit destroyed by her conversion. "Look at their troubled faces; they think that we are harbingers of mischief. Oh, me! What a reputation to have! But I declare it is funny." Whereupon she laughed softly, but unmistakably.

It was at this moment that Dr. Dennis's eyes rested on her.

"Oh, they are only here for material to make sport of," he said gloomily; "Miss Erskine might keep the boys quiet for a while if she chose to do so, I suppose."

"Or Miss Wilbur. Some of the boys in that class are in school, in her ward; they say she has grand order."

Dr. Dennis's face grew stern.

"No," he said, "don't ask *her;* at least we will not put them in a way to learn error, if we can teach them nothing good. Miss Wilbur is an infidel. I don't know what is to be done with that class, as you say. Poor Morris, I am afraid, will never be able to take it again; and he was utterly discouraged with them, anyway.

They get no good here that I can see; and they certainly do infinite mischief to the rest of the school."

"But at the same time, I suppose we cannot send them away?"

"Oh, certainly not. Well, suppose you see if Miss Erskine will sit there and try to awe them by her dignity for a while. And this week we must see what can be done; she won't try it, though, I presume."

It ended in the superintendent coming toward them at last. He didn't like to be too personal in his request, so he took the general way of putting a question, resting in the belief that each would refuse, and that then he could press the task on Miss Erskine.

"We are short of teachers today; would one of you be willing to sit with that class at your right and try to interest them a little? They are a sad set; very little can be done with them, but we have to try."

I shall have to confess that both Ruth and Marion were appalled. The one shrank as much as the other. If it had been a class in mathematics or philosophy, Marion would have been confident of her powers; but she felt so very ignorant of the Bible. She had come in, hoping and expecting a chance to slip into a grand Bible class, where she might learn some of the inner truths of that glorious lesson that she had been trying to study. But to teach it! This seemed impossible. As for Ruth, no thought of such an experience had as yet come to her. They, therefore, maintained a dismayed silence. Eurie was frank.

"I can't teach," she said; "I don't understand it myself. I shouldn't have the least idea what to say to anyone about the Bible lesson." And then they all turned and stared in a maze of surprise and perplexity at little fair-headed Flossy.

"I would like to try," she said simply; "I have thought about the lesson all the week; I am not sure that I can *teach* anything, but I should like to talk the story over with them if they will let me."

There was nothing for it but to lead this exquisite bit of flesh and blood, in her dainty summer toilet, before that rough and rollicking class of boys, old enough, some of them, to be called young men, but without an idea as to the manner of conduct that should honor that name. It would be hard to tell which was the most amazed and embarrassed, the superintendent or the girls whom Flossy left looking after her. They were quite sobered now; they did not want Flossy to come to grief. A tender feeling that was new and sweet had sprung up in the heart of each of them toward her.

"That innocent little kitten knows no more what she has undertaken than if she were a dove," said Marion, dismay and discomfort struggling in her face. "Why, she might as well be Daniel in the den of lions."

"Well," said Eurie, speaking gravely, "he came out all right, you know." Then she hailed the passing superintendent:

"Mr. Stuart, isn't there a Bible class that we can go in? We didn't come to look on. We want to study the lesson."

"Oh, why, yes, certainly," Mr. Stuart said, stammering and looking unutterable astonishment. "Where would they like to go? There were two vacant seats in Mr. Pembrook's class, and one in Judge Elmore's."

Ruth instantly chose Judge Elmore's, and left Marion and Eurie to make their way to the vacant places in Mr. Pembrook's class.

The young ladies of the class moved along to make

room for the newcomers, and the teacher carefully told them what chapter and verse were being studied. They found their places, and Mr. Pembrook searched laboriously for his. He had lost the spot on his lesson leaf where he had read the last question, and he was all at sea.

"Let me see," he said, "where *were* we?"

None of them seemed to know; at least they gave him no information. One of them tried to button a glove that was too small for her; one yawned behind her Bible, and the most utter indifference in regard to the lesson or the school seemed to prevail.

"Oh," said Mr. Pembrook, "here is where we were. I was just reading the thirtieth verse: 'As he spake these words, many believed on him.' Who spake them?"

"Jesus," one answered, speaking the word with a yawn.

"What did Jesus say next?"

The next young lady thus appealed to hurriedly looked up the place in her Bible and read:

"'Then said Jesus to those Jews which believed on him, If ye continue in my word, then are ye my disciples indeed.'"

"Well," said Mr. Pembrook, after a thoughtful pause, "there doesn't seem to be anything to say on that verse; it is all there. Will *you* read the next verse?"

Now the "you" whom he timidly addressed was our Marion. She doesn't understand even now why her heart should have throbbed so strangely; and her voice trembled as she read aloud the simple words.

"'And ye shall know the truth, and the truth shall make you free.'"

"Free from what?" she asked abruptly.

The class stared. Clearly the art of asking questions was an unknown accomplishment in that class. Mr.

Pembrook looked at her through his glasses; then he pushed his glasses up on his forehead. Finally he took them off and rubbed them carefully with the skirt of his coat before he essayed to answer.

"Why, my dear young lady, I suppose it means free from sin. The Lord Jesus Christ was speaking to his people, you know, to Christian people."

"Are Christian people free from sin?"

There was no note of cavil in Marion's voice. Her eyes were earnest and serious; and she waited, as one waits in honest perplexity to have a puzzle solved. But she was known as one who held dangerous, even infidel notions, and Mr. Pembrook, bewildered as to how to answer her, seemed to feel that probably a rebuke was what she needed.

"It is not for us to find fault with the words of the Lord Jesus Christ, my dear young lady. He spoke them, and they must mean what they say. We are to accept them in all sincerity and humility, remembering that what we know not now we shall know hereafter. That is the *Christian* way to do."

And then he cleared his throat and asked the next young lady to read the next verse.

Two bright spots glowed on Marion's cheeks. She bent her head low over her Bible, and it was with difficulty that she kept a rush of tears from filling her eyes. Had she seemed to cavil at the words of her Lord when she simply longed with all her soul to understand? *Did* the promise mean, You shall be free from sin? Had she a right to look forward to and hope for the time when sin should have no more dominion? Then that other sentence: "*Continue* in my word." Just what did it mean? Could one who was searching it eagerly and prayerfully, and trying to abide by its directions, be said to be continuing in it?

There were a dozen questions that she longed to ask. She had sought the Sabbath school this morning in search of help. She felt blind and lame, unable to take a step in any direction lest in her ignorance she should err, as already she had. Something in her way of speaking of these things must be radically wrong. She had misled this good man. It was no use to ask *him* questions.

As the lesson progressed there appeared other reasons why she need not question him. Clearly the good man knew nothing about his lesson save the questions contained on the bit of paper before him. It was entirely evident that he had not looked at the verses, nor thought of them until he came before his class.

It was equally plain that his scholars were entirely accustomed to this state of things, and were careful to follow his example. He could read a question at them from his lesson paper, and they could read an answer back to him from their Bibles, and this was all that either party expected of the other. Why these young ladies continued to come Sabbath after Sabbath and go over this weary routine of question and answer was a mystery to Marion.

She came away from the school in a most uncomfortable frame of mind. That to which she had looked forward all the week had proved a disappointment and a failure. She was almost inclined to say that she would have no more to do with Sunday schools; that they really were the humbug that she had always supposed them.

"Imagine my going to a philosophy class, knowing no more about the lesson than that old man did today!" she said to Eurie, as they walked down to the corner of Elm Street together.

"I know," said Eurie, speaking with unusual

thoughtfulness; "but suppose you *were* dull in the class, if it were known after all that you could make the most brilliant philosophical experiments you would probably be listened to with respect."

"What do you mean?" asked Marion, bewildered.

"Why, I mean that Deacon Pembrook can perform the experiments successfully. In other words, to come down to your comprehension, he succeeds in living so pure and careful a Christian life that he has the respect and confidence of everybody. What if he can't preach? He can practice. However, I am willing to admit that the dear old man would be more edifying if he would study his lesson a little. Wasn't it funny to think of calling that *teaching?*" And then this volatile young lady laughed. But her moralizing had done Marion good.

She said good morning more cheerily and went on her way thinking over the many things that she had heard in honor of Deacon Pembrook; so that by the time she had reached her boardinghouse, although his teaching would certainly make a very poor show, yet his sweet Christian life had come up to plead for him, and Marion was forced to feel that the truth had "made him free."

"But it is a real pity not to study his lesson," she said as she went about her gloomy-looking room. "Those girls didn't get a single idea to help them in any way. Some of them need ideas badly enough. Two or three of them are members of the church, I am sure. That Allie March is, but she has no ideas on *any* subject; you can see that in the grammar class."

And then Marion remembered that Allie March was in *her* grammar class; and Allie was a professed Christian. Could *she* help her? It was not pride in Marion, but she had to smile at the thought of herself being helped by so very third-rate a brain as that which Allie March possessed. And then she paused with her hand on the clothespress door, and her face glowed at the new and surprising thought that just then came to her.

"Would it not be possible for her, Marion Wilbur, to help Allie March, even in her Christian life!"

All that afternoon, though, she went about or sat down in her room with a sense of loneliness. No one to speak to who could understand and would believe in her, even in the Sunday school they were afraid of her. How could she help or be helped while this state of things lasted?

It was in the early twilight that, as she sat with her hat and sack on, waiting for Eurie, who had engaged to call for her to go to church, she strayed across a verse or two in her new possession, the Bible, that touched the point. It was where Saul "essayed to join himself to the disciples: but they were all afraid of him, and believed not that he was a disciple." Her experience precisely! They were afraid of her influence; afraid of her tongue; afraid of her example; and, indeed, what reason had they to feel otherwise? But she read on, that blessed verse wherein it says: "But Barnabas took him, and brought him to the apostles, and declared unto them how he had seen the Lord in the way, and that he had spoken to him." She was reading this for the second time when Eurie came.

"See here, Eurie, read this," she said as she passed her the Bible and made her final preparations for church. "Isn't that our experience? I mean I think it *is* to be ours. Judging from today as a foretaste, they will be afraid of us and believe not that we are disciples."

Eurie laughed, a quick little laugh that had an undertone of feeling in it, as she said:

"Well, then, I hope we shall find a Barnabas to vouch for us before long."

And Marion knew that she, too, felt the loneliness and the sense of belonging to no one. "We must help each other very much, we girls." This she said to herself as they went down the steps together.

2

Flossy "Begins"

FLOSSY Shipley's first day at Sabbath school was different. She went over to the class of boys, who were almost young men, with trepidation indeed, and yet with an assured sort of feeling that they would be quiet. Just how she was going to accomplish this she was not certain. She had studied the words of the lesson most carefully and prayerfully; indeed, they had been more in her mind all the week than had anything else. At the same time, she by no means understood how to teach those words and thoughts to the style of young men who were now before her.

Still, there was that in Flossy which always held the attention of the young men; she knew this to be the case, and, without understanding what her peculiar power was, she felt that she had it and believed that she could call it into service for this new work. They stared at her a little as she took her seat, then they nudged each other and giggled and looked down at their dusty boots, guiltless of any attempt at being black, and shuffled them in a way to make a disagreeable noise.

They knew Flossy—that is, they knew what street she lived on, and how the outside of her father's house looked, and what her standing in society was; they knew nothing of her in the capacity of a Sunday school teacher; and, truth to tell, they did not believe she *could* teach. She was a doll set up before them for them to admire and pretend to listen to. They did not intend to do it; she had nothing in common with them; they had a right to make her uncomfortable if they could, and they were sure that they could. This was the mood in which she found them.

"Good morning," she said brightly; and they glanced at each other, and shuffled their feet louder and some of them chuckled louder, while one of them said:

"It's rather late in the morning, isn't it? We got up quite a spell ago."

This passed for a joke, and they laughed aloud. At this point Flossy caught Dr. Dennis's distressed face turned that way. It was not reassuring; he evidently expected disastrous times in that corner. Flossy ignored the discourteous treatment of her "good morning" and opened her Bible.

"Do you know," she said with a soft little laugh, "that I haven't the least idea how to teach a Sunday school lesson? I never did such a thing in my life; so you mustn't expect wisdom from me. The very most I can do is to talk the matter over with you and ask you what you think about it."

Whereupon they looked at each other again and laughed; but this time it was a puzzled sort of laugh. This was a new experience. They had had teachers who knew extremely little about the lesson and proved it conclusively, but never once did they *own* it. Their plan rather had been to assume the wisdom of

Solomon, and in no particular to be found wanting in information. They did not know what answer to make to Flossy.

"Have you Bibles?" she asked them.

"No."

"Well, here are Lesson Leaves. These are pieces of the Bible, I suppose. Are they nice? I don't know anything about them. I have never been in Sunday school, you see; not since I was a little girl. What are these cards for, please?"

Now, they understood all about the management of the library cards, and the method of giving out books by their means, and Flossy was so evidently ignorant, and so puzzled by their attempts at explanation, and asked so many questions, and took so long to understand it that they really became very much interested in making it clear to her, and then in helping her carry out the program which they had explained; and every one of them had a queer sense of relationship to the school that they had not possessed before. They knew more than she did, and she was willing to own it.

"Now about this lesson," she said at last. "I really don't see how people teach such lessons."

"They don't," said one whom they called Rich Johnson. "They just pretend to, and they go around it, and through it, and ask baby questions, and pretend that they know a great deal; that's the kind of teaching that we are used to."

Flossy laughed.

"You won't get it today," she said, "for I certainly don't know a great deal, and I don't know how to pretend that I do. But I like to read about this talk that Christ had with the people; and I should have liked of all things to have been there and heard him. I would like to go now to the place where he was. Wouldn't you like to go to Jerusalem?"

What an awkward way they had of looking from one to the other and nudging each other. Rich Johnson seemed to be the speaker for the class. He spoke now in a gruff, unprepossessing voice:

"I'd enough sight rather go to California."

The others thought this a joke and laughed accordingly. Flossy caught at it.

"California," she said brightly. "Oh, I've been there. I don't wonder that you want to go. It is a grand country. I saw some of those great trees that we have heard about."

And forthwith she launched into an eager description of the mammoth tree; and as they leaned forward, and asked now and then an intelligent question, Flossy blessed the good fortune that had made her her father's chosen companion on his hasty trip to California the year before. What had all the trees in California to do with the Sabbath-school lesson? Nothing, of course; but Flossy saw with a little thrill of satisfaction that the boys were becoming interested in *her*.

"But for all that," she said, coming back suddenly, "I should like ever so much to go to Jerusalem. I felt so more and more, after I went to that meeting at Chautauqua and saw the city all laid out and a model of the very temple, you know, where Jesus was when he spoke these words."

They did not laugh this time; on the contrary, they looked interested. She could describe a tree, perhaps she had something else worth hearing.

"What's that?" said Rich. "That's something I never heard of."

And then Flossy laid her Bible in her lap, and began

to describe the living picture of the Holy Land, as she had seen and loved it at Chautauqua. Of course you know that she did *that* well. Was not her heart there? Had she not found a new love and life and hope while she walked those sunny paths that led to Bethany and to the Mount of Olives? Every one of the boys listened, and some of them questioned, and Rich said, when she paused:

"Well, now, that's an idea, I declare. I wouldn't mind seeing it myself."

And to each one of them came a glimmering feeling that there actually *was* such a city as Jerusalem, and such a person as Jesus Christ did really live and walk and talk here on the earth. Then Flossy took up her Bible again.

"But, of course, the next best thing to going to places and actually seeing people is to read about them and find out what the people said and did. I like these verses especially, because they mean us as well as those to whom they were spoken. Look at this verse. I have been all the week over it, and I don't see but I shall have to stay over it all my life. 'Then said Jesus, If ye *continue* in my word, then are ye my disciples indeed.' Just think how far that reaches! All through the words of Jesus. So many of them, so many things to do, and so many *not* to do; and then not only to begin to follow them, but to *continue;* day after day getting a little farther and knowing a little more. After all, it's very fascinating work, isn't it? If it *is* hard, like climbing a mountain, one gets nearer the top all the while; and when you do really reach the top, how splendid it is! Or, doing a hard piece of work, it's so nice to get nearer and nearer to the end of it and feel that you have done it."

One of the boys yawned. It was not so interesting

as the description of the miniature Jerusalem. One of them looked sarcastic. This was Rich.

"Do you suppose there ever was anybody like that?" he asked, and the most lofty incredulity was in his voice.

"Like what?"

"Why, that followed out that kind of talk. I know enough about the Bible to know they are mighty scarce. I'd go to Jerusalem on foot to see a real one. Where's the folks, I'd like to know, that live up to half of the things it says in the Bible? Why, they even say it *can't* be done, and that's why it seems all bosh to me. What was the use of putting it in there if it can't be done?"

Here was one who had evidently thought, and thought seriously, about these things. Is there a boy of seventeen in our country who has not? Flossy felt timid. How should she answer the sharp, sarcastic words? He had been studying inconsistencies and had grown bitter. The others looked on curiously; they had a certain kind of pride in Rich. He was their genius, who held all the teachers at bay with his ingenious tongue. But Flossy had been at a morning meeting in Chautauqua where there was talk on this very subject. It came back to her now.

"As for being *able* to do it," she said quickly, "I don't feel sure that we have anything to do with that until we have convinced ourselves that we have been just as good as we possibly could. Honestly, now, do you think you have been?"

"No," said Rich promptly; "of course not. And, what is more, I never pretended that I was."

"Well, I know *I* haven't been; I am perfectly certain that in a hundred ways I could have done better. Why, there is nothing that I could not have improved upon if I had tried. So, by our own confessions, what right have you and I to stumble over not being able to be perfect, so long as we have not begun to be as near it as we could?"

How was he to answer this?

"Oh, well," he said, "I haven't made any pretensions; I'm talking about those who have."

"That's exactly like myself; and, as nearly as I can see, we both belong to the class who knew our duty and had nothing to do with it. Now, I want to tell you that I have decided not to stand with that class any longer."

Flossy paused an instant, caught her breath, and a rich flush spread over her pretty face. This was her first actual "witnessing" outside of the narrow limits of her intimate three friends, who all sympathized.

"I gave myself to this Jesus when I was at Chautauqua," she said to him; "that I had stood one side and had nothing to do with his words all my life; just taken his favors in silence and indifference, but that for the future I was to belong to him. Now, of course, I don't know how many times I shall fail, nor how many things I shall fail in. The most I know is that I mean to 'continue.' After all, don't you see that the verse doesn't say if you are *perfect,* but simply 'If you continue.' Now, if I am trying to climb a hill, it makes a difference with my progress, to be sure, whether I stumble and fall back a few steps now and then. But for all that, I may continue to climb; and if I do, I shall be sure to reach the top. So now my resolution is to continue in his words all the rest of my life."

She did not ask Rich to do the same. She said not a word to him about himself. She said not a personal word to one of them, but every boy there felt himself asked to join her. More than that, not a boy of them but respected her. It is wonderful, after all, how rarely in this wicked world we meet with other than respect in answer to a frank avowal of our determination to be on the Lord's side. They were all quiet for an instant; and again Flossy caught a glimpse of Dr. Dennis's face. It looked full of perplexity and distrust. Was she telling them a fairy story or teaching them a new game of whist?

"Then there is such a grand promise in this lesson," Flossy went on. "I like it ever so much for that. 'And ye shall know the truth, and the truth shall make you free.'"

"Free from what?" asked Rich abruptly—the very question that Miss Marion Wilbur had asked in such anxiety. But Flossy was, in a measure, prepared for him. It chanced that she had asked Evan Roberts that self-same question.

"Why, free from the power and dominion of Satan; not belonging to him any more, and having a strength that is beyond and above anything earthly to lean upon, stronger than Satan's power can ever be."

Rich gave a scornful little laugh.

"He is an old fellow that I don't particularly believe in," he said loftily, as though that forever settled the question as to the existence of such a person. "I think a fellow is a silly coward who lays the blame of his wickedness off on Satan's shoulders; just as if Satan could make him do what he didn't choose to do! always supposing that there is such a creature."

Oh, wise and wily Flossy! She knew he was wrong. She knew he had contradicted his own logic, used but a few minutes before, but she did not attempt to prove it to him; for, in the first place, she felt instinctively that the most difficult thing in the world is to convince an ignorant person that he has been foolish and illogical in his argument. You may prove this to an intelligent mind that is accustomed to reason and to weigh the merits of questions, but it is a rare thing to find an uncultured brain that can follow you closely enough to be convinced of his own folly.

Flossy did not understand herself well enough to reason this out. It was simply a fine instinct that she had, perhaps it ought to be called "tact," that led her to be careful how she tried anything of this sort. Besides, there was another reason. She did not know how to set about doing it. It is one thing to see a sophistry, and another to take to pieces the filmy threads of which it is composed. She waived the whole subject and jumped to one on which there could be but one opinion.

"Well, then, suppose you were right, and everyone were free to be perfect if he would; that only reaches to the end of this life. We surely haven't been perfect— you and I, for instance—so our perfection cannot save us from the penalty of sin, and that is death. What a grand thing it would be to be free from that! You believe in death, don't you? And I suppose, like every other sensible person, you are afraid of death, unless you have found something that makes you free from its power."

Rich was still in a scornful mood.

"Should like to see anybody that is free from that!" he said sneeringly. "As near as I can make out, those persons who think they are good are just as likely to die as the rest of us."

"Ah, yes, but it isn't just that little minute of dying that you and I are afraid of; it is *afterward*. We are afraid of what will come next. You see, I know all about it, for I was awfully afraid; I had such a fear as I suppose you know nothing about. When it thundered, I shivered as if I had a chill, and it seemed to me as if every flash of lightning was going to kill me, and when I went on a journey I could enjoy nothing for the fear that there might be an accident and I might be killed. But I declare to you that I have found something that has taken the fear away. I do not mean that I would like to be killed, or that I am tired of living, or anything of the sort. I like to live a great deal better than I ever did before; I think the world is twice as nice, and everything a great deal pleasanter; but when I was coming home from Chautauqua I would waken in the night in the sleeping car, and I found to my surprise that, although I thought of the same thing— the possibility that there might be an accident that would cost me my life—yet I felt that horrible sense of fear and dread was utterly gone. I could feel that though death in itself might be sad and solemn, yet it was, after all, but the step that opened the door to joy. In short—" and here Flossy's face shone with a rare sweet smile—"I *know* that the truth, as it is in Jesus, has made me free."

Rich was utterly silent. What could he reply in the face of this simple, quiet "I *know*"? To say, "I don't believe it" would be the height of folly, and he realized it.

As for the rest, they had listened to this talk with various degrees of interest; the most of them amused that Rich should be drawn into any talk so serious, and he evidently so earnest.

Let me tell you a little about these young men. They were not from the very lowest depths of society; that is, they had homes and family ties, and they had enough to eat and to wear; in fact, they earned these latter, each for himself. There were two of them who had the advantage of the public schools and were fair sort of scholars. Rich Johnson was one of these and was therefore somewhat looked up to and respected by those even who would not have gone to school another day if they could.

But they were far enough out of the reach of Flossy Shipley; so far that she had never come in contact with one of them before in her life. She had no idea as to their names or their homes or their lives. She had no sort of idea of the temptations by which they were surrounded, nor what they needed. Perhaps this very fact removed all touch of patronage from her tone; as, when the bell rang, she found to her great surprise that the lesson hour was over, she turned back to them for a moment and said with that sparkling little smile of hers:

"I'm really sorry you hadn't a teacher today. I should have been glad to have taught the lesson if I had known how; but you see how it is; I have all these things to learn."

Now, Rich Johnson rather prided himself on his rudeness; a strange thing to pride oneself on, to be sure. But pride takes all sorts of curious forms, and he had actually rather gloried in his ability to say rude and cutting things at a moment's notice; words, you know, that the boys in his set called "cute." But he was at this time actually surprised into being almost gallant.

"We never had a better teacher," he said quickly. "If you are only just learning, you better try it again on us; we like the style enough sight better than the finished-up kind."

And then Flossy smiled again and thanked them and said she had enjoyed it. And then she did an unprecedented thing. She invited them all to call on her, in a pretty, graceful way, precisely as she would have invited a gentleman friend who had seen her home from a concert, the quiet, courteous invitation to her father's house, which is a mere matter of form among the young ladies of her set, but which to these boys was so astonishing as an invitation to the Garden of Eden.

They had not the slightest intention of accepting the invitation, but they felt, without realizing what made them feel so, a sudden added touch of self-respect. I almost think they were more careful of their words during the rest of that day than they would have been but for that invitation.

"Isn't Sunday school splendid?" Flossy said to Ruth Erskine as, with her cheeks in a fine glow of glad satisfaction that she had "begun," she joined Ruth in the hall.

"It was very interesting," said Ruth in her more quiet, thoughtful way. She was thoughtful during the entire walk home.

It was her lot to slip into one of those grand classes where Bible teaching means something more than simply reading over the verses. There had been good seed sown with a lavish hand, and there had been careful probing to see if it had taken root. Ruth had some stronger ideas about the importance of "continuing." She had a renewed sense of the blessedness of being made "free." She went home with a renewed desire to consecrate herself, and not only to enjoy, but to labor, that others might enter into that rest. Blessed are those teachers whose earnest Sabbath work produces such fruit as this!

3

BURDENS

UNDER the influence of the sermon and the prayers and the glorious music, life grew to be rose color to Marion before she reached home that Sabbath evening. She came home with springing step, and with her heart full of plans and possibilities for the future. Not even the dismalness of her unattractive room and desolate surroundings had power to drive the song from her heart. She went about humming the grand tune with which the evening service had closed:

> *In the cross of Christ I glory,*
> *Towering o'er the wrecks of time.*

As she sang, her whole soul thrilled with the joy of glorying in such a theme, and her last thought, as she closed her eyes for the night, was about a plan of work that she meant to carry out.

What could have happened to the night to so change the face of the world for her! It looked so utterly different in the morning. School was to open, and she shrank from it, dreaded it. The work looked all drudgery, and the plans she had formed the night before seemed impossibilities. The face of nature had changed wonderfully. In place of radiant sunshine there was falling a steady, dismal rain; the clouds bent low and looked like lead; the wind was moaning in a dismal way that felt like a wail; and nothing but umbrellas and waterproofs and rubber overcoats and dreariness were abroad.

The pretty, summery school dress that Marion had laid out to wear was hung sadly back in her wardrobe, and the inevitable black alpaca came to the surface. It seemed to her the symbol of her old life of dreariness, which she imagined had gone from her. It was not that she felt utterly dismal and desolate; it was not that she had forgotten her late experiences; it was not that she did not know that she had the Friend who is "the same yesterday, today, and forever"; it was simply that she could not feel it and joy in it as she had done only yesterday; and her religious life was too recent not to be swayed by feeling and impulse.

The fact that there was a clear sun shining above the clouds, and a strong and firm mountain up in the sunshine, on which it was her privilege to stand, despite what was going on below, she did not understand. She did not know what effect the weather and the sense of fatigue were having on her, and she felt not only mortified but alarmed that her joy had so soon gone out in cloud and gloom.

If she could only just run around the corner to see Eurie a minute, or up the hill to Flossy's home, how much it would help her; and the thought that she was actually looking to Flossy Shipley and Eurie Mitchell for help of any sort brought the first smile that she had indulged in that morning; she was certainly changed when she could look to them for comfort or sympathy.

Is there anyone reading this account of an everyday life who does not understand, by past experience, just how trying a first day at school is, when teachers and scholars have come out from the influence of a long summer vacation! Next week, or even tomorrow, they will have battled with and, in a measure, choked the spirit of disgust or homesickness or wariness, with which they come back from play to work; but today nothing seems quite so hard in all the world as to turn from the hundred things that have interested and delighted them and settle down to grammar and philosophy and algebra.

Teachers and scholars alike are apt to feel the depression of such circumstances; and when you add to the other discomforts that of a steady, pouring rain with a sound of fall in every whiff of wind, you will understand that Marion was to have comparatively little help from outside influences. She felt the gloom in her heart deepen as the day went on. She was astonished and mortified at herself to find that the old feelings of irritability and sharpness still held her in grasp; she was not free from *them,* at least.

Her tongue was as strongly tempted to be sarcastic, and her tone to be stern, as ever they had been. None of the scholars helped her. Those of them who were neither gloomy nor listless nor inclined to be cross were simply *silly;* they laughed on every possible occasion with or without an excuse; they devised ways and means to draw off the attention of these who made faint efforts to be studious; and, in short, were decidedly the most provoking of all the elements of the day. Marion found herself more than once curling her lip in the old sarcastic way at the inconsistencies and improprieties of those among her pupils who bore the name of Christian.

During the long recess she tried to go away by herself, in the hope that her heart might quiet down and rest itself on some of the new and solid ground on which she had so lately learned to tread. But they followed her; several of the teachers, in a gaiety of mood that was half affected to hide the homesickness of their hearts, and therefore infected no one else with a cheerful spirit. They were armed with a package of examination papers, given in by those scholars who aspired to a higher grade. They loudly called on Marion for assistance.

"You haven't had a single examination class yet; then it is clearly your duty to help the afflicted. 'Bear ye one another's burdens,' you know."

It was Miss Banks who said this, and she had barely escaped being Marion's intimate friend; as it was, she came nearer being familiar with her than with any other. She wondered now how it could have been that she had liked her! Her voice sounded so shrill and unwinning, and the quotation that she so glibly uttered was such a jar. However, she turned back with a wan attempt at a smile and said:

"I shall have enough examination papers of my own before night. How do yours range?" And she took half a dozen that were reached out to her.

"They range precisely as if we had a parcel of idiots in our care. The blunders that these aspiring young ladies and gentlemen make in orthography are enough to set one's teeth on edge."

"Orthography!" said Marion with a curling lip. "They are years too old for any such commonplace as that; it must be history, at least. Here is Allie March struggling for the advanced history class, and I venture to say she doesn't know who was president four years ago."

And then Marion suddenly remembered that Allie March was the one whom, in her glorified moments of only the day before, she had aspired to help forward in her Christian life. If she had seen that sneer and heard those sharp words would it have helped her, or inclined her ever to look that way for help? Then Marion and the rest gave themselves to silence and to work.

"What is the prospect for promotion?" Professor Easton said as he came and leaned over the desk before which they worked.

Miss Banks looked up with a laugh.

"It reminds one of one's childhood and Scripture-learning days: 'Many are called, but few are chosen.' There will be exceedingly few chosen from this class."

Why did those Bible quotations so jar Marion? It had been one of her weak points to quote them aptly and with stinging sarcasm. Perhaps that was one reason why she so keenly felt their impropriety now; she had been so long among the "called," and so very recently among the "chosen."

The possibility of having spent a lifetime without ever becoming one of those "chosen" ones seemed so fearful to her, and she felt that she had so narrowly escaped that end that she shivered and drew her little shawl around her as she glanced up quickly at Professor Easton.

He was a Christian man, a member of the First Church—would he have any reply to make to this irreverent application of solemn truth? No, he had only a laugh for reply; it might have been at Miss Banks's rueful face that he laughed, but Marion would have liked him better if he had looked *grave*. Miss Banks at that moment caught a glimpse of Marion's grave face.

"Miss Wilbur," she said quickly, "what on earth can have happened to you during vacation? I never in my life saw you look so solemn. Didn't I hear something about your going to the woods to camp meeting? How was that? I verily believe you spent your time on the anxious seat and have caught the expression. Did you find anyone to say to you, 'Come unto me?' I'm sure you 'labor' hard enough and look 'heavy laden,' doesn't she, Professor Easton? I really think we shall have to start a prayer meeting over her."

Marion threw down the paper she was correcting with a nervous start, and her voice sounded sharper than she meant.

"How is it possible, Miss Banks, that you can repeat those words in such a shockingly irreverent way? Surely you profess to have at least a *nominal* respect for the One who first uttered them!"

"Really!" said Miss Banks with an embarrassed laugh, astonishment and confusion struggling for the mastery on her flushed face. "'Is Saul also among the prophets?' There! I declare, I am quoting again. Is that wicked, too? Professor Easton, how is that? Miss Wilbur has been to camp meeting and is not responsible for her words, but you ought to be good authority. Is it wicked for me to quote Scripture? Haven't I as good a right to Bible verses as any of you? Here has Miss Wilbur been giving us lessons in that art for the last two years, and she suddenly deserts and takes to preaching at us. Is that fair, now? If it were not wicked I might say to her, 'Physician, heal thyself.'"

Marion bestowed a quick, searching, almost pleading glance on Professor Easton, and then looked down with a flushed and disappointed face. He was not equal to a bold spreading of his professed colors. He laughed, not easily, or as if he enjoyed the sharp words veiled so thinly by pleasantry, but as if he were in an awkward position and did not see his way out.

"You were just a little hard on Miss Wilbur in your selections, you must remember," he said at last. "People can always be excused for more or less somberness on the first day of the term."

And then he went away hurriedly, as if he desired to avoid anything further in that strain.

Hard on Miss Wilbur? Did he suppose she cared for such rapid nonsense? What surprised and hurt her was that he so utterly ignored the question at issue. Did he, a professed Christian of many years' standing, see no impropriety in this manner of quoting the very words of the Lord himself! Or hadn't he sufficient moral courage to rebuke it? Either conclusion was distasteful; especially distasteful to her, Marion found, because the one in question was Professor Easton. Hitherto she had held him a little above the ordinary. Was he then so *very* common after all?

This little occurrence did not serve to sweeten her day. The more so that after she had quieted down a little, at noon, she tried to join the other teachers as usual, and felt an air of stiffness or embarrassment or unnaturalness of some sort, in their manner to her. Twice, as she came toward them, Miss Banks, who was talking volubly, hushed into sudden and utter silence.

After that, Marion went into the upper hall and ate her lunch by herself. Matters grew worse, rather than better, as the afternoon session dragged its slow hours along. The air of the schoolroom seemed close and unbearable, and the moment a window was raised, the driving rain rushed in and tormented the victim who sat nearest to it.

Poor Marion, who was as susceptible to the temperature of rooms as a thermometer, tried each window in succession during the afternoon and came to the desperate conclusion that the rain came from all quarters of the leaden sky at once.

The spirit of unrest that pervaded the room grew into positive lawlessness as the day waned, and Marion's tone had taken even unusual sharpness; her self-command was giving way. Instead of helping, she had been positively an injury to Allie March; first by the sharpness of her reprimands, and then by sarcastic comments on her extreme dullness.

But the girl who had tried her the most during the entire day was the most brilliant, and, as a rule, the most studious scholar in her room. Every teacher knows that the good scholar who occasionally makes a failure is the one who exasperates the most; you are so utterly unprepared for anything but perfection on that one's part.

Not that Gracie Dennis was perfect; she was by far too noisy and decided for that; but she was, as a rule, ladylike in her manners and words, showing her careful teaching and her own sense of self-respect.

There had been little sympathy, however, between Marion and herself. She was too much like Marion in a haughty independence of manner to ever become that lady's favorite. Why, as to that, I am not sure that she *had* a favorite; there were many who liked her, and all respected her, but no one thought of expressing outright affection for Miss Wilbur.

As for Gracie Dennis, she had come nearer to outwitting her teacher than had any other young lady in the room, and she stood less in awe of her.

On this particular day, the spirit of disquiet seemed to have gotten entire possession of the girl; she had not given fifteen minutes to downright work but had dawdled and lounged in a most exasperating manner, and at times exhibited a dullness that was very hard to bear patiently, because Marion felt so certain that it was either feigned or the result of willful inattention. Several times Marion had to speak decidedly to the young ladies in her seat, once or twice directly to Grace herself, and at last, losing all patience with her, she took decided measures.

"Miss Dennis, I really have something to do besides watch you all the time. If you please, you may bring your book to the desk and take the seat beside me; then if you *must* whisper, I can afford you a special audience."

What an unheard of thing! Grace Dennis actually called to the platform, to the post of disgrace! The leading young lady in the school, and Dr. Dennis's only daughter! Some of the scholars looked aghast; some of the class who had long envied her were rude and cruel enough to indulge in an audible giggle.

As for Grace herself, hardly anyone could have been more amazed. It was many a day since, with all her love of fun, and her dangerous position as a leader, she had been obliged to receive a public reprimand; she had never in her life been called to that public seat, which was but one removed from being sent to Professor Easton's private office!

Her great handsome eyes dilated and flashed, and her cheeks glowed like fire. She half arose, then sat down again, and the school waited breathlessly, being about equally divided as to whether she would obey or rebel. Marion herself was somewhat in doubt, and in her excitement over the unwonted scene, concluded to make obedience a necessity.

"On the second thought, you may have your choice, Miss Dennis: You may come to the desk or repair at once to Professor Easton's room and state the cause of your appearance."

Again the hateful giggle! There were those who knew why being sent to Professor Easton was the worst thing that Gracie Dennis thought could happen to her. She arose again, and now she had the advantage of her teacher, for there were dignity and composure in her voice as she said:

"I believe I have never disobeyed your orders, Miss Wilbur; I certainly do not propose to do so now."

Then she came with composed step and took her seat beside Marion; but her eyes still glittered, and, as the business of the hour went on more quietly than any hour that had preceded it, Marion, as she caught glimpses now and then of the face bent over her Latin grammar, saw that it was flushed almost to a purple hue, and that the intense look in those handsome eyes did not quiet. She had roused a dangerous spirit.

To add to the embarrassment and the keenness of her rebuke, the door leading from the recitation room behind the platform suddenly opened, and Professor Easton himself came around to speak to Marion. He paused in astonishment as he caught sight of the culprit beside her and for an instant was visibly embarrassed; then he rallied, and, bowing slightly and very gravely, passed her by, and addressed Marion in a low voice.

As for Gracie, she did not once lift her eyes after the first swift glance had assured her who the caller was.

"I have made an enemy," thought Marion to herself as, her own excitement beginning to subside, she had time to reflect on whether she had done wisely. "She will never forgive me this public insult, as she will choose to call it. I see it in her handsome, dangerous eyes. And yet, I can hardly see how I could have done otherwise. If almost any of the others had given me half the provocation that she has today, I should have sent them to Professor Easton without question. Why should I hesitate in her favor? Oh, me, what a miserable day it has been! and I meant it to be such a good one! I wonder if my Christian life must be marked by such weary and ignominious failures as this? Gracie Dennis is one of the *Christian* young ladies. A lovely Christian she has shown, and, if I am not mistaken, will continue to show to me! I wonder if it amounts to nothing but a name, after all, with the most of them?"

And here Marion stopped this train of thought, because she suddenly remembered that she was not numbered among those on whom others were looking and wondering if their religion meant anything but name. Suppose that some had been looking at her in that light this day? How would they have decided?

She found that she was not willing to be judged by the same rule that she was almost unconsciously applying to Gracie Dennis. Then she went back over the day and tried to discover wherein she had failed and how she might have done what would have been better. Could she not, after all, have gotten along without so severe and public a rebuke to this young girl at her side?

She knew her temperament well. Indeed it was— she confessed it to herself—a good deal like her own. What would be a trifle to half the girls in the school, what would be forgotten by the best of them in a day or two, would burn in this girl's memory and affect

her after life and manner, almost in spite of herself—
the more so, because of that unfortunate call from
Professor Easton.

Marion knew by the swift glance which he gave at
this strange situation that it meant something to him.
Then it was doubly hard for Gracie. She began to feel
sorry for her; to wish that she might in some way
smooth over the chasm that she had builded between
them.

"She is very young," she said to herself with a little
sigh. "I ought not to have expected such wonderful
things of her. I wish I had managed differently; it is too
late now; I wonder how I shall get out of it all? Shall
I just let her go home without saying anything?"

All these troubled thoughts wandered through
Marion's brain during the intervals of quiet, when
nothing was heard save the scratch of pens, for the
entire room was engaged in a dictation exercise,
which was to determine their standing in the writing
class. At last there was quiet.

The demon of inattention had seemingly been
exorcised or subdued, for all were industriously at
work, and Marion had a chance to rest from the alert
watchfulness which had characterized the day.

All at work but Gracie. She still bent over her Latin
Grammar. She had not asked permission to join the
dictation class, and Marion had not volunteered it.
Truth to tell, she hardly dared venture to address her
at all. The eyes had lost some of their keen flash, and
the color seemed to be deepening, instead of subsid-
ing on her pretty soft cheeks.

Marion, as her eyes roved over the exercise book in
her hand, felt her heart arrested by these words among
the selections for dictation:

"Bear ye one another's burdens, and so fulfill the law of Christ."

They smote her like a blow from an unseen hand. What burdens of homesickness and ennui and weariness might not all these girls have had to bear today! Had she helped them? Had her manner been winning and hopeful and invigorating? Had her words been gentle and well chosen, as well as firm and decisive? Her answers to these questions stung her.

Moved by a sudden impulse, and not giving herself time to shrink from the determination, she bent forward a little and addressed Gracie:

"Read that, Gracie. I have not obeyed its direction today; have you? Do you think you have helped me to bear *my* burdens?"

Would Gracie answer her at all? Would her answer be cold and haughty; as nearly rude as she had dared to make it? Marion felt her heart throb while she waited. And she *had* to wait, for Gracie was utterly silent.

At last her teacher stole a glance at her. The great beautiful eyes were lifted to her face. The flash was passing out of them. In its place there was a puzzled, wondering, questioning look. And, when at last she spoke, her voice was timid, as if she were half frightened at her own words, and yet eager as one who must know:

"Miss Wilbur, you don't mean—oh, *do* you mean that *you* want to fulfill the law of Christ; that you own him?"

"That I own him and love him," Marion said, her cheeks glowing now as Gracie's did, "and that I want above all things to fulfill his law, and yet that I have miserably failed, even this first day."

Among Marion's sad thoughts that day had been:

"There is no one to know, or to care, whether I am different or not. If I could only *tell* someone—some Christian who would be glad—but who is there to tell? Professor Easton is a Christian, but he doesn't care enough about the Lord Jesus to rebuke those who profane his name; he has let me do it in his presence, and smiled at my wit. And these girls (and here Marion's lip had curled), they don't know what they mean by their professions."

She was unprepared for what followed. Gracie Dennis, graceful, queenly in her dignity, and haughty, even in her mirth, said suddenly, in a voice which quivered with gladness:

"Oh, I am so glad; *so* glad! Oh, Miss Wilbur, I don't know how to be thankful enough!" And then she raised her head suddenly, and her glowing lips just touched Marion's cheek.

It was so unusual for Marion to be kissed. Her friends at Chautauqua had been those who rarely indulged in that sort of caress—never, at least, with her. And, while, as I told you, many of them liked, and all of them respected her, it was yet an unheard-of thing for the scholars to caress Miss Wilbur. And then, too, Gracie Dennis was by no means lavish of her kisses. This made the token seem so much more. It felt almost like a benediction.

Gracie's next words were humbling to her:

"Miss Wilbur, will you forgive me? I didn't mean to annoy you. I don't know what has been the matter with me."

But, long before this, the last laggard had finished her line and was staring in undisguised astonishment at the scene enacted on the platform.

Marion rallied her excited thoughts. "Dear child," she said, "we have each something to forgive. I think

I have been too severe with you. We will try to help each other tomorrow."

Then she gave the next sentence as calmly as usual. But she went home that night through the rain with a quick step and with joy in her heart. It was not *all* profession. It meant something to those girls; to Grace Dennis it meant everything. It was enough to make her forget her passion, and her wounded pride, and to make her face actually radiant with joy.

It should mean more to *her*. She had failed that day. She had not been, in any sense, what she meant to be; what she ought to have been. But there was a blessed verse: "Who forgiveth *all* thine iniquities."

What a salvation! Able to forgive transgression, to cover sin, to remember it no more. It all seemed very natural to her tonight; very like an infinite Savior, one infinitely loving.

She began to realize that even poor *human* love could cover a multitude of sins. How easy it seemed to her that it would be to overlook the mistakes and shortcomings of Gracie Dennis, after this!

4

COL. BAKER'S SABBATH EVENING

AMONG Marion Wilbur's gloomy thoughts during that trying Monday were these: "Some lives are a good deal harder to bear than others. It would be nonsense for some people to talk about crosses. There are Ruth and Flossy; what do they know about annoyances or self-denials? Such homes as theirs and such occupations as theirs have very little in common with hard, uncongenial work such as mine. Eurie Mitchell has less easy times; but then it is home, and father, and mother, and family friends. She isn't all alone. None of them can sympathize with me. I don't see how Flossy Shipley is ever to grow, if 'crosses are a fruitful condition of the Christian life.' I'm sure she can do as she pleases, and when she pleases."

Thus much Marion knew about other lives than hers. The actual truth was that Flossy's shadows began on Sabbath evening, while Marion was yet on the heights.

It was just as they stepped from the aisle of the church into the wide hall that Col. Baker joined her. This was not a new experience. He was very apt to join her. No other gentleman had been a more frequent or more enjoyable guest at her father's house. Indeed, he was so familiar that he was as likely to come on the Sabbath as on any other day and was often in the habit of calling to accompany Flossy to any evening service where there was to be a little grander style of music than usual, or a special floral display.

In fact he had called this very evening on such an errand, but it was after Flossy had gone to her own church. So her first meeting with him since her Chautauqua experiences was in that hall belonging to the First Church.

"Good evening," he said, joining her without the formality of a question as to whether it would be agreeable; his friendship was on too assured a footing for the need of that formality. "You are more than usually devoted to the First Church, are you not? I saw you in the family pew this morning. I felt certain of being in time to take you to the South Side tonight. St. Stephen's Church has a grand choral service this evening. I was in at one of the rehearsals, and it promised to be an unusually fine thing. I am disappointed that you did not hear it."

Here began Flossy's unhappiness. Neither Marion nor Ruth could have appreciated it. To either of those it would have been an actual satisfaction to have said to Col. Baker, in a calm and superior tone of voice:

"Thanks for your kindness, but I have decided to attend my own church service regularly after this, and would therefore not have been able to accompany you if I had been at home."

But for Flossy, such an explanation was simply dreadful. It was so natural, and would have been so easy, to have murmured a word of regret at her absence and expressed disappointment in having missed the choral.

But for that address to the children, given under the trees at Chautauqua, by Dr. Hurlburt, she would have said these smooth, sweet-sounding words as sweetly as usual without a thought of conscience. But had not he shown her, as plainly as though he had looked down into her heart and seen it there, that these pleasant, courteous phrases which are so winning and so false were among her besetting sins? Had he not put her forever on her guard concerning them? Had she not promised to wage solemn war against the tendency to so sin with her graceful tongue? Yet how she dreaded the plain speaking!

How would Marion's lips have curled over the idea of such a small matter as that being a cross! And yet Flossy could have been sweet and patient and tender to the listless, homesick schoolgirls and kissed away half their gloom and thought it no cross at all. Verily there is a difference in these crosses, and verily, "the heart knoweth his own bitterness."

Col. Baker was loth to leave the subject:

"Aren't you being unusually devout today?" he asked. "I heard of you at Sabbath school; I was certain after that effort, I should find you at home, resting. What spell came over you to give the First Church so much of your time?"

"One would think, to hear you, that I never went to church on Sabbath evening," Flossy said. And then to a certain degree conscience triumphed. "I have not been very often, it is true; but I intend to reform in that respect in the future. I mean to go whenever I can, and I mean to go always to the First Church."

Col. Baker looked at her curiously in the moon-light.

"Is that an outgrowth of your experience in the woods?" he asked.

"Yes," Flossy said simply and bravely.

He longed to question further, to quiz her a little, but something in the tone of the monosyllable prevented. So he said:

"I am at least surprised at part of the decision. I thought part of the work of those gatherings was to teach fellowship and unity. Why should you desert other churches?"

"There is no desertion about it. I do not belong to other churches, and nobody has reason to expect me at any of them; but my pastor has a right to expect me to be in my pew."

"Oh; then it is the accident of the first choice that must determine one's sitting in church for all future time?"

"With me it has been only an accident," she said simply. "I suppose there are people who had better reasons for selecting their church home. But I am very well satisfied with my place." And then Flossy was very glad that they were nearing her father's house. The gladness did not last, however. There hung over it another cross. This Col. Baker had been in the habit of being invited to enter, and of spending an hour or more in cozy chat with the family. Nothing confidential or special in these Sabbath-evening calls; they seemed simply to serve to pass away a dull hour. They had been pleasant to Flossy. But it so happened that the hours of the Sabbath had grown precious to her; none of them was dull; every moment of them was needed.

Besides, in their walk up the hill from the auditorium one evening, Evan Roberts had said in answer to a wonderment from her that so little was accomplished by the Sabbath services throughout the land:

"I think one reason is the habit that so many people have of frittering away any serious impression or solemn thought they may have had by a stream of small talk in which they indulge with their own family or their intimate friends, after what they call the Sabbath is past. Do you know there are hundreds of people, good, well meaning—in fact, Christians— who seem to think that the old Puritan rules in regard to hours hold yet, in part. It begins at eight or nine o'clock, when they have their nap out; and at the very latest it closes with the minister's benediction after the second service; and they laugh and talk on the way home and at home as if the restraints of the day were over at last."

How precisely he had described the Sabbath day of the Shipley family. With what a sense of relief had she often sat and chatted with Col. Baker at the close of what had been to her an irksome day and felt that at last the sense of propriety would not be shocked if they laughed and bantered with each other as usual.

Things were different now. But poor Flossy's face flushed, and her heart beat hard over the trial of *not* asking Col. Baker to come in. Silly child! Ruth would have said, and her calm, clear voice would not have hesitated over the words: "Col. Baker, I cannot ask you in this evening, because I have determined to receive no more calls, even from intimate friends, on the Sabbath. On any other evening I shall be happy to see you."

As for Marion, she would have decidedly enjoyed saying it. But Flossy, she could never have explained it to him. Her voice would have trembled too much, and her heart beat too hard. The very most that she could do was to keep her lips closed. No invitation from her should pass them, and this in itself was five times more of a cross than it would have been for either of the others to have spoken.

However, it did no good. Col. Baker's friendship was on too assured a footing to wait for ceremony. He had received too many invitations of that nature to even notice the omission now. Though Flossy paused and turned toward him he did not notice it, but himself opened the door for her and passed in at her side, talking still about some matter connected with his plans for the evening, that had been overthrown by her strange propensity for church.

She did not hear him at all; she was both grieved and annoyed. If only she dared go directly to her room! If she had been Ruth Erskine it would have been done in a moment.

They sat down in the back parlor, and it was made evident to Flossy that the entertainment of Col. Baker would be considered her special duty. The library door was closed, and the sound of subdued voices there told that Kitty Shipley and her suitor were having a confidential talk. Kitty wouldn't help, then. Mrs. Shipley had retired, and Mr. Shipley sat at the droplight reading the journal. He glanced up at their entrance, gave Col. Baker the courteous and yet familiar greeting that welcomed him as a special friend of the house, and then went on with his reading. As for her brother, Charlie, he had not come in, and probably would not for hours to come.

What was there for Flossy to do but to take a seat and talk to Col. Baker? Yet how she shrank from it! She wanted to be alone, to go over in her heart all the sweet and blessed experiences of the day, for this day had helped her much. She wanted to think about those boys in the school, and form plans for their future, and try to decide whether it could be that they would really like her for a teacher, and whether Dr. Dennis would let her undertake the class. Why would not Col. Baker go home?

"What is the matter with you?" he asked, studying her face curiously, and with a doubtful sound in his voice. "I don't believe that strange freak of yours did you any good."

"It did me more good than anything that ever happened to me in my life," Flossy said positively.

If she could only have explained to him just what the nature of that good was! Possibly she might have tried, only there sat her father. Who could tell when his interest in the *Times* would cease, and he give attention to her? Flossy could not understand why she should be so afraid of her father in this matter; but she was very much afraid.

The talk they had was of that kind known as "small." To Flossy it seemed exceedingly small, and she did not know how to make it otherwise. She began to wonder if she and Col. Baker really had any ideas in common; yet Col. Baker could talk with gentlemen, and talk well. It was simply the habit of being frippery with the ladies that made his words seem so foolish to Flossy.

Contrary to her expectation, her brother, Charlie, suddenly appeared on the scene; and for a time she was privileged to slip into the background. Charlie had been to hear the choral, and Col. Baker was very anxious to know as to its success. You would have supposed them to be talking about a prima-donna concert. At last Charlie turned to Flossy with the trying question:

"Sis, why didn't you go to the choral? I thought you were coming for her, Baker. Didn't you tell me so?"

"I came, but was too late. Miss Flossy had already betaken herself to the First Church."

"So *you* missed the choral?"

"Well, only part of it. I went for an hour; then I left and went in search of your sister, to discover if I could what special attractions First Church had for her tonight."

Now this fashion of going to one service until he was tired, and then quietly slipping out in search of something more attractive, was peculiar to Col. Baker. Flossy had known of his doing it on several different occasions. The very most that she had thought about it had been that it was making oneself very conspicuous. She didn't believe she would like to do it, even if she were a man. But tonight the action had taken an irreverent shade that it never had before. She discovered that she utterly disapproved of it. There seemed to be many things in Col. Baker that met with her disapproval. Meantime the talk went on.

"Did you find the attraction?" Charlie asked.

Col. Baker shrugged his handsome shoulders.

"I confess I couldn't find it in the sermon. It was one of the Doctor's sharpest and bluest efforts. That poor man has the dyspepsia, I feel certain. Seems to me he develops an increased ability for making people miserable."

Now, Col. Baker fully expected to draw forth by this remark one of Flossy's silvery laughs, which, to tell the truth, were becoming sweeter to his ears than any choral.

He was surprised and annoyed at the steady look of thoughtful, not to say distressed, gravity that she gave him out of those soft blue eyes of hers. He did not know what to make of this Flossy; he was feeling the change in her more decidedly than anyone else had done. He waited for Flossy's answer, and she gave it at last, in a grave, rebuking tone of voice:

"I liked the sermon very much."

"Did you, indeed? I confess I am astonished. I gave you the credit of possessing a more tender heart. Frankly, then, I didn't. I must say I don't like to go to church to be made uncomfortable."

"Did you find that sentence in the paper?" Flossy asked, a little gleam of mischief in her eyes. "Because, if you did, I should have thought you would have considered it answered very well by the comments."

"As a rule, I am not obliged to resort to the papers to find remarks to quote," Col. Baker said with an attempt at gaiety, which but half concealed the evident annoyance that he felt. "But I judge the paper found someone suffering in the same way. Pray, what was the answer?"

"Why, the writer said that he supposed no one liked to be uncomfortable; but whether it was the sermon that should change, or the life, in order to remove the discomfort, was a question for each to decide for himself."

"Sharp!" said Charlie, laughing; "you've got hit, Baker."

"Oh no," he said, "not at all. Don't you see, the author kindly accorded permission for each person to decide the question for himself? Now I have it decided so far as I am concerned. I prefer a change in the sermon. Oh, Dr. Dennis is a good man; no one doubts it; but he is too severe a sermonizer. His own church officers admit that. He is really driving the young people away from the church. I should not be greatly surprised if there had to be a change in that locality very soon. The spirit of the times demands more liberality and a larger measure of Christian charity."

Col. Baker was really too well educated a man to have allowed himself to use these terms parrotlike, without knowledge or thought as to their meaning; but the truth was, he cared so little about church and Christian charity, and all those phrases, as to have very little idea of what he meant himself when he used them.

But pretty little Flossy had never argued with him, never been known to argue with anybody. Why should he not occasionally awe her with his high-sounding words? It is a pity that Ruth or Marion had not been there to take up the theme; and yet it is doubtful if arguments would have had any weight with him. The truth was, he did not need to be convinced. Probably Flossy's perfect gravity and dignity and silence did more to answer him than any keen words could have done.

5

NEW MUSIC

CHARLIE arose suddenly and went toward the piano. Things were becoming uncomfortably grave.

"Sis," he said, "can't you give us some new music? Try this new piece; Baker hasn't heard you sing it. I don't think it is remarkable, but it is better than none. We seem to have a very small list of music that will pass the orthodox line for Sunday use."

Both he and Flossy had sighed over the dearth of pretty things that were suited to Sunday. The one in question was one of the worst of its kind—one of that class which Satan seems to have been at work getting up for the purpose of lulling to rest weak consciences. Sickly, sentimental ideas, expressed in words that are on the very verge of silly; and yet with just enough solemn sounding phrases in them, thrown in here and there, to allow them to be caught up by a certain class and pronounced "sacred song." Flossy had herself selected this one, and before her departure for Chautauqua had pronounced it very good. She had not looked at it since she came home. Charlie spread it open for her on the piano, then returned to the sofa to enjoy the music. Flossy's voice was sweet and tender; no power in it, and little change of feeling, but pleasant to listen to, and capable of being tender and pathetic. She looked over the sacred song with a feeling of aversion almost amounting to disgust. The pitiful attempts at religion sounded to her recently impressed heart almost like a caricature. On the piano beside her lay a copy of *Gospel Songs*; open, so it happened, at the blessed and solemn hymn "How Much Owest Thou?" Now a coincidence that seemed remarkable, and at once startled and impressed Flossy, was that Dr. Dennis's text for the evening had been the words "How much owest thou unto my Lord?" She hesitated just a moment, then she resolutely pushed aside the sheet music, drew the book toward her, and without giving herself time for a prelude, gave herself to the beautiful and well-remembered words:

> *"How much owest thou?*
> *For years of tender, watchful care,*
> *A father's faith, a mother's prayer:*
> *How much owest thou?*
>
> *"How much owest thou?*
> *For calls, and warnings loud and plain,*
> *For songs and sermons heard in vain:*
> *How much owest thou?*
>
> *"How much owest thou?*
> *Thy day of grace is almost o'er,*
> *The judgment time is just before:*
> *How much owest thou?*
>
> *"How much owest thou?*
> *Oh, child of God, and heir of heaven,*

> *Thy soul redeemed, thy sins forgiven:*
> *How much owest thou?"*

Flossy had heard Mr. Bliss, with his grand and glorious voice, ring that out on a certain evening at Chautauqua, where all the associations of the hour and place had been solemn and sacred. It might have been in part these memories, and the sense of something missed, that made her have a homesick longing for the place and song again, that gave to her voice an unusually sweet and plaintive sound. Every word was plain and clear and wonderfully solemn; but when she reached the words

> *"Oh, child of God, and heir of heaven,*
> *Thy soul redeemed, thy sins forgiven"*

There rang out a note of triumph that filled the room and made the hearts of her listeners throb with surprise and wonder. Long before the song was closed, her father had laid aside the *Times,* and, with spectacles pushed above his eyes, was listening intently. Absolute silence reigned for a moment, as Flossy's voice died out in sweetness; then Charlie, clearing his throat, said:

"Well! I said I didn't consider the song remarkable. But I take it back; it is certainly remarkable. Did you ever hear anything that had so changed since you last met it?"

Col. Baker did not at once reply. The very first line had struck him, for the reason that above most men, he had reason to remember a "mother's prayer." There were circumstances connected with that mother of his that made the line doubly startling to him. He was agitated by the wonderful directness of the solemn words, and he was vexed that they agitated him; so when he did speak, to conceal his feeling, he made his voice flippant.

"It is a remarkable production, worthy of camp meeting, I should say. But, Miss Flossy, allow me to congratulate you. It was sung with striking effect."

Flossy arose suddenly from the piano and closed the book of hymns.

"Col. Baker," she said, "may I ask you to excuse me this evening? I find I am not in a mood to enjoy conversation; my brother will entertain you, I am sure."

And before Col. Baker could recover from his astonishment sufficiently to make any reply at all, she had given him a courteous bow for good-night and escaped from the room.

The situation was discussed by the Shipley family at the next morning's breakfast table. Flossy had come down a trifle late, looking pale and somewhat sober, and was rallied by Kitty as to the cause.

"Her conscience is troubling her a little, I fancy," her father said, eyeing her closely from under heavy brows. "Weren't you just a little hard on the colonel last night, Daughter? He is willing to endure considerable from you, I guess; but I wouldn't try him too far."

"What was the trouble, Father? What has Flossy done now? I thought she was going to be good at last?"

"Done! You may well ask what, Miss Kitty. Suppose the friend you had shut up in the library had been informed suddenly that you were not in a mood to talk with him, and then you had decamped and left him to the tender mercies of two men?"

"Why, Flossy Shipley! You didn't do that, did you?

Really, if I were Col. Baker, I would never call on you again."

"I don't see the harm," Flossy said sharply. "Father and Charlie were both there. Surely that was company enough for him. I hadn't invited him to call."

"Oh, undoubtedly he calls on purpose to see Father and Charlie! He has not been so attentive to the family during your absence, I can assure you. We haven't as much as had a peep at him since you went away. Flossy, I hadn't an idea you could be so rude. I declare, I think that Wilbur girl is demoralizing you. They say she has no idea of considering people's feelings; but then, one expects it of her class."

Mrs. Shipley came to Flossy's aid:

"Poor child, I don't blame her for slipping away. She was tired. She had been to church twice, and to Sunday school at noon, without any lunch, too. Flossy, you mustn't indulge in such an absurd freak another Sunday. It is too much for you. I am sure it is not strange that you wanted to get away to rest."

Then the father:

"I daresay, you were tired, as your mother says; in fact, though, I must say I think I never saw you looking better than you were last evening. But it was a trifle thoughtless, Daughter, and I want you to be more careful in the future. Col. Baker's father was my oldest and most valued friend, and I want his son to be treated with utmost consideration and to feel that he is always welcome. Since he has so special a friendship for you, you must just remember that his position in society is one of the highest, and that you are really decidedly honored. Not that I am rebuking you, Flossy dear, only putting you on your guard; for remember that you carry a very thoughtless little head on your pretty shoulders."

And then he leaned over and patted the thoughtless head and gave the glowing cheek such a loving, fatherly kiss.

As for poor Flossy, the bit of steak she was trying to swallow seemed to choke her; she struggled bravely to keep back the tears that she felt were all ready to fall. The way looked shadowy to her; she felt like a deceitful coward. Here were they, making excuses for her—tired, thoughtless, and the like. Oh, for courage to say to them that she had not been tired at all, and that she thought about that action of hers longer than she had thought about anything in her life, up to a few weeks ago.

If she could only tell them out boldly and plainly that everything was changed to her, that she looked at life from a different standpoint; and that, standing where she did now, it looked all wrong to spend the last hours of the Sabbath in entertaining company. But her poor little tongue, all unused to being brave, so shrank from this ordeal, and the lump in her throat so nearly choked her, that she made no attempt at words.

So the shadows that had fallen on her heart grew heavier as she went about her pretty room. She foresaw a troubled future. Not only must the explanation come, but she foresaw that her changed plans would lie right athwart the views and plans of her father.

What endless trouble and discomfort would this occasion! Also, there were her pet schemes for Sunday school, including those boys for whom she had already planned a dozen different things.

Her mother had frankly expressed her opinion, and, although it is not the age when parents say, nor were Flossy's parents of the sort who would ever have said, "You *must* do thus, and you *shall* not do so," still, she foresaw endless discussions; sarcastic raillery from

Kitty and Charlie; persuasions from her mother; earnest protests from her father and a general air of lack of sympathy or interest about them all.

These things were to Flossy almost more than, under some circumstances, the martyr's stake would have been to Marion Wilbur. Then she, too, as she went about doing sundry little things toward making her room more perfect in its order, took up Marion's fashion of pitying herself, and looking longingly at the brightness in some other life.

Not Marion's, for she was all alone and had great responsibilities, and no one to shield her or help her or comfort her; that was dreadful. Not Ruth's, for her life was so high up among books and paintings and grandeur that it looked like cold elegance and nothing else.

She wouldn't have lived that life; but there was Eurie Mitchell, in a little home that had always looked sunny and cheerful when she had taken occasional peeps into it—somewhat stirred up, as became a large family and small means, but with a cleanly, cheery sort of stir that was agreeable rather than otherwise.

And there were little children to love and care for—children who put their arms around one's neck and said, "I love you," a great many times a day.

Flossy, having never tried it, did not realize that if the fingers had been sticky or greasy or a trifle black, as they were apt to be, it would be an exceeding annoyance to her. She saw what people usually do see about other people's cares and duties, only the pretty, pleasant side. To have felt somewhat of the other side, she should have spent that Monday with Eurie.

To Eurie a Monday rain was a positive affliction; it necessitated the marshaling of tubs and pails into the little kitchen and the endurance of Mrs. Maloney's

presence in constant contact with dinner arrangements—on pleasant days Mrs. Maloney betook herself
to the open air.

Then, in the Mitchell family there was that trial to
any woman of ordinary patience, a small girl who
"helped—" worked for her board mornings and evenings and played at school the rest of the time.

Sallie Whitcomb, the creature who tried Eurie, was
rather duller than the most of her class and had her
days or spells when she seemed utterly incapable of
understanding the English language. This day was very
apt to be Monday; and on this particular Monday of
which I write, the spell was on her in full force.

To add to the bewilderments of the day, Dr. Mitchell, after a very hurried breakfast, had departed, taking
the household genius with him to see a patient and
friend, who was worse.

"I don't know how you will manage," Mrs. Mitchell had said as she paid a hasty visit to the kitchen.
"There is bread to mix, you know, and that yeast
ought to be made today; and then the starch you must
look after or it will be lumpy; and oh, Eurie, do see
that your father's handkerchiefs are all picked up; he
leaves them around so. You must keep an eye on the
baby, for he is a trifle hoarse this morning; and Robbie
mustn't go in the wind—mustn't eat a single apple, for
he isn't at all well; you must see to that, Eurie—I
wouldn't have you forget him for anything. See here,
when the baby takes a nap, see that the lower sash is
shut—there is quite a draught through the room. I
don't know how you are to get through. You must
keep Jennie from school to take care of the children,
and do the best you can. If Mrs. Craymer hadn't sent
for me, I wouldn't go this morning, much as I want to
see her, but I think I ought to, as it is."

"Of course," Eurie said cheerily. "Don't worry about us, Mother; we'll get through somehow. I'll see to Mrs. Maloney and all the rest."

"Well, be careful about the bread; don't let it get too light, and don't for anything put it in too soon; it was a trifle heavy last week, you know, and your father dislikes it so. Never mind much about dinner; your father will have to go to two or three places when he gets back from the Valley, and I can get up a warm bite for him while he is gone."

And with a little sigh and a regretful look back into the crowded, steamy kitchen, Mrs. Mitchell answered her husband's hurried call and ran. So Eurie was left mistress of the occasion.

It looked like a mountain to her. The dishes were piled higher than usual, for the Sabbath-evening lunch had made many that had not been washed. And Sallie, who should have been deep into them already, was at that moment hanging on the gate she had gone to shut and watching the retreating tail of the doctor's horse.

"Sallie!" Eurie called, and Sallie came, looking bewildered and indolent, eating an apple as she walked.

"Now, Sallie, you must hurry with the dishes; see how soon you can get them all out of the way. I have the bread to mix and a dozen other things to do, and I can't help you a bit."

At the same time she had an inward consciousness that the great army of dishes would never marshal into place till she came to their aid.

This was the beginning, not a pleasant one, and the bewilderments of the morning deepened with every passing half hour.

What happened? Dear me, what *didn't?* Inexperienced Eurie, who rarely had the family bread left on her hands, went to mixing it before getting baking tins ready, and Sallie left her dishes to attend to it, and dripped dishwater over them and the moldingboard and on Eurie's clean apron in such an unmistakable manner that the annoyed young lady washed her hands of dough and dumped the whole pile of tins unceremoniously into the dishwater.

"They are so greasy I can't touch them!" she said in disdain, "and have drops of dishwater all over them, and besides here is the core of an apple in one. I wonder, Sallie, if you eat apples while you are washing the dishes! Put some wood in the stove. Jennie, can't you come here and wipe these dishes? We won't get them out of the way before Mother comes home."

Jennie appeared at the door, book in hand.

"How can I leave the baby, Eurie? Robbie says he can't play with him—he feels too sick. I think something ought to be done for Robbie; his cheeks are as red as scarlet."

Whereupon Eurie left dishes and bread and went in to feel of Robbie's pulse and ask how he felt and got a pillow for him to lie on the lounge; and the baby cried for her and had to be taken a minute; so the time went—time always goes like lightning in the kitchen on Monday morning. When that bread was finally set to rise, Eurie dismissed Sallie from the dishpan in disgust with orders to sweep the room, if she could leave her apple long enough.

6

DISTURBING ELEMENTS

THE next anxiety was the baby, who contrived to tumble himself over in his high chair and cried loudly. Eurie ran. Dr. Mitchell was always so troubled about bumps on the head. She bathed this in cold water and in arnica and petted and soothed and pacified as well as she could a child who thought it a special and unendurable state of things not to have mamma and nobody else. Between the petting she administered wholesome reproof to Jennie.

"If you hadn't been reading instead of attending to him, this would not have happened. I wish I had told Mother to lock up all the books before she went. You are *great* help; worthwhile to stay from school to busy yourself in a book."

"I haven't read a dozen pages this morning," Jennie said with glowing cheeks. "He was sitting in his high chair, just as he always is, and I had stepped across the room to get a picture book for Robbie. How could I know that he was going to fall? I don't think you are very kind, anyway, when I am helping all that I can and losing school besides." And Miss Jennie put on an air of lofty and injured innocence.

"I believe she is sweeping right on the bread," said Eurie, her thoughts turned into another channel. "Go and see, Jennie."

Jennie went, and returned as full of comfort as any of Job's friends.

"She swept right straight at it; and she left the door open, and the wind blew the cloth off, and a great hunk of dust and dirt lies right on top of one loaf, and the clothes are boiling over on the others. Nice bread you'll have!"

Before this sentence was half finished, Eurie sat the baby on the floor and ran, stopping only to give orders that Jennie should not let him go to sleep for anything.

The doorbell was the next sound that tried her nerves. The little parlor where they had lingered late, she and Nellis, last evening, when they had a pleasant talk together, the pleasantest she had ever had with that brother; now she remembered how it looked; how he had said as he glanced back when they were leaving:

"Eurie, I hope you won't have any *special* calls before you get around to this room in the morning; it looks as though there had been an upheaval of books and papers here."

Books, and papers, and dust, and her hat and sack, and Jennie's gloves, and Robbie's playthings; she had forgotten the parlor.

Meantime, Jennie had rushed to the door, and now returned, holding the kitchen door open, and talking loud enough to be heard distinctly in the parlor.

"Eurie, Leonard Brooks is in the parlor. He says he wants to see you for just a minute, and I should think that is about as long as he would care to stay; it looks like sixty in there."

"Oh, dear me!" said Eurie, and she looked down at her dress. It had long black streaks running diagonally across it, and dishwater and grease combined on her apron; a few drops of arnica on her sleeves and hands did not improve the general effect.

"Jennie, why in the world didn't you tell him that I was engaged, and couldn't see him this morning?"

"Why, how should I know that you wanted me to say so to people? You didn't tell me. He said he was in a hurry. He isn't alone, either; there is a strange gentleman with him."

Worse and worse.

"I won't go," said Eurie.

"But you will *have* to. I told him you were at home and would be in in a moment. Go on, what do you care?"

There was no way but to follow this advice; but she *did* care. She set the starch back on the stove and washed her hands and waited while Sallie ran upstairs and hunted a towel; then she went, flushed and annoyed, to the parlor. Leonard Brooks was an old acquaintance, but who was the stranger?

"Mr. Holden, of New York," Leonard said. "They would detain her but a moment, as she was doubtless engaged"; and then Leonard looked mischievously down at the streaked dress. He was not used to seeing Eurie look so entirely awry in the matter of her toilet.

Mr. Holden was going to get up a tableau entertainment and needed home talent to help him; he, Leonard, had volunteered to introduce him to some of the talented ladies of the city, and had put her first on the list. Eurie struggled with her embarrassment and answered in her usual way:

"He can see at a glance that I merit the compliment. If myself and all my surroundings don't show a marked talent for disorder, I don't know what would."

Mr. Holden was courteous and gallant in the extreme. He took very little notice of the remark; ignored the state of the room utterly; apologized for the unseemly hour of their call, attributing it to his earnest desire to secure her name before there was any other engagement made; "might he depend on her influence and help?"

Eurie was in a hurry. She smelled the starch scorching; Robbie was crying fretfully, and the baby was so quiet she feared he was asleep; the main point was to get rid of her callers as soon as possible. She asked few questions and knew as little about the projected entertainment as possible, save that she was pledged to a rehearsal on the coming Wednesday at eight o'clock. Then she bowed them out with a sense of relief; and, merely remarking to Jennie that she wished she could coax Robbie and the baby into the parlor and clear it up a little before anybody more formidable arrived, she went back to the scorched starch and other trials.

From that time forth a great many people wanted Dr. Mitchell. The bell rang and rang and rang. Jennie had to run, and Eurie had to run to Baby. Then came noon, bringing the boys home from school, hungry and in a hurry; and Eurie had to go to Sallie's help, who was struggling to get the table set and something on it to eat.

Whereupon the bread suddenly announced itself ready for the oven by spreading over one-half of the bread cloth with a sticky mess. Then the bell rang again.

"I hope that is someone who will send to the Valley

for Father right away; then we shall have Mother again."

This was Eurie's half-aloud admission that she was not equal to the strain. Then she listened for Jennie's report. The parlor door being opened, and somebody being invited thither; and that room not cleared up yet! Then came Jennie with her exasperating news.

"It is Dr. Snowdon from Morristown, and he wants Father for a consultation; says he is going to take him back with him on the two o'clock train, and he wants to know if you could let him have a mouthful of dinner with Father? He met Father at the crossing half a mile below, and he told him to come right on."

"And where is Mother?" said Eurie, pale and almost breathless under this new calamity.

"Why, he didn't say; but I suppose she is with Father. He stopped to call at the Newtons'. I guess you will have to hurry, won't you?"

Jennie was provokingly cool and composed; no sense of responsibility rested upon her.

"Hurry!" said Eurie. "Why, he can't have any dinner here. We haven't a thing in the house for a stranger."

"Well," said Jennie, balancing herself on one foot, "shall I go and tell him that he must take himself off to a hotel?"

"Nonsense!" said Eurie; "you know better." Then she whisked into the kitchen. Twenty minutes of one, and the train went at ten minutes of two, and nothing to eat, and Dr. Snowdon (of all particular and gentlemanly mortals without a wife, or a house, or any sense of the drawbacks of Monday) to eat it! Is it hardly to be wondered at that the boys voted Eurie awfully cross?

"Altogether, it was just the most horrid time that

ever anybody had." That was the way Eurie closed the account of it, as she sat curled on the foot of Marion's bed with the three friends, who had been listening and laughing, gathered around her in different attitudes of attention.

"Oh, you can laugh, and so can I, now that it is over," Eurie said. "But I should just like to have seen one of you in my place; it was no laughing matter, I can tell you. It was just the beginning of vexations, though; the whole week, so far, has been exasperating in every respect. Never anything went less according to planning than my program for the week has."

Each of her auditors could have echoed that, but they were silent. At last Marion asked:

"But how did you get out of it? Tell us that. Now, a dinner of any kind is something that is beyond me. I can imagine you transfixed with horror. Just tell us what you did."

"Why, you will wonder who came to my rescue; but I tell you, girls, Nellis is the best fellow in the world. If I was half as good a Christian as he is without any of that to help him, I should be a thankful mortal. I didn't expect him, thought he had gone away for the day; but when he came he took in the situation at a glance. Half a dozen words of explanation set him right. 'Never mind,' he said. 'Tell him we didn't mean to have dinner so early, but we flew around and got them a bite—then let's do it.' 'But what will the bite be?' I asked, and I stood looking up at him like a ninny who had never gotten a meal in her life. 'Why, bread, and butter, and coffee, and a dish of sauce, and a pickle, or something of that sort'; and the things really sounded appetizing as he told them off. 'Come,' he said, 'I'll grind the coffee, and make it; I used to be a dabster at that dish when I was in college. Jennie, you set the table, and Ned will help; he's well enough for that, I know.'

"And in less time than it takes to tell it, he had us all at work, baby and all; and, really, we managed to get up quiet a decent meal, out of nothing, you understand; had it ready when Father drove up; and he said it was as good a dinner as he had had in a week. But, oh, me! I'm glad such days don't come very often. You see, none of you know anything about it. You girls with your kitchens supplied with first-class cooks, and without any more idea of what goes on in the way of work before you are fed than though you lived in the moon, what do you know about such a day as I have described? Here's Marion, to be sure, who has about as empty a purse as mine; but as for kitchens, and wash days, and picked-up dinners, she is a novice."

"I know all about those last articles, so far as eating them is concerned," Marion said grimly. "I know things about them that you don't, and never will. But I have made up my mind that living a Christian life isn't walking on a featherbed, whether you live in a palace or a fourth-rate board house, and teach school. I shouldn't wonder if there were such things as vexations everywhere."

"I don't doubt it," Ruth Erskine said, speaking more quickly than was usual to her. The others had been more or less communicative with each other. It wasn't in Ruth's nature to tell how tried and dissatisfied she had been with herself and her life and her surroundings all the week. She was not sympathetic by nature. She couldn't tell her inward feelings to anyone, but she could endorse heartily the discovery that Marion had made.

"Well, I know one thing," said Eurie, "it requires twice the grace that I supposed it did to get through with kitchen duties and exasperations and keep one's temper. I shall think, after this, that Mother is a saint when she gets through the day without boxing our ears three or four times around. Come, let's go to meeting."

It was Wednesday evening, and our four girls had met to talk over the events of the week and to keep each other countenance during their first prayer meeting.

"It is almost worse than going to Sunday school," Eurie said as they went up the steps, "except that we can help ourselves to seats without waiting for any attentions which would not be shown."

Now the First Church people were not given to going to prayer meeting. It is somewhat remarkable how many First Churches there are to which that remark will apply. The chapel was large and inviting, looking as though in the days of its planning many had been expected at the social meetings, or else it was built with an eye to festivals and societies. The size of the room only made the few persons who were in it seem fewer in number than they were.

Flossy had been to prayer meeting several times before with a cousin who visited them, but none of the others had attended such a meeting since they could remember. To Eurie and Ruth it was a real surprise to see the rows of empty seats. As for Marion, she had overheard sarcastic remarks enough in the watchful and critical world in which she had moved to have a shrewd suspicion that such was the case.

"I don't know where to sit," whispered Flossy, shrinking from the gaze of several heads that were turned to see who the newcomers were. "Don't you suppose they will seat us?"

"Not they," said Eurie. "Don't you remember Sunday? We must just put the courageous face on and march forward. I'm going directly to the front. I always said if ever I went to prayer meeting at all, I shouldn't act as though I was ashamed that I came." Saying which she led the way to the second seat from the desk, directly in line with Dr. Dennis's eyes.

That gentleman looked down at them with troubled face. Marion looked to see it light up, for she said in her heart:

"Gracie has surely told him my secret."

She knew little about the ways in the busy minister's household. The delightful communion of feeling that she had imagined between father and daughter was almost unknown to them. Very fond and proud of his daughter was Dr. Dennis; very careful of her health and her associations; very grateful that she was a Christian, and so, safe.

But so busy and harassed was his life, so endless were the calls on his time and his patience and his sympathy, that almost without his being aware of it, his own family were the only members of his church who never received any pastoral calls.

Consequently, a reserve like unto that in too many households had grown up between himself and his child, utterly unsuspected by the father, never but half owned by that daughter. He thought of her religious life with joy and thanksgiving; when she went astray, was careful and tender in his admonition; yet of the inner workings of her life, of her reaching after higher and better living, of her growth in grace, or her days of disappointment and failure and decline, he knew no more than the veriest stranger with whom she never spoke.

For while Grace Dennis lived and reverenced her father more than she did any other earthly being, she acknowledged to herself that she could not have told him even of the little conversation between her teacher and herself. She could, and did, tell him all about the lesson in algebra, but not a word about the lesson in Christian love.

So on this evening his face expressed no satisfaction in the presence of the strangers. He was simply disturbed that they had formed a league to meet here with mischief ahead, as he verily believed.

He arose and read the opening hymn; then looked about him in a disturbed way. Nobody to lead the singing. This was too often the case. The quartet choir rarely indeed found their way to the prayer meeting; and when the one who was a church member occasionally came to the weekly meeting, for reasons best known to herself, apparently the power of song for which she received so good a Sabbath-day salary had utterly gone from her, for she never opened her lips.

"I hope," said Dr. Dennis, "that there is someone present who can start this tune; it is simple. A prayer meeting without singing loses half its spiritual force." Still everyone was dumb. "I am sorry that I cannot sing at all," he said again, after a moment's pause. "If I could, ever so little, it would be my delight to consecrate my voice to the service of God's house."

Still silence. All this made Marion remember her resolves at Chautauqua.

"What tunes do people sing in prayer meeting?" she whispered to Eurie.

"I don't know, I am sure," Eurie whispered back. And then the ludicrous side happened to forcibly strike that young lady, just then she shook with laughter and shook the seat. Dr. Dennis looked down at her with grave, rebuking eye.

"Well," he began, "if we cannot sing—"

And then, before he had time to say further, a soft, sweet voice, so tremulous it almost brought tears to think what a tremendous stretch of courage it had taken, quivered on the air.

7

Prayer Meeting and Tableaux

IT WAS Flossy who had triumphed again over self and a strong natural timidity. Her voice trembled but for an instant, then it was literally absorbed in the rich, full tones which Marion allowed to roll out from her throat—richer, fuller, stronger than they would have been had she not again received this sharp rebuke from the timid baby of their party. But that voice of hers! I wish I could describe it to you. It is not often that one hears such a voice. Such a one had never been heard in that room, and the few occupants were surely justified in twisting their heads to see from whence it came.

It was still a new thing to Marion to sing such words as were in that hymn; and in the beauty of them, and the enjoyment of their richness, she lost sight of self and the attention she was attracting and sang with all her heart. It so happened that every one of the three friends could help her not a little, so our girls had the singing in their own hands for the evening.

When the next hymn was announced, Marion leaned forward, smiling a little, and covered with her firm, strong hand the trembling little gloved hand of Flossy, and herself gave the key note in clear, strong tones that neither faltered nor trembled.

"You've taken up your little cross bravely," she whispered afterward. "Shown me my duty and shamed me into it; the very lightest end of it shall not rest on you anymore."

Notwithstanding the singing, and finding that it could be well done, Dr. Dennis took care to see that there should be much of it, that meeting dragged. The few who were in the habit of saying anything, waited until the very latest moment, as if hopeful that they might find a way of escape altogether, and yet, when once started, talked on as though they had forgotten how to arrange a suitable closing, and must therefore go on. Then the prayers seemed to our newcomers and new-beginners in prayer very strange and unnatural.

"Do you suppose Mr. Helm really feels such a deep interest in everything under the sun?" queried Eurie. "Or did he pray for all the world in detail because that is the proper way to do? Someway, I don't feel as if I could ever learn to pray in that way. I believe I shall have to ask for just what I want and then stop."

"If you succeed in keeping to the latter part of your determination you will do better than the most of them," Marion said. "I can't help thinking that the worst feature of it is the keeping on, long after the person wants to stop. Now, I tell you, girls, that is not the way they prayed at Chautauqua, is it?"

"Well," said Flossy, "it is not the way Dr. Dennis prays, either; but then, he has a theological education; that makes a difference, I suppose."

"No, it doesn't, you mouse, make a speck of difference. That old Uncle Billy, as they call him, who sat down by the door in the corner, hasn't a theological education, nor any other sort of education. Did he speak one single sentence according to rule? Yet, didn't you notice his prayer? Different from most of the others. He meant it."

"But you wouldn't say that some of the others meant it?" Ruth said, speaking hesitatingly and questioningly.

"No," Marion answered slowly. "I suppose not, of course; yet there is something the matter with them. It may be that the ones who make them may feel them, but they don't succeed in making me feel."

"Well, honestly," said Eurie, "I'm disappointed. I have heard that people who were really Christians liked to go to prayer meeting better than anywhere else, but I feel awfully wicked about it. But, as true as I live, I have been in places that I thought were ever so much pleasanter than it was there this evening. Now, to tell the plain truth, some of the time I was dreadfully bored. I'm specially disappointed, too, for I had a plan to trying to coax Nellis into going with me, but I really don't know whether I want him to go or not."

But this talk was when they were on their way homeward. Before that, as they went down the steps, Eurie said:

"What plans have you for the evening, girls? Won't you go with me?"

And then she went back to that tormenting Monday, and told of Leonard Brooks's call with his friend Mr. Holden, and of the tableau entertainment to which she was pledged. They had all heard more or less of it, and all in some form or other had received petitions for help, but none of them had come in direct contact with it, save Eurie, and it appeared that the rest of them had given the matter very little attention. Still, they were willing to go with Eurie and see what was to be seen. At least they walked on in that direction.

Dr. Dennis and his daughter were directly behind them. As they neared a brightly lighted street corner, he came up to Eurie and Marion, who were walking together, with a pleasant good-evening. Something in Marion's manner of singing the hymn had interested him, and also he was interested in learning, if he could, what motive had brought them to so unusual a place as the prayer meeting.

"It is a lovely evening for a walk," he said. "But, Miss Wilbur, you don't propose to take it alone, I hope! Isn't your boarding place at some distance?"

She was not going directly home, Marion explained, not caring to admit the loneliness, and also what evidently seemed to Dr. Dennis the impropriety of having to traverse the street alone so often that it had failed to seem a strange thing to her. Eurie volunteered further information:

"We are going up to Annesley's Hall, to make arrangements for the tableau entertainment."

Now, it so happened that Dr. Dennis knew more about the tableau entertainment than Eurie did, and his few minutes of feeling that perhaps he had misjudged these girls departed at once; so did his genial manner.

"Indeed!" he said in the coldest tone imaginable and almost immediately dropped back with his daughter.

There was a gentleman hurrying down the walk, evidently for the purpose of overtaking him. At this moment he pronounced the doctor's name.

"Walk on, Grace, I will join you in a moment," the

girls heard Dr. Dennis say, and Grace stepped forward alone.

Marion glanced back. But a few weeks ago it would have been nothing to her that Grace Dennis or anyone else walked alone, so that she had no need for their company. But the law of unselfishness, which is the very essence of a true Christian life, was already beginning to work unconsciously in this girl's heart, and it made her turn now and say to Grace with winning voice:

"Have you lost your companion? Come and walk with us until you can have him again. Miss Mitchell, Miss Dennis."

It was a fact that, though Eurie was of the same church with Grace Dennis, and though she knew Grace by sight and bowed to her in the daytime, their familiarity with each other was not so sufficient as to ensure a gaslight recognition.

"We know each other," Grace said brightly, "at least we ought to. We do when we see each other plainly enough. I have been meaning to call with Papa, Miss Mitchell, but I haven't been able to, yet; I am only a schoolgirl, you know."

Eurie preferred to ignore the calling question; she had little sympathy with that phase of fashionable life; so she plunged at once into another subject.

"Are you going to the hall tonight, Miss Dennis, to help in getting up the tableau entertainment?"

Something in the quick way in which Grace Dennis said, "Oh no," made Marion anxious to question further.

"Why not?" she asked. "Miss Mitchell says they want all the ladies of talent; I'm sure you and I ought to be there. I can imagine you in a splendid tableau, Gracie; perhaps you would better go and help. To be sure, I haven't been really invited myself, but I guess I can get on somehow. Won't you go with us now?"

"I can't, Miss Wilbur. I should like to go; I enjoy tableaux ever so much; but Papa does not approve of making tableaux of Scripture scenes. You know, ministers have to be in advance on all these subjects."

Grace spoke in an apologetic tone, and with a flushed face, as one who had been obliged into saying a rude thing, and must make it sound as best she could.

"Are they to be Scripture scenes?" Eurie asked; and in the same breath added: "Why does he disapprove?"

"I don't think I could give his reasons. He thinks them irreverent, sometimes, I fancy; but I am not sure. I never heard him say very much on the subject; but I know quite well that he would not like me to go. Don't you know, Miss Mitchell, that clergymen always have to stand aloof from so many things, because they are set up as examples for others to follow?"

"But what is the use of it if others don't follow?" said quick-witted Eurie. "We must look into this question. I have never thought of it. It will have to be put down with that long list of subjects on which I have never had any thoughts; that list swells every day."

At this point Dr. Dennis somewhat decidedly summoned his daughter to his side, and it was after they had turned onto another street that the girls took the prayer meeting into consideration.

They were still talking of it when they reached the hall. Quite a company was assembled, including Eurie's brother, who was to meet her there, and Col. Baker, who had come for the purpose of meeting Flossy, much to her discomfiture. Mr. Holden and Leonard Brooks came over to the seat which they had taken, and the former was presented to the rest of the party.

"This is capital!" Nellis Mitchell said. "Holden, I congratulate you. I knew Flossy would help, and possibly Miss Wilbur; but I will confess to not even hoping for you, Miss Erskine."

"If your hopes are necessary to the completion of this scheme, I advise you not to raise them high so far as I am concerned, for they will have a grievous fall. I am the most indifferent of spectators." This from Ruth, in her most formal and haughty tone. Nellis Mitchell was not one of her favorites.

"Oh, you will help us, will you not?" Mr. Holden asked in a tone so familiar and friendly that Ruth flushed as she answered:

"Thank you, no."

Whereupon Mr. Holden discovered himself to be silenced.

"Never mind," Leonard Brooks said, "we have enough helpers promised to make the thing a grand success. Eurie, let me show you the picture of one which we have planned for you; the scenic effect is really very fine—Oriental, you know; and you will light up splendidly in that picture."

"Thank you," said Eurie, in an absentminded tone; and she had to be twice recalled from her thoughts before she turned to look at the plate spread before her. On the instant an angry flush arose, spreading itself over her face as she looked. "You do not mean that you are to present this?" she said at length.

"Why not?" asked Leonard, in astonishment. Mr. Holden hastened to explain:

"It is not often chosen for tableaux, I admit; but on that account is all the more desirable. We want to get away from the ordinary sort. This is magnificent in its working up. I had it in New York last winter, and it was one of the finest presented."

"It will not be presented with my help." Eurie's tone was so cold and haughty that Marion turned toward her in surprise, and for the first time glanced at the plate.

"Why, Miss Mitchell!" Mr. Holden exclaimed, "I am surprised and grieved if I have annoyed you by my selection. I was thinking how well you would light up an Oriental scene. Is it the representation of the Savior that you dislike? I cannot see why that should be objectionable. It is dealing with him as a mere man, you know. It is simply an Oriental dress of a male figure that we want to represent, and this figure of Christ as he sat at the well is so exceedingly minute and so carefully drawn that it works up finely."

"Christ at the well of Samaria!" read Flossy, now bending over the book, and her eyes and cheeks told the story of her aversion to the idea. "Who *would* be willing to personate the Savior?"

Mr. Holden was prompt with his answer:

"I have had not the slightest difficulty in that matter. My friend, Col. Baker here, expressed himself as entirely willing to undertake it. Why, my dear young ladies, you see it is nothing but the masculine form of dress that we want to bring out. There is really nothing more irreverent in it than there is in your looking at this picture here tonight."

"Then we will not look longer at the picture," Eurie said, drawing back suddenly, the color on her face deepening into crimson. "It is useless for you to undertake an argument with me. I will be very plain with you, and inform you that, aside from the irreverent nature of the tableau, I consider myself insulted in being chosen to make a public representation of that character. I am certainly absolved from my promise, Mr. Holden; and I beg you to withdraw my name from your list at once."

Mr. Holden turned the leaf on the offending picture. He was amazed and grieved; he had looked at the picture purely in an artistic light; he supposed all people looked thus at tableau pictures; it was certainly a compliment that he meant to pay, and not the shadow of a discourtesy; but since they looked at it in that singular manner, of course it should be withdrawn from the lists; nothing further should be said about it. Let him show them, just allow him to show them, one plate which was the very finest in scenic effect of anything that he had ever gotten up. The name of it was "The Ancient Feast."

Eurie turned hotly away, but Flossy and Ruth looked. It was a representation of Belshazzar at his impious feast, at the time when he was arrested by the handwriting on the wall. Ruth Erskine curled her handsome lip into something like a sneer.

"Does Col. Baker kindly propose to aid you in representing the hand of God?" she said in her haughtiest tones. "He is so willing to lend himself to the other piece of sacrilege that one can hardly expect him to shrink even from this."

Mr. Holden promptly closed his book.

"There is some mistake," he said, "I supposed the ladies and gentlemen gathered here came in for the purpose of helping, not for ridiculing. Of course if we differ so entirely on these topics we can be of very little help to each other."

"So I should judge," Marion said. "And, that being the case, shall we go?"

"What nonsense!" said Leonard Brooks, following after the retreating party but speaking only in a low tone and addressing Eurie. "One expects such lofty humbug from Miss Erskine, and even from Miss Wilbur—the tragic is in her line; but I thought you would enter into and enjoy the whole thing. I told Holden that you would be the backbone of the matter."

"Thank you," said Eurie, her voice half choked with indignation and wounded pride. "And I presume you assisted in the selection of the characters that I should personate! As I said, I consider myself insulted. Please allow me to pass."

Much excited, and some of them very much ashamed, they all found themselves on the street again, Nellis Mitchell being the only one of the astonished gentlemen who had bethought himself, or had had sufficient courage to join them.

"Well, what next?" he said.

"Nell," said Eurie, "what do you think of that?"

Nellis shrugged his shoulders.

"It is not according to my way of thinking," he said; "but they told me you had promised, and I thought if you had, with your eyes open, it was none of my business. I congratulate you on being fairly out of it. That Holden is a scamp, I believe."

"And Col. Baker was going to take that character," said Flossy to herself. And Eurie, in her heart, felt grieved and hurt that her friend of long standing, Leonard Brooks, could have said and done just what he had; he could never be to her as though he had not said and done those things. As for Marion, all she said was:

"I begin to have a clearer idea of what Grace Dennis and her father mean."

8

DR. DENNIS'S STUDY

THEY walked on in absolute silence for a few minutes, each busy with her own thoughts. Eurie was the first to speak:

"Girls, I propose we go and call on Dr. Dennis."

Ruth and Marion uttered exclamations of dismay, or it might have been of surprise. Flossy spoke:

"You don't mean *now?*"

"Now, this minute. We have an hour at our disposal, and we are all together. Why not, and have it over with? I tell you, that man is afraid of us! And when you come to think of it, why should he not be? What have we ever done to help his work; and how much we may have done to hinder it! I never realized how much, until this present moment. It enrages me to think how many enterprises, like this one, I have been engaged in without giving it a thought. Just imagine how such things must look to Dr. Dennis!"

"But, Eurie, you have never been mixed in with anything like that performance, as it is to be! What do you mean by admitting it?" It was Ruth who spoke, in some heat; the association rankled in her heart.

"Not precisely that sort of thing, I admit; but what must be the reputation I have earned, when I can be so coolly picked out for such work? I tell you, girls, I am angry. I suppose I ought to be grateful, for my eyes have certainly been opened to see a good many things that I never saw before; but it was a rough opening. Shall we go to the parsonage or not?"

"Oh, dear! I don't feel in the least like it," Flossy said timidly.

"Do you ever expect to *feel* like it?" Eurie asked, still speaking hotly. "For myself, I must say that I do. I am tired of my place; I want to be admitted, and belong somewhere. It is entirely evident to me that I don't belong where I did. I have discovered that a great many things about me are changed. I feel that I shall not assimilate well. Let me get in where I can have a chance. I want to belong to that Sunday school, for instance; to be recognized as a part of it, and to be counted in a place. So do you, Flossy, I am sure; why not settle the matter?"

Yes, Flossy certainly wanted to belong to that Sunday school; more than that, she wanted to belong to that class. Her heart had been with it all the week. If there was a hope that she might be permitted to try it for a while, she was willing even to call on Dr. Dennis, though that act looked awfully formidable to her.

"I suppose it is very silly not to want to go this evening, as well as any time," she admitted at last.

"Of course it is," Marion said energetically. "Let us turn this corner at once, and in two minutes more we shall have rung his bell; then that will settle the question. Nothing like going ahead and doing things without waiting to get into the mood."

"See here," said Nellis Mitchell, speaking for the first time. "Please to take into consideration what you propose to do with me? I take it that you don't want me to make this call with you. My sister has been remarkably bewildering in her remarks, but I gather that it is something like a confidential talk that you are seeking with the doctor, into which I am not to be admitted."

"I forgot that you were along," said Eurie with her usual frankness. "No, Nell, we don't want you to call with us; not this time."

"I might ask for a separate room, and make my call on Miss Grace. At least I might try it; but I doubt her father's permitting such a tremendous action. So, really, I don't see quite what you are to do with me. I am entirely at your disposal."

"See here, Nell, couldn't you call for us, in half an hour, say? Girls, *could* we stay half an hour, do you suppose? We shall have to do something of the kind; it won't do for us to go home alone. I see what we can do, Nell. You go to Father's office, and wait just a little while; if we are not there in half an hour, you can call for us at Dr. Dennis's; and if we find we are not equal to a call of that length, we will come to the office; will that do?"

The obliging brother made a low bow of mock ceremony, assured her that he was entirely at her service, that she might command him and he would serve to the best of his knowledge and ability, made a careful minute of the present time, in order to be exact at the half hour, and as they laughingly declined his offer to ring the doctor's bell for them, he lifted his hat to them with the lowest of bows, and disappeared around the corner.

"He is such a dear fellow!" said Eurie, looking fondly after him.

"I don't see in what respect," muttered Ruth in an

aside to Flossy. Ruth had a special aversion to this young man; possibly it might have been because he treated her with the most good-humored indifference, despite all her dignity and coldness.

Meantime, in Dr. Dennis's study, his daughter was hovering around among the books, trying to bring order out of confusion on the shelves and table, and at the same time find a favorite volume she was reading. The doctor turned on a brighter flame of gas, then lowered it, and seemed in a disturbed state of mind. At last he spoke:

"I don't know that my caution is needed, daughter—I have no reason to think that it is, from anything in your conduct at least; but I feel like saying to you that I have less and less liking for those young ladies, who seem, since their unfortunate freak of attending that Chautauqua meeting, to have banded themselves together. I can hardly imagine why; they are certainly unlike enough. But I distrust them in almost every way. I am sorry that you are at school under Miss Wilbur's influence; not that I dread her influence on you, except in a general way."

At this point Grace opened her bright lips to speak; there was an eager sentence glowing on her tongue, but her father had not finished his:

"I know all that you can say; that you have nothing to do with her religious or nonreligious views, and that she is a splendid teacher. I don't doubt it; but I repeat to you that I distrust all of them. I don't know why they have seen fit to come to our Sabbath school and to our meeting this evening, unless it be to gain an unhappy influence over some whom they desire to lead astray. I can hardly think so meanly of them as that, either. I do not say that such was their motive, but simply that I do not understand it, and am afraid of it;

and I desire you to have just as little to do with any of them as ordinary civility will admit. Hitherto I have thought of Ruth Erskine as simply a leader of fashion and of Flossy Shipley as the tool of the fashionable world; but I am afraid their dangerous friends are leading them to be more. The tableau affair, tonight, I have investigated to a certain degree, and I consider it one of the worst of its kind. I would not have you associated with it for—well, any consideration that I can imagine; and yet, if I mistake not, I heard them urging you to join them."

Again Grace essayed to speak, but the pealing of the doorbell interrupted her.

"Who is it, Hannah?" Dr. Dennis questioned, as that personage peeped her head in at the door.

"It is four young ladies, Dr. Dennis, and they want to see you."

Grace arose to depart.

"Do you know any of them, Hannah?" the doctor asked.

"Well, sir, one of them is the Miss Wilbur who teaches, and I think another is Dr. Mitchell's daughter. I don't know the others."

"Show them in here," said Dr. Dennis promptly. "And, Daughter, you will please remain. They have doubtless come to petition me for your assistance in the tableaux, and I have not the least desire to be considered a household tyrant or to have them suppose that you are my prisoner. I would much rather that you should give them your own opinions on the subject like a brave little woman."

"But Father," Grace said, and there was a gleam of mischief in her eye, "I haven't any opinions on this subject. The most that I can say is that you don't wish me to have anything to do with them; and so, like a dutiful daughter, I decline."

"Well, then," he said, smiling back on her in a satisfied way, "show them how gracefully you can play the part of a dutiful daughter. While you are so young, and while I am here to have opinions for you, the dutiful part cheerfully done is really all that is necessary."

And this was the introduction that the four girls had to the pastor's study. How shy they felt! Ruth could hardly ever remember of feeling so very much embarrassed. As for Eurie, she began to feel that distressing sense of the ludicrous creeping over her, and so was horribly afraid that she should laugh. Marion went forward to Grace, and in the warm, glad greeting that this young girl gave, felt her heart melted and warmed.

Dr. Dennis, confident in the errand that had brought them, decided to lead the conversation himself, and give them no chance to approach the topic smoothly.

"Have you done up the tableaux so promptly?" he asked. And while he addressed his question to Marion, Eurie felt that he *looked* right at her.

Marion's answer was prompt and to the point.

"Yes, sir, we have. Miss Mitchell was the only one of us who was pledged; and I believe she was entirely dissatisfied with the character of the entertainment and withdrew her support."

"Indeed!" Dr. Dennis's manner of pronouncing this word was, in effect, saying, "Is it possible that there can be an entertainment of so questionable a character that Miss Mitchell will withdraw from it?"

At least that was the way the word sounded to Eurie, but she had been roused to unusual sensitiveness. The effect was to rouse her still further, to put to flight every trace of embarrassment and every desire to laugh. She spoke in a clear, strong voice:

"Dr. Dennis, we shall be talking at cross purposes if we do not make some explanation of our object in calling this evening. We feel that we do not belong in the society where you are classing us; in fact, we do not belong anywhere. Our views and feelings have greatly changed within a short time. We want to make a corresponding change in our associations; at least, so far as is desirable. Our special object in calling just now is that we know it will soon be time for the communion in your church, and we have thought that perhaps we ought to make a public profession of our changed views."

Was ever a man more bent on misunderstanding plain English than was Dr. Dennis this evening? He looked at his callers in an astonished and embarrassed way for a moment, as if uncertain whether to consider them lunatics or not; and then said, addressing himself to Eurie:

"My dear young lady, I fear you are laboring under a mistake as to the object in uniting with the Church of Christ, and the preparation necessary. You know, as a church, we hold that something more than a desire to change one's social relations should actuate the person to take such a step; that, indeed, there should be a radical change of heart."

Poor Eurie! She thought she had been *so* plain in her explanation. She flushed and commenced a stammering sentence; then paused, and looked appealingly at Ruth and Marion.

Finally she did what, for Eurie Mitchell to do, was unprecedented, lost all self-control, and broke into a sudden and passionate gust of tears.

"Eurie, don't!" Marion said; to her it was actual pain to see tears. As for Dr. Dennis, he was very much at his wits' end, and Ruth's embarrassment grew upon her every moment. Flossy came to the rescue.

"Dr. Dennis," she said, and he noticed even then that her voice was strangely sweet and winning, "Eurie means that we love Jesus, and we believe he has forgiven us and called us by name. We mean we want to be his and to serve him forever; and we want to acknowledge him publicly, because we think he has so directed."

How simple and sweet the story was, after all, when one just gave up attempting to be proper and gave the quiet truth. Ruth was struck with the simplicity and the directness of the words; she began to have not only an admiration but an unfeigned respect for Flossy Shipley. But you should have seen Dr. Dennis's face. It is a pity Eurie could not have seen it at that moment; if she had not had hers buried in the sofa pillow, she would have caught the quick glad look of surprise and joy and heartfelt thankfulness that spoke in his eyes. He arose suddenly and, holding out his hand to Flossy, said:

"Let me greet you and thank you and ask you to forgive me, in the same breath. I have been very slow to understand and strangely stupid and unsympathetic. I feel very much as I fancy poor doubting Thomas must have done. Forgive me; I am so astonished and so glad that I don't know how to express the feeling. Do you speak for all your friends here, Miss Flossy? And may I ask something about the wonderful experience that has drawn you all into the ark?"

But Flossy's courage had forsaken her; it was born of sympathy with Eurie's tears. She looked down now, tearful herself, and trembling like a leaf. Ruth found voice to answer for her.

"Our experience, Dr. Dennis, can be summed up in one word—Chautauqua."

Dr. Dennis gave a little start; another astonishment.

"Do you mean that you were converted during that meeting?"

Marion smiled.

"We do not know enough about terms to really be sure that that is the right one to use," she said; "at least, I do not. But we do know this, that we met the Lord Jesus there, and that, as Flossy says, we love him and have given our lives into his keeping."

"You cannot say more than that after a hundred years of experience," he said quickly. "Well, dear friends, I cannot, as I said, express to you my gratitude and joy. And you are coming into the church and are ready to take up work for the Master, and live for him? Thank the Lord."

Little need had our girls to talk of Dr. Dennis's coldness and dignity after that. How entirely his heart had melted! What a blessed talk they had! So many questions about Chautauqua, so much to tell that delighted him. They had not the least idea that it was possible to feel so much at ease with a minister as they grew to feel with him.

The bell rang and was answered, and yet no one intruded on their quiet, and the talk went on, until Marion, with a sudden recollection of Nellis Mitchell, and their appointment with him, stole a glance at her watch and was astonished into the announcement:

"Girls, we have been here an hour and a quarter!"

"Is it possible!" Ruth said, rising at once. "Father will be alarmed, I am afraid."

Dr. Dennis rose also.

"I did not know I was keeping you so," he said. "Our theme was a fascinating one. Will you wait a moment and let me make ready to see you safely home?"

But it appeared, on opening the door, that Nellis Mitchell occupied an easy chair in the parlor, just across the hall.

"I'm a patient young man, and at your service," he said, coming toward them as they emerged. "Please give me credit for promptness. I was here at the half hour."

As they walked home, Nellis, with his sister on one arm and Flossy Shipley on the other, said:

"Now, what am I to understand by this sudden and violent intimacy at the parsonage? Miss Flossy, my sister has hitherto made yearly calls of two seconds' duration on the doctor's sister when she is not home to receive them."

"A great many things are to be different from what they have hitherto been," Flossy said with a soft, little laugh.

"So I begin to perceive."

"Nell," said Eurie, turning back when she was halfway up the stairs, having said good night, "are you going to help them with those tableaux?"

"Not much," said Nellis.

And Eurie, as she went on, said:

"I shouldn't be surprised if Nell felt differently about some things from what he used to. Oh, I wonder if I can't coax him in?"

9

A WHITE SUNDAY

AMONG other topics that were discussed with great interest during that call at Dr. Dennis's was the Sunday school, and the place that our girls were to take in it. Flossy was not likely to forget that matter. Her heart was too full of plans concerning "those boys."

Early in the talk she overwhelmed and embarrassed Dr. Dennis with the request that she might be allowed to try that class. Now if it had been Ruth or Marion who had made the same request, it would have been unhesitatingly granted. The doctor had a high opinion of the intellectual abilities of both these young ladies, and now that they had appeared to consecrate those abilities, he was willing to receive them.

But this little summer butterfly with her small sweet ways and winning smile! He had no more idea that she could teach than that a hummingbird could; and of all classes in the school, to expect to do anything with those large, wild boys! It was preposterous.

"My dear friend," he said, and he could hardly keep from smiling, even though he was embarrassed, "you have no idea what you are asking! That is altogether the most difficult class in the school. Some of our best teachers have failed there. The fact is, those boys don't *want* to be instructed; they are in search of fun. They are a hard set, I am really afraid. I wouldn't have you tried and discouraged by them. We are at a loss what to do with them, I will admit; for no one who can do it seems willing to try them. In fact, I am not sure that we have anyone who *can*. I understand your motive, Miss Flossy, and appreciate your zeal; but you must not crush yourself in that way. Since you have been out of the Sunday school for so many years, and, I presume, have not made the Bible a study—unhappily, it is not used as a textbook in many of our schools—would it not be well for you to join some excellent Bible class for a while? I think you would like it better and grow faster, and we really have some superior teachers among the Bible classes."

And while he said this, the wise doctor hoped in his heart that she would not be offended with his plain speaking, and that some good angel would suggest to Marion Wilbur the propriety of trying that class of boys.

Flossy was not offended, though Marion Wilbur, spoken to in the same way, would have been certain to have felt it. Little Flossy, though sorely disappointed, so much so that she could hardly keep the tears from rising, admitted that she did not know how to teach, and that, of course, she ought to study the Bible and would like ever so much to do so.

It so happened that the other girls were more than willing to be enrolled as pupils; indeed, had not an idea of taking any other position. So, after a little more talk, it was decided that they all join Dr. Dennis's class, every one of them expressing a prompt preference for that class above the others. In his heart Dr. Dennis entirely approved of this arrangement, for he wanted the training of Flossy and Eurie, and he meant to make teachers of the other two as soon as possible.

Now it came to pass that an unlooked-for element came into all this planning—none other than the boys themselves. They had ideas of their own, and they belonged to that part of the world which is hard to govern. They would have Miss Flossy Shipley to be their teacher, and they would have no one else; she suited them exactly, and no one else did.

"But, my dear boys," Dr. Dennis said, "Miss Shipley is new to the work of teaching; she is but a learner herself; she feels that her place is in the Bible class, so that she may acquire the best ways of presenting lessons."

"Did she say she wouldn't teach us?" queried Rich Johnson with his keen eyes fixed on the doctor's face.

What could that embarrassed but truthful man do but slowly shake his head, and say hesitatingly:

"No, she didn't say that; but I advised her to join a Bible class for a while."

"Then we want her," Rich said stoutly. "Don't we, boys? She just suits us, Dr. Dennis; and she is the first one we ever had that we cared a snap for. We had just about made up our minds to quit it; but, on the whole, if we can have her, we will give it another trial."

This strange sentence was uttered in a most matter-of-fact business way, and the perplexed doctor, quite unused to dealing with that class of brain and manners, was compelled to beat a retreat and come to Flossy with his novel report. A gleam of satisfaction, not to say triumph, lit up her pretty face, and, aglow with smiles and blushes, she made her way with alacrity to her chosen class. Teacher and scholars thoroughly suited to each other; surely they could do some work during that hour that would tell on the future. Meantime, the superintendent was having his perplexities over in another corner of the room. He came to Dr. Dennis at last for advice.

"Miss Hart is absent today; her class is almost impossible to supply; no one is willing to try the little midgets."

"Miss Hart," Dr. Dennis repeated thoughtfully; "the primary class, eh? It is hard to manage; and yet, with all the subteachers present, one would think it might be done."

"They are not all present," Mr. Stuart said. "They never are."

Dr. Dennis ignored this remark.

"I'll tell you what to do," he said with a sudden lighting up of his thoughtful face. "Get Miss Wilbur to go in there; she is equal to the emergency, or I am much mistaken."

Mr. Stuart started in unqualified astonishment.

"I thought," he said, recovering his voice, "that you seriously objected to her as a teacher in Sabbath school?"

"I have changed my mind," Dr. Dennis said with a happy smile, "or, the Lord has changed her heart. Ask her to take the class."

So two of our girls found work.

Another thing occurred to make that Sabbath a memorable one. The evening was especially lovely, and, there happening to be no other attraction, a much larger number than usual of the First Church people got out to the second service. Our girls were all present, and, what was unusual, other representatives from their families were with them.

Also, Col. Baker had obliged himself to endure the

infliction of another sermon from Dr. Dennis, in order that he might have the pleasure of a walk home in the glorious moonlight with Miss Flossy.

The sermon was one of special solemnity and power. The pastor's recent communion with newborn souls had quickened his own heart and increased the longing desire for the coming of the Spirit of God into their midst. At the sermon's close, he took what, for the First Church, was a very wide and startling departure from the beaten track. After a tender personal appeal, especially addressed to the young people of his flock, he said:

"Now, impelled by what I cannot but feel is the voice of the Lord Jesus, by his Spirit, I want to ask if there are any present who feel so much of a desire to be numbered with the Lord's friends that they are willing to ask us to pray for them, to the end that they may be found of him. Is there one in this audience who, by rising and standing for but a moment, will thus simply and quietly indicate to us such a desire and willingness?"

Who ever heard of the First Church pastor doing so strange a thing? His people had voted for festivals and concerts and lectures and picnics and entertainments of all sorts and shades. They had taken rising votes, and they had voted by raising the hand; they had made speeches, many of them, on the questions to be presented; they had added their voice to the pastor's explanations; they had urged the wisdom and the propriety of the question presented; they had said they earnestly hoped the matter would meet careful attention; and no one in the church had thought such proceedings strange. But to ask people to rise in their seats, and thus signify that they were thinking of the question of eternal life and home and peace and unutterable blessedness—what innovation was this?

Much rustling and coughing took place; then solemn silence prevailed. Not a deacon there, or officer of any sort, had the least idea of audibly hoping that the pastor's words would receive thoughtful attention; not a person arose; the silence was felt to be embarrassing and oppressive to the last degree.

Dr. Dennis relieved them at last by reading the closing hymn. During the reading, when startled thoughts became sufficiently composed to flow in their accustomed channels, many, almost unconsciously to themselves, prepared speeches which they meant to utter the moment their lips were unsealed by the pronouncing of the benediction.

"A very strange thing to do."

"What could Dr. Dennis be thinking of?"

"A most unwise effort to force the private lives of people before the public."

"An unfortunate attempt to get up an excitement."

"Well meant, but most ill-timed and mistaken zeal, which would have a reaction that would do harm."

These and a dozen other mental comments that roved through people's brains, while they were supposed to be joining in the hymn of praise, were suddenly cut short by the sound of Dr. Dennis's voice again—not in benediction, as surely they had a right to expect by this time, but with another appeal.

"I am still of the impression that there are those present who are doing violence to their convictions of right and to good judgment by not responding to my invitation. Let us remember to pray for all such. Now, I want to ask if there are any in this congregation who have lately proved the truth of the doctrine that there is a Savior from sin, and a peace that the world cannot give. If there are those present who have decided this question recently, will they rise for a moment, thus testifying to the truth of the words which have been spoken this evening, and thus witnessing that they have chosen the Lord Jesus for their portion?"

Another sensation! Dr. Dennis must have taken leave of his senses! This was more embarrassing than the last. The wise ones were sure that there had been no conversions in a long time. So far as they knew and believed, entirely other thoughts were occupying the minds of the people.

Then, into the midst of this commotion of thought, there stole that solemn hush, almost of heartbeatings, which betokens a new revelation that astonishes and thrills and solemnizes.

There were persons standing. Ladies! One—two—three. Yes, one in the gallery. There were four of them! Who were they? Why, that little, volatile Flossy Shipley was one! How strange! And that girl in the gallery was the teacher at one of the ward schools. It had been rumored that she was an infidel!

Who in the world was that beside Judge Erskine? It couldn't be his daughter! Yet it certainly was. And behold, in the doctor's pew stood Eurie, the young lady who was so free and careless in her manners and address that, were it not for the fact that she was the doctor's daughter, her very respectability would have stood a chance of being questioned!

As it was, there were mothers in the church who were quite willing that their daughters should have as little to do with her as possible. Yet, tonight their daughters sat beside them, unable to rise in any way to testify to the truth of the religion of Jesus Christ; and Eurie Mitchell, with grave, earnest face, in which decision and determination were plainly written, stood up to testify that the Lord was true to his promises.

Gradually there dawned upon the minds of many who knew these girls the remembrance that they had been together to that great Sunday school meeting at Chautauqua. How foolish the scheme had seemed to them when they heard of it; how sneeringly they had commented on the absurdity of such supposed representatives from the Sunday school world.

Surely this seeming folly had been the power of God and the wisdom of God. There were those in the First Church, as, indeed, there are many in every church of Christ, who rejoiced with all their souls at the sound of this good news.

There was another thing that occurred that night over which the angels, at least, rejoiced. There was another witness. He was only a poor young fellow, a day laborer in one of the machine shops, a newcomer to the city. He knew almost nobody in that great church where he had chanced to be a worshiper, and, literally, no one knew him.

When the invitation was first given, he had shrunken from it. Satan, with ever-ready skill, and with that consummate wisdom which makes him as eager after the common day laborers as he is among the wealthy and influential, had whispered to him that the pastor did not mean such as he; no one knew him, his influence would be nothing. This church was too large and too grand, and it was not meant that he should make himself so conspicuous as to stand alone in that great audience room and testify that the Lord Jesus had called him.

So he sat still; but as one and another of those young ladies arose quietly with true dignity and sweet composure testifying to their love for the Lord, John Warden's earnest soul was moved to shame at his own shrinking, and from his obscure seat, back under the gallery, he rose up, and Satan, foiled that time, shrunk away.

As for our girls, they held no parley with their consciences, or with the tempter; they did not even think of it. On the contrary, they were glad, every one, that the way was made so plain and so easy to them. Each of them had friends whom they especially desired to have know of the recent and great change that had come to their lives. With some of these friends they shrank unaccountably from talking about this matter. With others of them they did not understand how to make the matter plain.

But here it was explained for them, so plainly, so simply, that it seemed that everyone must understand, and their own future determination as to life was carefully explained for them. There was nothing to do but to rise up and, by that simple act, subscribe their names to the explanation—so making it theirs.

I declare to you that the thought of its being a cross to do so did not once occur to them. Neither did the thought that they were occupying a conspicuous position affect them. They were used to conspicuous positions; they had been twice as prominent in that very church when other subjects than religion had been under consideration.

At a certain festival, years before, they had every one taken part in a musical entertainment that brought them most conspicuously before an audience three times the size of the evening congregation. So you see they were used to it.

And, as for the fancy that it becomes a more conspicuous and unladylike matter to stand up for the

Lord Jesus Christ than it does to stand up for anything else under the sun. Satan was much too wise and knew his material entirely too well to suggest any such absurdity to them.

Flossy had been the only one of their number in the least likely to be swayed by such arguments. But Flossy had set herself with earnest soul and solemn purpose to follow the light wherever it should shine, without allowing her timid heart time for questioning, and the father of all evil finds such people exceedingly hard to manage.

"How do you do," said Dr. Dennis to John Warden two minutes after the benediction was fully pronounced. "I was very glad to see you tonight. I am not sure that I have ever met you? No? I thought so; a stranger? Well, we welcome you. Where do you board?"

And a certain black book came promptly out of the doctor's pocket. John Warden's name and street and number and business were written therein, and John Warden felt for the first time in his life as though he had a Christian brother in that great city, and a name and a place with the people of God.

Another surprise awaited him. Marion and Eurie were right behind him. Marion came up boldly and held out her hand:

"We seem to have started on the road together," she said. "We ought to shake hands and wish each other a safe journey."

Then she and Eurie and John Warden shook each other heartily by the hand; and Flossy, standing watching, led by this bolder spirit into that which would not have occurred to her to do, slipped from her place beside Col. Baker and, holding her lavender-kidded little hand out to his broad brown palm, said with a grace and a sweetness that belonged to neither of the others: "I am one of them." Whereupon John Warden was not sure that he had not shaken hands with an angel.

10

THE RAINY EVENING

A COOL, rainy evening, one of those sudden and sharp reminders of autumn, came to us in the midst of summer. The heavy clouds had made the day shut down early, and the rain was so persistent that it was useless to plan walks or rides, or entertainments of that nature. Also it was an evening when none but those who are habitual callers at special homes are expected.

One of these was Col. Baker. The idea of being detained by rain from spending the evening with Flossy Shipley did not occur to him; on the contrary, he rejoiced over the prospect of a long and uninterrupted talk. The more indifferent Flossy grew to these long talks, the more eager was Col. Baker to enjoy them. The further she slipped away from him, the more eagerly he followed after. Perhaps that is human nature; at least it was Col. Baker's nature.

In some of his plans he was disappointed. Mrs. Shipley was gone for a three-days' visit to a neighboring city, and Flossy was snugly settled in the back parlor, entertaining her father.

"Show him right in here," directed her father, as

soon as Col. Baker was announced. Then to Flossy: "Now we can have a game at cards as soon as Charlie comes in. Where is he?"

Rainy evenings, when four people could be secured sufficiently disengaged to join in his favorite amusement, were the special delight of Mr. Shipley. So behold them, half an hour after, deep in a game of cards, Col. Baker accepting the situation with as good a grace as he could assume, notwithstanding the fact that playing cards, simply for amusement, in that quiet way in a back parlor, was a good deal of a bore to him; but it would be bad policy to tell Mr. Shipley so. Their game was interrupted by a ring of the doorbell.

"Oh, dear!" said Mr. Shipley, "I hope that is no nuisance on business. One would think nothing but business would call people out on such a disagreeable night."

"As, for instance, myself," Col. Baker said laughingly.

"Oh, you. Of course, special friends are an exception."

And Col. Baker was well pleased to be ranked among the exceptions. Meantime, the ringer was heralded.

"It is Dr. Dennis, sir. Shall I show him in here?"

"I suppose so," Mr. Shipley said gloomily, as one not well pleased; and he added, in undertone, "What on earth can the man want?"

Meantime, Col. Baker, with a sudden dexterous move, unceremoniously swept the whole pack of cards out of sight under a paper by his side.

It so happened that Dr. Dennis's call was purely one of business; some item connected with the financial portion of the church, which Dr. Dennis desired to report in a special sermon that was being prepared.

Mr. Shipley, although he was so rarely an attendant at church and made no secret of his indifference to the whole subject of personal religion, was yet a power in the financial world, and, as such, recognized and deferred to by the First Church.

Dr. Dennis was in haste, and beyond a specially cordial greeting for Flossy and an expression of satisfaction at her success with the class the previous Sabbath, he had no more to say, and Mr. Shipley soon had the pleasure of bowing him out, rejoicing in his heart as he did so that the clergyman was so prompt a man.

"He would have made a capital businessman," he said, returning to his seat. "I never come in contact with him that I don't notice a sort of executive ability about him that makes me think what a success he might have been."

There was no one to ask whether that remark meant that he was at present supposed to be a failure. There was another subject which presently engrossed several of them.

"Now be so kind as to give an account of yourself," Charlie Shipley said, addressing Col. Baker. "What on earth did you mean by making a muddle of our game in that way? I was in a fair way for winning. I suppose you won't own that that was your object."

Col. Baker laughed.

"My object was a purely benevolent one. I had a desire to shield your sister from the woebegone lecture she would have been sure to receive on the sinfulness of her course. If he had found her playing cards, what would have been the result?"

Mr. Shipley was the first to make answer, in a somewhat testy tone:

"Your generosity was uncalled for, Colonel. My

daughter, when she is in her father's house, is answerable to him, and not to Dr. Dennis or any other divine."

"I don't in the least understand what you are talking about," said mystified Flossy. "Of what interest could it have been to Dr. Dennis what I am doing; and why should he have delivered a lecture?"

Col. Baker and Charlie Shipley exchanged amused glances, and the former quoted, significantly:

"Where ignorance is bliss, 'tis folly to be wise." Then he added, as Flossy still waited with questioning gaze: "Why, Miss Flossy, of course you know that the clergy think cards are synonyms for the deadly sin, and that to hold one in one's hand is equivalent to being poisoned, body and soul?"

"I am sure I did not know it. Why, I knew, of course, that gambling houses were not proper; but what is the harm in a game of cards? What can Dr. Dennis see, for instance, in our playing together here in this room, and simply for amusement?"

Col. Baker shrugged his handsome shoulders. That shrug meant a great deal, accomplished a great deal. It was nearly certain to silence a timid oppose; there was something so expressively sarcastic about it; it hid so much one felt sure Col. Baker *might say* if he deemed it prudent or worthwhile. It had often silenced Flossy into a conscious little laugh. Tonight she was in earnest; she paid no attention to the shrug, but waited, questioningly, for her answer, and as it was her turn to play next, it seemed necessary to answer her if one wanted the game to go on.

"I am sure I don't know," Col. Baker said at last. "I have very little idea what he would consider the harm; I am not sure that *he* would be able to tell. It is probably a narrow, straitlaced way that the cloth have of looking at this question, in common with all other questions, save prayer meetings and almsgiving. Their lives are very much narrowed down, Miss Flossy."

Flossy was entirely unsatisfied. She had a higher opinion of Dr. Dennis's "breadth" than she had of Col. Baker's; she thought his life had a very much higher range; she was very much puzzled and annoyed. Her father came into the conflict:

"Come, come, Flossy, how long are you going to keep us waiting? It is of no particular consequence what Dr. Dennis thinks or does not think. He has a right to his own opinions. It is a free country."

Ah, but it did make a tremendous difference to Flossy. She had accepted Dr. Dennis as her pastor; she had determined to look to him for help and guidance in this new and strange path on which her feet had so lately entered.

She wondered if Col. Baker could be right. Was it possible that Dr. Dennis disapproved of cards played at home in this quiet way! If he did, why did he? And, another puzzling point, how did Col. Baker know it? They two certainly did not come in contact that they should understand each other's ideas.

She went on with her cardplaying, but she played very badly. More than once Col. Baker called her with good-humored sarcasm, and her father spoke impatiently. Flossy's interest in the game was gone; instead, her heart was busy with this new idea. She went back to it again in one of her pauses in the game.

"Col. Baker, don't you really know at all what arguments clergymen have against cardplaying for amusement?"

Again that expressive shrug; but it had lost its power over Flossy, and its owner saw it and made haste to answer her waiting eyes.

"I really am not familiar with their weapons of warfare; probably I could not appreciate them if I were; I only know that the entire class frowns upon all such innocent devices for passing a rainy evening. But it never struck me as strange, because the fact is, they frown equally on all pastimes and entertainments of any sort; that is, a certain class do—fanatics, I believe, is the name they are known by. They believe, as nearly as I am capable of understanding their belief, that life should be spent in psalm singing and praying."

Whereupon Flossy called to mind the witty things she had heard, and the merry laughs which had rung around her at Chautauqua, given by the most intense of these fanatics; she even remembered that she had seen two of the most celebrated in that direction playing with a party of young men and boys on the croquet ground, and laughing most uproariously over their defeat. It was all nonsense to try to compass her brain with such an argument as that; she shook her head resolutely.

"They do no such thing; I know some of them very well; I don't know of any people who have nicer times. How do you know these things, Col. Baker?"

Col. Baker essayed to be serious:

"Miss Flossy," he said, leaning over and fixing his handsome eyes impressively on her face, "is it possible you do not know that, as a rule, clergymen set their faces like a flint against all amusements of every sort? I do not mean that there are not exceptions, but I do mean most assuredly that Dr. Dennis is not one of them. He is as rigid as it is possible for mortal man to be.

"Herein is where the church does harm. In my own opinion, it is to blame for the most, if not for all, of the excesses of the day; they are the natural rebound of nerves that have been strained too tightly by the over-tension of the church."

Surely this was a fine sentence. The Flossy of a few weeks ago would have admired the smooth-sounding words and the exquisitely modulated voice as it rolled them forth. How had the present Flossy been quickened as to her sense of the fitness of things. She laughed mischievously. She couldn't argue; she did not attempt it. All she said was, simply:

"Col. Baker, on your honor, as a gentleman of truth and veracity, do you think the excesses of which you speak occur, as a rule, in those whose lives have been very tightly bound by the church, or by anything else, save their own reckless fancies?"

Charlie Shipley laughed outright at this point. He always enjoyed a sharp thing wherever heard, and without regard to whether he felt himself thrust at or not.

"Baker, you are getting the worst of it," he said gayly. "Sis, upon my word, that two weeks in the woods has made you real keen in argument; but you play abominably."

"There is no pleasure in the game now!" This the father said, throwing down his cards somewhat hastily. "Flossy, I hope you will not get to be a girl of one idea—tied to the professional conscience. What is proper for you could hardly be expected to be just the thing for Dr. Dennis; and you have nothing to do, as I said before, with what he approves or disapproves."

"But, Father," Flossy said, speaking somewhat timidly, as she could not help doing when she talked about these matters to her father, "if we call clergymen our spiritual guides and look up to them to set examples for us to follow, what is the use of the example if we don't follow it at all but conclude they are simply doing things for their own benefit?"

"I never call them my spiritual guides, and I have not the least desire to have my daughter do so. I consider myself capable of guiding my own family, especially my own children, without any help."

This was said in Mr. Shipley's stiffest tone. He was evidently very much tried with this interruption to his evening's entertainment. Whatever might be said of the others, he was certainly very fond of cards. He, however, threw down the remaining ones, declaring that the spirit of the game was gone.

"Merged into a theological discussion," Charlie said with a half laugh, half sneer; "and of all the people to indulge in one, this particular circle would be supposed to be the last."

"Well, I am certainly very sorry that I was the innocent cause of such an upheaval," Col. Baker said in the half-serious, half-mocking tone that was becoming especially trying to Flossy. "It seems that I unwittingly burst a bombshell when I overturned those cards. I hadn't an idea of it. Miss Flossy, what can I do to atone for making you so uneasy? I assure you it was really pure benevolence on my part. What can I do to prove it?"

"Nothing," Flossy said, smiling pleasantly. She was very much obliged. He had awakened thought about a matter that had never before occurred to her. She began to think there were a good many things in her life that had not been given very much thought. She meant to look into this thing, and understand it if she could. Indeed, that was what she wanted of all things to do.

Nothing could be simpler and sweeter, and nothing

could be more unlike the Flossy of Col. Baker's former acquaintance.

"I shouldn't wonder a bit if you had roused a hornet's nest about your ears," Charlie Shipley said to his friend. "Now I tell you, you may not believe it, but my little sister is just exactly the stuff out of which they made martyrs in those unenlightened days when anybody thought there was enough truth in anything to take the trouble to suffer for it. She can be made by skillful handling into a very queen of martyrs, and if you fall in the ruins, it will be your own fault."

But he did not say this until Flossy had suddenly and unceremoniously excused herself, and the two gentlemen were alone over their cigars.

"Confound that Chautauqua scheme!" Col. Baker said, kicking an innocent hassock half across the room with his indignant foot. "That is where all these new ideas started. I wish there was a law against fanaticism. Those young women of strong mind and disagreeable manners are getting a most uncomfortable influence over her, too. If I were you, Charlie, I would try to put an end to that intimacy."

Charlie whistled softly.

"Which do you mean?" he asked at last. "The Erskine girl, or the Wilbur one? I tell you, Baker, with all the years of your acquaintance, you don't know that little Flossy as well as you think you do. Let me tell you, my man, there is something about her, or in her, that is capable of development, and that is being developed (or I am mistaken), that will make her the leader, in a quiet way, of a dozen decided and outspoken girls like those two, and of several men like yourself besides, if she chooses to lead you."

"Well, confound the development then! I liked her better as she was before."

"More congenial, I admit; at least I should think so; but not half so interesting to watch. I have real good times now. I am continually wondering what she will do next."

11

━━ ◆ ━━

THE NEXT THING

WHAT she did next that night was to sit with her elbows in her lap and her chin resting on her hands and stare into vacancy for half an hour. She was very much bewildered. Col. Baker had awakened a train of thought that would never slumber again. He need not hope for such a thing. Her brother Charlie saw deeper into her nature than she did herself. She was tenacious of an idea; she had grasped at this one, which, of itself, would perhaps never have occurred to her.

Hitherto she had played at cards as she had played on the piano or worked at her worsted cats and dogs or frittered away an evening in the smallest of small talk or done a hundred other things, without thought of results, without so much as realizing that there were such things as results connected with such trifling commonplaces.

At least, so far as the matter of cards was concerned, she would never do so again. Her quiet had been disturbed. The process of reasoning by which she found herself disturbed was very simple. She had discovered, as if by accident, that her pastor—as she loved to call Dr. Dennis, lingering on the word, now that it had such a new meaning for her—disapproved of cardplaying, not only for himself but for her; at least that Col. Baker so supposed.

Now there must be some foundation for this belief of his. Either there was something in the nature of the game which Col. Baker recognized, and which she did not, that made him understand, as by instinct, that it would be disapproved by Dr. Dennis, or else he had heard him so express himself, or else he was totally mistaken and was misrepresenting that gentleman's character.

She thought all this over as she sat staring into space, and she went one step further—she meant to discover which of these three statements were correct. If Dr. Dennis thought it wrong to play cards, then he must have reasons for so thinking. She accepted that at once as a necessity to the man. They must also have been carefully weighed reasons, else he would not have given them a place in his creed. This also was a necessity to a nature like his.

Clearly there was something here for her to study; but how to set about it? Over this she puzzled a good deal; she did not like to go directly to Dr. Dennis and ask for herself; she did not know how to set to work to discover for herself the truth; she could pray for light, that to be sure; but having brought her common sense with her into religious matters, she no more expected light to blaze upon her at the moment of praying for it than she expected the sun to burst into the room despite the closing of blinds and dropping of curtain, merely because she prayed that it might shine.

Clearly, if she wanted the sun, it was her part to open the blinds and draw back curtains; clearly, if she wanted mental light, it was her part to use the means that God had placed at her disposal. This much she realized. But not being a self-reliant girl, it resulted in her saying to Eurie Mitchell when she slipped in the next evening to spend an hour:

"I wish we girls could get together somewhere this evening; I have something to talk over that puzzles me a great deal."

You are to understand that the expression "we girls" meant the four who had lived Chautauqua together; from henceforth and forever "we girls," who went through the varied experiences of life together that were crowded into those two weeks, would be separated from all other girls, and their intercourse would necessarily be different from any other friendships, colored always with that which they had lived together under the trees.

"Well," said Eurie, quick, as usual, to carry out what another only suggested, "I'm sure that is easily managed. We can call for Ruth, and go around to Marion's den; she is always in, and she never has any company."

"But Ruth nearly always has," objected Flossy, who had an instant vision of herself among the fashionable callers in the Erskine parlor, unable to get away without absolute rudeness.

"I'll risk Ruth if she happens to want to come with us," Eurie said, nodding her head sagely. "She will dispose of her callers in some way; strangle them, or what is easier and safer, simply ignore their existence and beg to be excused. Ruth is equal to any amount of well-bred rudeness; all that is necessary is the desire to perform a certain action, and she will do it."

This prophecy of Eurie's proved to be the case. Nellis Mitchell was called into service to see the girls safely over to the Erskine mansion, where they found two gentlemen calling on Ruth and her father. No sooner did she hear of their desire to be together, than, feeling instant sympathy with it, she said, "I'll go in five minutes." Then they heard her quiet voice in the parlor:

"Father, will you and our friends excuse me for the remainder of the evening, and will you enjoy my part of the call and yours too? I have just had a summons elsewhere that demands attention."

"Isn't that perfect in its propriety, besides bringing things to the exact point where she wants them to be?" whispered Eurie to Flossy as they waited in the hall. "Oh, it takes Ruth to manage."

"I wonder," said Flossy with her faraway look, and half-distressed, wholly perplexed curve of the lip—"I wonder if it is strictly *true;* that is what troubles me a good deal."

Oh, Dr. Hurlburt! Your address to the children that summer day under the trees was the germ of this shoot of sensitiveness for the strict truth that shall bloom into conscientious fruit.

It was by this process that they were all together in Marion's den, as Eurie called her stuffed and uninviting little room. Never was mortal more glad to be interrupted than she, as she unceremoniously tossed aside schoolbooks and papers and made room for them around the table.

"You are a blessed trio," she said exultantly. "What good angel put it into your hearts to come to me just now and here? I am in the dismals; have been down all day in the depths of swampland, feeling as if I hadn't a friend on earth and didn't want one; and here you are, you blessed three."

"But we didn't come for fun or to comfort you, or anything of that sort," explained Flossy earnestly, true to the purpose that had started her. "We came to talk something over."

"I don't doubt it. Talk it over then, by all means. I'll talk at it with all my heart. We generally do talk something over, I have observed, when we get together; at least we do of late years. Which one wants to talk?"

Thus introduced, Flossy explained the nature of her perplexities; her occupation the evening before; the interruption from Dr. Dennis; the sweeping action of Col. Baker, and the consequent talk.

"How do you suppose that is true?" she said, suddenly breaking off at the point where Col. Baker had assured her that all clergymen looked with utter disfavor on cards.

Marion glanced from one to another of the faces before her with an amused air; none of them spoke.

"It is rather queer," she said at last, "that I have to be authority, or that I seem to be the only one posted, when I have but just emerged from a state of unbelief in the whole subject. But I tell you truly, my blessed little innocent, Col. Baker is well posted; not only the clergy but he will find a large class of the most enlightened Christians look with disapproval on the whole thing in all its variations."

"Why do they?" This from Flossy with a perplexed and troubled tone.

"Well," said Marion, "now that question is more easily asked than answered. It requires an argument."

"An argument is just what I want; I like to have things explained. Before that, though, one thing that puzzles me is how should Col. Baker be so familiar with the views of clergymen?"

"That is a curious fact, my mousie; you will find it, I fancy, in all sorts of strange places. People who are

ISABELLA ALDEN

not Christians seem to have an intuitive perception of the fitness of things. It is like dancing and theatergoing, and a dozen other questions. It is very unusual to meet people who do not sneer at Christians for upholding such amusements; they seem to realize an incongruity between them and the Christian profession. It was just as plain to me, I know, and I have sneered many a time over cardplaying Christians, and here you are, dear little Flossy, among them, just for the purpose of teaching me not to judge."

Ruth, for the first time, took up the subject:

"If your statement is true, Marion, how is it that so many professed Christians indulge in these very things?"

"Precisely the question that I just asked myself while I was talking. By what means they become destitute of that keen insight into consistencies and inconsistencies the moment they enter the lists as Christian people is more than I can understand, unless it is because they decide to succumb to the necessity of doing as other people do and let any special thinking alone as inconvenient and unprofitable. I don't know how it is; only you watch this question and think about it, and you will discover that just so surely as you come in contact with any who are active and alert in Christian work, whose religion you respect as amounting to something, you are almost sure to see them avoiding all these amusements. Whoever heard of a minister being asked to spend an evening in social cardplaying! I presume that even Col. Baker himself knows that that would be improper, and he would be the first to sneer."

"Of course," Ruth said, "ministers were expected to be examples for other people to follow."

"Well, then," Flossy said, her perplexity in no way lessened, "ought we not to follow?"

Whereupon Marion clapped her hands.

"Little Flossy among the logicians!" she said. "That is the point, Ruth Erskine. If the example is for us to follow, why don't we follow? Now, what do you honestly think about this question yourself?"

"Why," said Ruth hesitatingly, "I have always played cards, in select circles, being careful, of course, with whom I played, just as I am careful with whom I associate, and, contrary to your supposition, I have always supposed those people who frowned on such amusements to be a set of narrow-minded fanatics. And I didn't know that Christian people did frown on such amusements; though, to be sure, now that I think of it, there are certain ones who never come to card parties nor dancing parties. I guess the difficulty is that I have never thought anything about it."

Marion was looking sober.

"The fact is," she said gravely, "that with all my loneliness and poverty and general forlornness, I have had a different bringing up from any of you. My father did not believe in any of these things."

"And he was a Christian man," Flossy said quickly. "Then he must have had a reason for his belief. That is what I want to get at. What was it?"

"He found it in an old book," said Marion, looking at her brightly, through shining eyes. "He found most of his knowledge and his hope and joy in that same book. The Bible was almost the only book he had, and he made much of that."

"And yet you hated the Bible?" Eurie said this almost involuntarily, with a surprised tone.

"I hated the way in which people lived it, so different from my father's way. I don't think I ever really discarded the book itself. But I was a fool; I don't mind owning that."

Flossy brought them back to the subject.

"But about this question," she said. "The Bible was just where I went for help, but I didn't find it; I looked in the concordance for cards and for amusements, and for every word which I could think of that would cover it, but I couldn't find anything."

Marion laughed again. This little morsel's ignorance of the Bible was to this girl, who had been an avowed infidel for more than a dozen years, something very strange.

"The Bible is a big book, darling," she said, still laughing. "But, after all, I fancy you will find something about the principle that governs cards, even if you cannot find the word."

Meantime, Ruth had been for some minutes regarding Eurie's grave face and attentive eyes with no small astonishment in her gaze. At this point she interrupted:

"Eurie Mitchell, what can be the matter with you? Were you ever known to be so quiet? I haven't heard you speak on this theme, or any other, since you came into the room; yet you look as though you had some ideas, or you choose to advance them. Where do you stand on this card question?"

"We never play cards at home," Eurie said quickly, "and we never go where we know they are to be played."

Flossy turned upon her the most surprised eyes. Dr. Mitchell's family was the most decidedly unconventional and free and easy of any represented there. Flossy had supposed that they, of all others, would make cards a daily pastime.

"Why not?" she asked briefly and earnestly, as one eager to learn.

"It is on Nell's account," Eurie said, still speaking very gravely. "Nell has but one fault, and that is cardplaying; he is just passionately fond of it; he is tempted everywhere. Father says Grandfather Mitchell was just so, and Nell inherits the taste. It is a great temptation to him, and we do not like to foster it at home."

"But home cardplaying is so different; that isn't gambling." This from Flossy, questioningly.

"Nell learned to play at home," Eurie said quickly. "That is, he learned at Grandfather Mitchell's home when he was a little boy. We have no means of knowing whether he would have been led into gambling but for that early education. I know that Robbie shall never learn if we can help it; we never mean to allow him to go where any sort of cards are played, so long as we have him under control."

All this was utterly new to Flossy.

"Then, if your little Robbie should come with other children to see me, and I should teach them a game of cards to amuse them, I might be doing you a positive injury," she said thoughtfully.

"I certainly should so consider it," Eurie said with quickness and with feeling. "Girls, I speak vehemently on this subject always; having one serious lesson at home makes people think."

"It is a question whether we have any right to indulge in an amusement that has the power to lead people astray," Ruth said, grave and thoughtful, "especially when it is impossible to tell what boy may be growing up under that influence to whom it will become a snare."

Marion added:

"Flossy, do you begin to see?"

"I see in every direction," Flossy said. "There is no telling when we may be doing harm. But, now, let me be personal; I play with Father a great deal; he is an old man, and he has no special temptation, certainly. I have heard him say he never played for anything of more value than a pin in his life. What harm can there possibly be in my spending an evening with him in such an amusement, if it rests and entertains him?"

"Imagine some of your Sunday school boys accepting your invitation to call on you and finding you playing a social game with your father; then imagine them quoting you in support of their game at the billiard saloon that same evening a little later," Marion said quickly. "You see, my little Flossy, we don't live in nutshells or sealed cans; we are at all times liable to be broken in upon by people whom we may influence and whom we may harm. I confess I don't want to do anything at home that will have to be pushed out of sight in haste and confusion because someone happens to come in. I want to be honest, even in my play."

Over this Flossy looked absolutely aghast. Those boys of hers, they were getting a strong hold upon her already; she longed to lead them. Was it possible that by her very amusements she might lead them astray? Another point was that Nellis Mitchell could never be invited to join them in a game. She had invited him often, and she winced at the thought. Did his sister think she had helped him into temptation? Following these trains of thought, she was led into another, over which she thought aloud.

"And suppose any of them should ask me if I ever played cards? I should have to say yes."

"Precisely," said Marion. "And don't you go to thinking that you can ever hide behind that foolish little explanation, 'I play simply for amusement; I think it is wrong to play for money.' It won't do; it takes logical brains to see the difference, and some even of those *won't* see it; but they can readily see that, having plenty of money, of course you have no temptation to play cards for it, and they see that with them it is different."

12

SETTLING QUESTIONS

"THERE is Bible for that doctrine too."

"Where?" Flossy asked, turning quickly to Marion.

"In this verse: 'If meat make my brother to offend, I will eat no flesh while the world standeth.' Don't you see you never can know which brother may be made to offend?"

"And it is even about so useful a thing as food," said Flossy, looking at her in amazement; she had never heard that verse before in her life. "About just that thing; and nothing so really unnecessary to a complete life as cardplaying may be."

"Col. Baker sneers at the inconsistency of people who have nothing to do with cards and who play croquet." Eurie said this with cheeks a little heightened in color; she had come in contact with Col. Baker on this very question.

Ruth looked up quickly from the paper on which she was scribbling.

"I think myself," she said, "that if it should seem necessary to me to give up cards entirely, consistency would oblige me to include croquet and all other games of that sort."

"I shouldn't feel obliged to do any such thing," Marion said promptly; "at least, not until I had become convinced that people played croquet late into the night in rooms smelling of tobacco and liquor and were tempted to drink freely of the latter and pawn their coats, if necessary, to get money enough to carry out the game. You see, there is a difference."

"Yet people can gamble in playing croquet," Eurie said thoughtfully.

"Oh yes, and people can gamble with pins, or in tossing up pennies. The point is, they are not in the habit of doing it; and pins suggest no such thing to people in general; neither do croquet balls; while the fact remains that the ordinary use of cards is to gamble with them; and comparatively few of those who use them habitually confine themselves to quiet home games. People are in danger of making their brothers offend by their use; we all know that."

"If that is true, then just that one verse from the Bible ought to settle the whole question." There was no mistaking the quiet meaning in Flossy's voice; it was as good as saying that the whole question was settled for her. Marion regarded her with evident satisfaction; her manner was all the more fascinating, because she was so entirely unconscious that the way of looking at questions, rather than this firm manner of settling questions, was not common, even among Christians. "Can you show me the verse in your Bible?" she presently asked.

"I can do that same with the greatest pleasure," Marion said, bringing forward a new and shining concordance. "I really meant to have a new dress this fall; I say that, Ruthie, for your special comfort; but the truth is, there was an army of Bible verses that I learned in my youth trooping up to me, and I had such a desire to see the connection and find out what they were all about that I was actually obliged to sacrifice the dress and get a concordance. I have lots of comfort with it. Here is the verse, Flossy."

Flossy drew the Bible toward her with a little sigh.

"I wish I knew an army of verses," she said. "Seems to me I don't know any at all." Then she went to reading.

"I know verses enough," Eurie said, "but they seem to be in a great muddle in my brain. I can't remember that any of them were ever explained to me; and it isn't very often that I find a place where any of them will fit in."

"They do fit in, though, and with astonishing closeness, you will find, as you grow used to them. I have been amazed at that feature of the Bible. Some of the verses that occur in the selections for parsing are just wonderful; they seem aimed directly at me. What have you found, Flossy?"

"Wonderful things," said Flossy, flushing and smiling.

"You are reading backward, aren't you? I know those verses; just you let me read them, substituting the object about which we are talking and see how they will fit. You see, girls, this astonishing man, Paul by name—do you happen to know his history?— more wonderful things happened to him than to any other mortal, I verily believe. Well, he was talking about idols, and advising his Christian friends not to eat the food that had been offered to idols; not that it would hurt them, but because—well, you'll see the 'because' as I read. I'll just put in our word, for an illustration, instead of meat. 'But cards commendeth us not to God: for neither if we play, are we the better; neither if we play not, are we the worse. But take heed lest by any means this liberty of yours become a stumblingblock to them that are weak. For if any man see thee which hast knowledge sit at cards, shall not the conscience of him which is weak be emboldened to sit at cards also? And through thy knowledge shall the weak brother perish, for whom Christ died? But when ye sin so against the brethren, and wound their weak conscience, ye sin against Christ. Wherefore, if cards make my brother to offend, I will play no cards while the world standeth, lest I make my brother to offend.' Doesn't that fit?"

"Let me look at that," said Eurie suddenly, drawing the Bible to her. "After all," she said after a moment, "what right have you to substitute the word *cards?* It is talking about another matter."

"Now, Eurie Mitchell, you are too bright to make such a remark as that! If the Bible is for our help as well as for Paul's, we have surely the right to substitute the noun that fits our present needs. We have no idols nowadays; at least they are not made out of wood and stone; and the logic of the question is as clear as sunlight. We have only to understand that the matter of playing cards is a snare and a danger to some people, and we see our duty clearly enough, because, how are we ever to be sure that the very person who will be tempted is not within the reach of our influence? What do you think, Flossy? Is the question any clearer to you?"

"Why, yes," Flossy said slowly, "that eighth verse settles it: 'But meat commendeth us not to God: for neither, if we eat, are we the better; neither if we eat not, are we the worse.' It certainly can do no one any harm if I let cards alone, and it is equally certain that

Isabella Alden

it may do harm if I play them. I should think my duty was clear."

"I wonder what Col. Baker will say to that duty?" queried Eurie, thinking aloud rather than speaking to anyone. "He is very much given over to the amusement, if I am not mistaken."

Flossy raised her eyes and fixed them thoughtfully on Eurie's face, while a flush spread all over her own pretty one. Was it possible that she had helped to foster this taste in Col. Baker? How *many* evenings she had spent with him in this way. *Was* he very much addicted to the use of cards, she wondered; that is, outside of their own parlor? Eurie seemed to know something about it.

"What makes you think so?" she asked at last.

"Because I know so. He has a great deal to do with Nell's infatuation. He was the very first one with whom Nell ever played for anything but fun. Flossy Shipley, you surely know that he derives a good deal of his income in that way?"

"I certainly did *not* know it," Flossy said with an increasing glow on her cheeks. The glow was caused by wondering how far her own brother, Charlie, had been led by this man.

"Girls," said Marion, concluding that a change of subject would be wise, "wouldn't a Bible-reading evening be nice?"

"What kind of an evening can that be?"

Marion laughed.

"Why, a reading together out of the Bible about a certain subject, or subjects, that interested us, and about which we wanted to inform ourselves. Like this, for instance. I presume there are dozens of texts that bear on this very question. It would be nice to go over them together and talk them up."

130

Flossy's eyes brightened.

"I would like that exceedingly," she said. "I need the help of you all. I know so very little about the Bible. We have musical evenings and literary evenings; why not Bible evenings? Let's do it."

"Apropos of the subject in hand; before we take up a new one, what do you think of this by way of illustration?" Ruth asked as she threw down on a table a daintily written epistle. There was an eager grasping after it by this merry trio, and Eurie, securing it, read aloud. It was an invitation for the next evening to a select gathering of choice spirits for the purpose of enjoying a social evening at cards.

"What do you propose to do with it?" Marion asked, as Eurie balanced the note on her hand with an amused face; the illustration fitted so remarkably into the talk.

"Decline it," Ruth said briefly. And then added, as an afterthought, "I never gave the subject any attention in my life. I am, perhaps, not entirely convinced now, only I see as Flossy does that I shall certainly do no harm by declining; whereas it seems I may possibly do some by accepting; therefore, of course, the way is clear."

She said it with the utmost composure, and it was evident that the idea of such a course being disagreeable to her or of her considering it a cross to decline had not occurred to her. She cared nothing at all about these matters and had only been involved in them as a sort of necessity belonging to society. She was more than willing to be "counted out."

As for Flossy, she drew a little sigh of envy. She would have given much to have been constituted like Ruth Erskine. She knew that the same like invitation would probably come to her, and she knew that she would decline it; but, aside from loss of the pleasure and excitement of the pretty toilet and the pleasant evening among her friends, she foresaw long and wearisome discussions with Col. Baker, with Charlie, with her father; sarcastic remarks from Kitty and her lover, and a long train of annoyances. She dreaded them all; it was so easy to slip along with the current; it was so hard to stem it and insist on going the other way.

As for Marion Wilbur, she envied them both; a chance for them to dash out into a new channel and make some headway, not the everlasting humdrum sameness that filled her life.

Flossy was fascinated with the Bible words that were so new and fresh to her.

"Those verses cover a great deal of ground," she said, slowly reading them over again. "I can think of a good many things which we call right enough that, measured by that test, would have to be changed or given up. But, Marion, you spoke of dancing and theatergoing. I can't quite see what the verses have to do with either of those amusements; I mean not as we, and the people in our set, have to do with such things. Do you think every form of dancing is wicked?"

"What wholesale questions you ask, my morsel! And you ask them precisely as though I had been made umpire and you must abide by my decisions, whatever they are. Now, do you know I never believed in dancing? I had some queer, perhaps old-fashioned, notions about it all my life. Even before there was any such thing as a conscientious scruple about it, I should not have danced if I had had a hundred chances to mingle in just the set that you do; so perhaps I am not the one of whom to ask that question."

"I should think you were just the one. If you have

examined it and know why you think so, you can surely tell me and give me a chance to see whether I ought to think as you do or not."

"*I* need posting, decidedly, on that question," Eurie said, throwing off her earnestness and looking amused. "If there is any one thing above another that I do thoroughly enjoy, it is dancing; and I give you all fair warning, I don't mean to be coaxed out of it very easily. I shall fight hard for that bit of fun. Marion doesn't know anything about it, for she has never danced; but the rest of you know just what a delicious exercise it is; and I don't believe, when it is indulged in reasonably and at proper places, there is any harm at all in it. If I am to give it up, you will have to show me strong reasons why I should."

"All this fits right in with my idea," Marion said. "Nothing could be more suitable for our first Bible reading. Let us take an evening for it and prepare ourselves as well as we can beforehand and examine into the Bible view of it. Eurie, you will be expected to be armed with all the scriptural arguments in its favor. I'll try for the other side. Now, Ruth and Flossy, which side will you choose?"

"Neither," Ruth said promptly. "I am interested in the subject and shall be glad to be informed as to what the Bible says about it, if any of you are smart enough to find anything that will bear on the subject; but I believe the Bible left that, as well as some other things, to our common sense, and that each of us have to decide the matter for ourselves."

"All right," said Marion, "we'll accept you on the noncommittal side. Only, remember you are to try to prove from the Bible that it has left *us* to decide this matter for ourselves."

"I shall take every side that I find," Flossy said. "What I want to know is the truth about things."

"Without regard as to whether the truth is so fortunate as to agree with your opinion or not?" said Marion. "You will, probably, be quite as likely to find the truth as any of us. Well, I like the plan; there is work in it, and it will amount to something. When shall it be?"

"Next Friday," said Flossy.

"No," said Ruth; "Friday is the night of Mrs. Garland's lawn party."

"A dancing party," said Eurie. "Good! Let us come together on Thursday evening. If there is a dancing party just ahead, it will make us all the more zealous to prove our sides; I shall be, at least, for I want to go to Mrs. Garland's."

13

Looking for Work

DR. DENNIS had just gone into his study to make ready for the evening prayer meeting when he heard his doorbell ring. He remembered with a shade of anxiety that his daughter was not yet out of school, and that his sister and housekeeper was not at home. It was more than likely that he would be interrupted.

"What is it, Hannah?" he asked, as that person appeared at his door.

"It is Miss Erskine, sir. I told her that Miss Dennis was out of town, and Miss Grace was at school, and she said it was of no consequence; she wanted to see the minister himself. Will I tell her that you are engaged?"

"No," said Dr. Dennis promptly. The sensation was still very new, this desire on the part of any of the name of Erskine to see him. His preparation could afford to wait.

Two minutes more and Ruth was in the study. It was a place in which she felt as nearly embarrassed as she ever approached to that feeling. She had a specific purpose in calling, and words arranged wherewith to commence her topic; but they fled from her as if she had been a schoolgirl instead of a finished young lady in society; and she answered the doctor's kind enquiries as to the health of her father and herself in an absent and constrained manner. At last this good man concluded to help her.

"Is there anything special that I can do for you today?" he asked with a kindly interest in his tone that suggested the feeling that he was interested in her plans, whatever they were, and would be glad to help.

"Yes," she said, surprised into frankness by his straightforward way of doing things; "or, at least, I hope you can. Dr. Dennis, ought not every Christian to be at work?"

"Our great Example said: 'I must work the works of him that sent me, while it is day.'"

"I know it; that very verse set me to thinking about it. That is what I want help about. There is no work for me to do; at least, I can't find any. I am doing just nothing at all, and I don't in the least know which way to turn. I am not satisfied with this state of things; I can't settle back to my books and my music as I did before I went away; I don't enjoy them as I used to; I mean, they don't absorb me; they seem to be of no earthly use to anyone but myself, and I don't feel absolutely certain that they are of any use to me; anyway, they are not Christian work."

"As to that, you are not to be too certain about it. Wonderful things can be done with music; and when one is given a marked talent for it, as I hear has been the case with you, it is not to be hidden in a napkin."

"I don't know what I can do with music, I am sure," Ruth said skeptically. "I suppose I must have a good deal of talent in that direction; I have been told so ever since I can remember; but beyond entertaining my friends, I see no other special use for it."

"Do you remember telling me about the songs which Mr. Bliss sang at Chautauqua, and the effect on the audience?"

"Yes," said Ruth, speaking heartily, and her cheeks glowing at the recollection, "but he was wonderful!"

"The same work can be done in a smaller way," Dr. Dennis said, smiling. "I hope to show you something of what you may do to help in that way before another winter passes; but, in the meantime, mere entertainment of friends is not a bad motive for keeping up one's music. Then there is the uncertain future ever before us. What if you should be called upon to teach music someday?"

A vision of herself toiling wearily from house to house in all weathers, and at all hours of the day, as she had seen music teachers do, hovered over Ruth Erskine's brain, and so utterly improbably and absurd did the picture seem when she imagined it as having any reference to her that she laughed outright.

"I don't believe I shall ever teach music," she said positively.

"Perhaps not; and yet stranger things than that *have* happened in this changeful life."

"But, Dr. Dennis," she said with sudden energy, and showing a touch of annoyance at the turn which the talk was taking, "my trouble is not an inability to employ my time; I do not belong to the class of young ladies who are afflicted with ennui." And a sarcastic curve of her handsome lip made Ruth look very like the Miss Erskine that Dr. Dennis had always known. She despised people who had no resources within themselves. "I can find plenty to do, and I enjoy doing it; but the point is, I seem to be living only for myself, and that doesn't seem right. I want Christian work."

To tell the truth Dr. Dennis was puzzled. There was so much work to do, his hands and heart were always so full and running over, that it seemed strange to him for anyone to come looking for Christian work; the world was teeming with it.

On the other hand, he confessed to himself that he was utterly unaccustomed to hearing people ask for work; or, if the facts be told, to having anyone do any work.

Years ago he had tried to set the people of the First Church to work; but they had stared at him and misunderstood him, and he confessed to himself that he had given over trying to get work out of most of them. While this experience was refreshing, it was new, and left him for the moment bewildered.

"I understand you," he said, rallying. "There is plenty of Christian work. Do you want to take a class in the Sunday school? There is a vacancy."

Ruth shook her head with decision.

"That is not at all my forte. I have no faculty for teaching children; I am entirely unused to them and have no special interest in them and no sort of idea how they are to be managed. Some people are specially fitted for such work; I know I am not."

"Often we find our work much nearer home than we had planned," Dr. Dennis said, regarding her with a thoughtful air. "How is it with your father, Miss Erskine?"

"My father?" she repeated; and she could hardly have looked more bewildered if her pastor had asked after the welfare of the man in the moon.

"Are you trying to win him over to the Lord's side?"

Utter silence and surprise on Miss Erskine's part. At last she said:

"I hardly ever see my father; we are never alone except when we are on our way to dinner or to pay formal calls on very formal people. Then we are always in a hurry. I cannot reach my father, Dr. Dennis; he is immersed in business and has no time nor heart for such matters. I should not in the least know how to approach him if I had a chance; and, indeed, I am sure I could do no good, for he would esteem it an impertinence to be questioned by his daughter as to his thoughts on these matters."

"Yet you have an earnest desire to see him a Christian?"

"Yes," she said, speaking slowly and hesitatingly; "of course I have that. To be very frank, Dr. Dennis, it is a hopeless sort of desire; I don't expect it in the least; my father is peculiarly unapproachable; I know he considers himself sufficient unto himself, if you will allow the expression. In thinking of him, I have felt that a great many years from now, when he is old, and when business cares and responsibilities have in a measure fallen off and given him time to think of himself, he might then feel his need of a Friend and be won; but I don't even hope for it before that time."

"My dear friend, you have really no right to set a different time from the one that your Master has set," her pastor said earnestly. "Don't you know that his time is always *now?* How can you be sure that he will choose to give your father a long life and leisure in old age to help him to think? Isn't that a terrible risk?"

Ruth Erskine shook her decided head.

"I feel sure that my work is not in that direction," she said. "I could not do it; you do not know my father as well as I do; he would never allow me to approach him. The most I can hope to do will be to hold what he calls my new views so far into the background that he will not positively forbid them to me. He is the only person I think of whom I stand absolutely in awe. Then I couldn't talk with him. His life is a pure, spotless one, convincing by its very morality; so he thinks that there is no need of a Savior. I do pray for him; I mean to as long as he and I live; but I know I can do nothing else; at least not for many a year."

How was Dr. Dennis to set to work a lady who knew so much that she could not work? This was the thought that puzzled him. But he knew how difficult it was for people to work in channels marked out by others. So he said encouragingly:

"I can conceive of some of your difficulties in that direction. But you have other friends who are not Christians?"

This being said inquiringly, Ruth, after a moment of hesitation, answered it:

"I have one friend to whom I have tried to talk about this matter, but I have had no success. He is very peculiar in his views and feelings. He agrees to everything that I say and admits the wisdom and reasonableness of it all, but he goes no further."

"There are a great many such people," Dr. Dennis said with a quick sigh. He met many of them himself. "They are the hardest class to reach. Does your friend believe in the power of prayer? I have generally found the safest and shortest way with such to be to use my influence in inducing them to begin to pray. If they admit its power and its reasonableness, it is such a very simple thing to do for a friend that they can hardly refuse."

"I don't think he ever prays," Ruth said, "and I

don't believe he would. He would think it hypocritical. He says as much as that half the praying must be mockery."

"Granting that to be the case, does he think he should therefore not offer real prayer? That would be a sad state. Because I have many hypocrites in my family whose words to me are mockery, therefore no one must be a true friend."

"I know," said Ruth, interrupting. "But I don't know how to reach such people. Perhaps he may be your work, Dr. Dennis, but I don't think he is mine. I don't in the least know what to say to him. I refer to Mr. Wayne."

"I know him," Dr. Dennis said, "but he is not inclined to talk with me. I have not the intimacy with him that would lead him to be familiar. I should be very certain, if I were you, that my work did not lie in that direction before I turned from it."

"I am certain," Ruth said with a little laugh. "I don't know how to talk to such people. I should feel sure of doing more harm than good."

"But, my dear Miss Erskine, I beg your pardon for the reminder, but since you are thrown much into his society, will it not be necessary for you, as a Christian, to talk more or less about this matter? Should not your talk be shaped in such a way as to influence him, if you can?"

"I don't think I understand," Ruth said doubtfully. "Do you mean that people should talk about religion all the time they are together?"

During this question Dr. Dennis had drawn his Bible toward him and been turning over the leaves.

"Just let me read you a word from the Guidebook on this subject: 'Only let your conversation be as becometh the gospel of Christ.' 'As he which hath called you is holy, so be ye holy in all manner of conversation.' 'Seeing then that all these things shall be dissolved, what manner of persons ought ye to be in all holy conversation and godliness?' What should you conclude as to Christian duty in the matter of daily conversation?"

Ruth made no answer to this question, but sat with an earnest, thoughtful look fixed on her pastor's face.

"Who follows that pattern?" she asked at last.

"My dear friend, is not our concern rather to decide whether you and I shall try to do it in the future?"

Someway this brought the talk to a sudden lull. Ruth seemed to have no more to say.

"There is another way of work that I have been intending to suggest to some of you young ladies," Dr. Dennis said after a thoughtful silence. "It is something very much neglected in our church—that is the social question. Do you know we have many members who complain that they are never called on, never spoken with, never noticed in any way?"

"I don't know anything about the members," Ruth said. "I don't think I have a personal acquaintance with twenty of them—a calling acquaintance, I mean."

"That is the case with a great many, and it is a state of things that should not exist. The family ought to know each other. I begin to see your work clearer; it is the young ladies, to a large extent, who must remedy this evil. Suppose you take up some of that work, not neglecting the other, of course. 'These ought ye to have done, and not to leave the other undone,' I am afraid will be said to a good many of us. But this is certainly work needing to be done, and work for which you have leisure."

He hoped to see her face brighten, but it did not. Instead she said:

"I hate calling."

"I daresay; calling that is aimless and, in a sense, useless. It must be hateful work. But if you start out with an object in view, something to accomplish that is worth your while, will it not make a great difference?"

Ruth only sighed.

"I have so many calls to make with Father," she said wearily. "It is the worst work I do. They are upon fashionable, frivolous people, who cannot talk about *anything*. It is worse martyrdom now than it used to be. I think I am peculiarly unfitted for such work, Dr. Dennis."

"But I want you to try a different style of calls. Go alone; not with your father, or with anyone who will trammel your tongue; and go among a class of people who do not expect you and will be surprised and pleased, and helped, perhaps. Come, let me give you a list of persons whom I would like to have you call on at your earliest opportunity. This is work that I am really longing to see done."

A prisoner about to receive sentence would hardly have looked more gloomy than did Ruth. She was still for a few minutes, then she said:

"Dr. Dennis, do you really think it is a person's duty to do that sort of work for which he or she feels least qualified, and which is the most distasteful?"

"No," said Dr. Dennis promptly. "My dear Miss Erskine, will you be so kind as to tell me the work for which you feel qualified, and for which you have no distaste?"

Again Ruth hesitated, looked confused, and then

laughed. She began to see that she was making a very difficult task for her pastor.

"I don't feel qualified for anything," she said at last. "And I feel afraid to undertake anything. But at the same time, I think I ought to be at work."

"Now we begin to see the way clearer," he said smiling, and with encouragement in his voice. "It may seem a strange thing to you, but a sense of unfitness is sometimes one of the very best qualifications for such work. If it is strong enough to drive us to the blessed Friend who has promised to make perfect our weakness in this as in all other efforts, and if we go out armed in His strength, we are sure to conquer. Try it. Take this for your motto: 'As ye have opportunity.' And, by the way, do you know the rest of that verse? 'Especially unto them who are of the household of faith.' It is members of the household that I want you to call on, remember."

Ruth laughed again and shook her head. But she took her list and went away. She had no more that she wanted to say just then; but she felt that she had food for thought.

"I may try it," she said as she went out, holding up her list, "but I feel that I shall blunder and do more harm than good."

Dr. Dennis looked after her with a face on which there was no smile. "There goes one," he said to himself, "who thinks she is willing to be led, but, on the contrary, she wants to lead. She is saved but not subdued. I wonder what means the great Master will have to use to lead her to rest in his hands, knowing no way but his?"

14

AN UNARMED SOLDIER

MANY things intervened to keep Ruth Erskine from having much to do with that list which her pastor had given her. She read it over indeed and realized that she was not familiar with a single name.

"What an idea it will be for me to go blundering through the city, hunting up people whom I shall not know when I find."

This she said as she read it over; then she laid it aside and made ready to go out to dinner with her father to meet two judges and their wives and daughters who were stopping in town.

During that day she thought many times of the sentences that had been read to her out of that plain-looking, much-worn Bible on Dr. Dennis's study table. The only effect they had on her was to make her smile at the thought of the impossibility of anything like a religious conversation in such society as that!

"How they would stare," she said to herself, "if I should ask them about a prayer meeting! I have half a mind to try it. If Father were not within hearing I would, just to see what these finished young ladies would say."

But she did not try it; and the evening passed, as so many evenings had, without an attempt on her part to carry out any of the thoughts which troubled her. She looked forward to one bit of work which she expected to fall to her share, at least she liked to call it work.

That card party to which she had been invited; she would be expected to attend in company with Mr. Wayne; she meant to decline, and her father would be surprised and a trifle annoyed, for it was at a place where, not liking the people well enough himself to be social, he desired his daughter to atone for his deficiency. But she would steadily refuse. She did not shrink from this effort as Flossy did; on the contrary, she half enjoyed the thought of being a calm and composed martyr.

But, quite to her discomfort, the martyrdom was not permitted; at least it took a different form. Mr. Wayne was obliged to be out of town and sent profuse regrets, assuming that, of course, it would be a sore disappointment to her.

Her father took sufficient notice of it to make one or two efforts to agreeably supply his place and, failing in that, assured his daughter that rather than have her disappointed, he would have planned to accompany her himself if he had known of Mr. Wayne's absence in time. The actual cross that it would have been to explain to her father that she did not desire to go, and the reasons therefore, she did not take up; but the occurrence served to annoy her.

Two days afterward she was busy all the morning with her dressmaker, getting a special dress ready for a wedding among the upper circles. She had been hurried and worried and was so nearly out of patience as her calmness ever allowed her to be. Still she remembered that it was the prayer-meeting evening, that she should see Dr. Dennis, and that he would be likely to ask her about the people on that list. She ought to go that afternoon and try what she could do.

Once since her call on Dr. Dennis she had met him as he was going down Clinton Street, and he had turned and joined her for a few steps while he said:

"I have been thinking about another friend of yours that I should be very glad to see influenced in the right direction. His sister is trying, I presume; but other people's sisters sometimes have an influence. Young Mitchell, the doctor's son, is a young man of real promise; he ought to be on the Lord's side."

"You are mistaken in supposing him to be a friend of mine," Ruth said with promptness and emphasis. "We have the most distant speaking acquaintance only, and I have a dislike for him amounting to absolute aversion." There was that in Ruth Erskine's voice when she chose to let it appear that said, "My aversion is a very serious and disagreeable thing."

"Yes," the doctor said quietly, as one in no degree surprised or disturbed; "yet he has a soul to be saved, and the Lord Jesus Christ died to save him."

There was no denying this; and certainly it would not look well in her to say that she had no desire to have part in his salvation; so she kept silence. But there followed her a disagreeable remembrance of having negatived every proposition whereby the doctor had hoped to set her at work. She decided, disagreeable as it was, to make a vigorous assault on those families, thereby showing him what she could do.

To this end she arrayed herself in immaculate calling attire—with a rustle of silk and a softness of ruffle, and a daintiness of glove that none but the wealthy can assume, and, in short, with that unmistakable air about everything pertaining to her that marks the lady of fashion. These things were as much a part of Ruth Erskine as her hair and eyes were. Once ready, her dress, perhaps, gave her as little thought as her eyes or hair did. But she looked as though that must have been the sole object of thought and study in order to produce such perfect results.

Her preparation for her new and untried work had been none of the best. As I said, the morning had been given to the cares of the dressmaker and the deceitfulness of trimmings, so much so that her Bible reading even had been omitted, and only the briefest and most hurried of prayers, worthy of the days when prayer was nothing to her but a formal bowing of the head on proper occasions, had marked her need of help from the Almighty Hand. These thoughts troubled her as she went down the street. She paused irresolutely before one of the principal bookstores.

"I ought to have some tracts," she said doubtfully to herself. "They always take tracts when they go district visiting; I know that from hearing Mrs. Whipple talk. What is this but a district visiting? Only Dr. Dennis has put my district all over the city; I wonder if he could have scattered the streets more if he had tried? Respectable streets, though, all of them; better than any Mrs. Whipple ever told about."

Then she tried to select her tracts; but when one has utter ignorance of such literature, and a few minutes at a crowded counter in which to make a selection, it is not likely to be very select. She finally gave up any attempt at choice, beyond a few whose titles seemed inviting, chose a package at random, and hastened on her way.

"Mrs. C. Y. Sullivan" was the first name on her list, and, following her directions, she came presently to the street and number. A neat brick house with a modern air about it and its surroundings; a bird singing in a cage before the open window and pots of flowers blooming behind tastefully looped white curtains; not at all the sort of a house that Ruth had imagined she would see.

It did not suit her ideas of district visiting, crude though those ideas were. However, she rang the bell. Having commenced the task she was not one to draw back, though she admitted to herself that she never felt more embarrassed in her life. Nor did the embarrassment lessen when she was shown into the pretty, tasteful parlor, where presently Mrs. Sullivan joined her.

"I am Miss Erskine," Ruth said, rising as Mrs. Sullivan, a tall woman of some degree of dignity, after a slight bow, waited as if she would know her errand. Unfortunately Ruth had no errand, save that she had come out to do her duty and make the sort of call that Dr. Dennis expected her to make. Her embarrassment was excessive! What *could* she do or say next? Why did not Mrs. Sullivan take a chair, instead of standing there and looking at her like an idiot?

"Do you get out to church every Sabbath?" she asked suddenly, feeling the need of saying something.

Mrs. Sullivan looked as though she thought she had suddenly come in contact with a lunatic.

"Do I get out to church?" she repeated. "That depends on whether I decide to go or not. May I ask why you are interested?"

What had become of Ruth's common sense? Why couldn't she have said, in as natural a way as she would have talked about going to a concert, that she was interested to know whether she enjoyed such a privilege? Why couldn't she have been herself in talking about these matters, as well as at any other time? Does anyone know why such a sense of horrible embarrassment creeps over some people when their conversation takes the least tinge of religion—people who are wonderfully self-possessed on all other themes?

"Well," said Ruth, in haste and confusion, "I merely inquired; I mean no offence, certainly; will you have a tract?" And she hastily seized one from her package, which happened to be entitled "Why are you not a Christian?"

"Thank you," Mrs. Sullivan said, drawing back, "I am not in special need of reading matter; we keep ourselves supplied with religious literature of a kind that suits our tastes. As to tracts, I always keep a package by me to distribute when I go among the poor. This one would not be particularly appropriate to me, as I trust I am a Christian."

Dear me! how stiff and proper they both were! And in their hearts how indignant they both felt. What about? Could either of them have told?

"I wonder what earthly good that call did?" Ruth asked herself, as with glowing cheeks and rapid steps, she made her way down the street. "What could have been Dr. Dennis's object in sending me there to call? I thought I was to call on the poor. He didn't say anything about whether they were poor or not, now I think of it; but I supposed, of course, that was what he meant. Why need she have been so disagreeable, anyway? I am sure I didn't insult her."

And I tell you truly that Miss Erskine did not know that she had seemed disagreeable in the extreme to Mrs. Sullivan, and that she was at that moment raging over it in her heart.

Extremely disgusted with her first attempt, and almost ready to declare that it should be the last, Ruth still decided to make one more venture—that inborn dislike which she had for giving up what had once been undertaken, coming to her aid in this matter.

Another pretty little house, white and green blinds, and plant in bloom; the name on the door and on her list was "Smith." That told her very little. She was ushered into what was evidently the family sitting room, and a pretty enough room it was; occupied just now by three merry girls, who hushed their laugh as she entered, and by a matronly lady, whom one of them called *Mother.*

Ruth had never made calls before when she had the least tinge of embarrassment. If she could have divested herself on the idea that she was a district visitor out distributing tracts, she would not have felt so now; but as it was, the feeling grew upon her every instant. Pretty little Miss Smith had decidedly the advantage of her, as she said promptly:

"Good afternoon, Miss Erskine; Mother, this is Judge Erskine's daughter"; and then proceeded to introduce her friends.

Now, if Ruth could have become unprofessional, all might have been well; but she had gone out with a sincere desire to do her duty; so she took the offered seat near Mrs. Smith and said:

"I called this afternoon, at Dr. Dennis's request, to see if there was anything that I could do for you."

Mrs. Smith looked politely amazed.

"I don't think I quite understand," she said slowly; while in the daughter's bright eyes there gleamed mirth and mischief.

"I do," she said quickly. "Dr. Dennis is very kind. Miss Erskine, I am very anxious to have a blue silk dress, trimmed in white lace, to wear to the party next week; could you manage it for me, do you think?"

"Caroline!" spoke Mrs. Smith in a surprised and reproving tone, while Ruth looked her indignant astonishment.

"Well, Mother, she said she called to see if we wanted anything, and I certainly want that."

"There is some mistake," Mrs. Smith said, speaking kindly and evidently pitying Ruth's dreadful embarrassment. "You have mistaken the house, I presume; our name is such a common one. You are out on an errand of charity, I presume? We are glad to see you, of course, but we are not in need of anything but friends. I believe you attend the same church with ourselves; we ought to know each other, of course. So we shall profit by the mistake after all. My daughter is a wild little girl and lets her sense of fun get the better of her politeness sometimes; I hope you will excuse her."

What was to be said? Why could not Ruth get rid of her horrible embarrassment and rally to meet this kind and frank greeting? In vain she tried to command her tongue; to think of something to say that would be proper under these strange circumstances. How had she misunderstood Dr. Dennis! Why should these people be called on? Why should they feel that they were being neglected when they were in need of nothing?

It was all a mystery to her; and the world is full of people who do not understand a sense of loneliness, whose lives are so full of friendships and engagements and society, that they imagine all other people are like themselves except that class known as the poor, who need old clothes and cold pieces and tracts!

That was all that Ruth Erskine knew. She could not

recover from her astonishment and confusion; she made her stay very short, indeed, apologizing in what she was conscious was an awkward way for her intrusion, and then went directly toward home, resolving in great firmness that she had made her last calls on people selected from that horrible list.

She was more than embarrassed; she was utterly dismayed and disheartened. Was there, then, nothing for her to do? It had been a real honest desire to be up and doing which had sent her to Dr. Dennis; it had been a real cross, and one keenly felt to take up this work about which she had started. What an utter failure! What could he have meant? How was she expected to help those people? They needed nothing; they were Christian people; they were pleasantly circumstanced in every way. She had not the least idea how to be of any help to them. There was nothing for her to do. She felt humbled and sad.

Yet that young lady was joined in a few minutes by Nellis Mitchell, who cordially volunteered to shield her dainty summer toilet from certain drops of rain that began to fall, and so walked six entire blocks by her side, pleasant and genial as usual, and not a word said she to him about the great topic to which her life was consecrated. He even helped her by himself referring to the evening meeting and saying that he should have to escort Eurie as far as the door if this rain continued, and she did not so much as think to ask him to come further and enjoy the meeting with them. She did not like Nellis Mitchell, you will remember.

Also that same evening she spent an hour after prayer meeting in conversation with her friend, Mr. Wayne, and she said not a single word to him about this matter. She could not talk with him, she told

herself; he did not understand her, and it did no good.
Some time when he was in a less complaisant mood,
she could do something for him, but not now. She was
not very companionable, however; her mind was
dwelling on her afternoon disappointment.

"It was the most horrid time I ever had in my life!"
she told Marion, after going over an account of the
experience. "I shall not be caught in that way again."

And Marion, unsympathetic girl that she was,
laughed much and long.

"What a creature you are!" she said at last. "I
declare, it is funny that people can live in the world
and know so little about their fellow mortals as you
and Flossy do. She knows no more about them than a
kitten does, and you know no more than the moon.
You sail right above all their feelings and ideas. It
served you right, I declare. What earthly right had you
to go sailing down on people in that majestic fashion
and asking questions as if they were Roman Catholics
and you were the priest?"

"I don't see what in the world you mean!" Ruth
said, feeling exceedingly annoyed.

"Well, my dear young woman, you ought to see;
you can't expect to get through the Christian world
even without having a due regard for common sense.
Just suppose the president's wife should come sweeping into your parlor, asking you if you went to church,
and if you would have a tract. I am afraid you would
be tempted to tell her it was none of her business."

"The cases are not at all parallel," Ruth said, flushing deeply. "I consider myself on quite an equal
footing with the president's wife or any other lady."

Whereupon Marion laughed with more abandon
than before.

"Now, Ruth Erskine," she said, "don't be a goose.

Do use your common sense; you have some, I am sure. Wherein are these people whom you went to see on a lower footing than yourself? Granting that they have less money than you do, or even, perhaps, less than I have, are you ready to admit that money is the question that settles positions in society?"

15

MARION'S PLAN

"MISS Wilbur! Miss Wilbur! Can't we go in Miss Lily's class today? Our teacher isn't here."

"Miss Wilbur, they are crowding us off the seat; there isn't room for no more in this class."

"Miss Wilbur, my sister Nellie can't come today; she has the toothache. Can I go in Kitty's class?"

Every one of these little voices spoke at once; two of the owners thereof twitched at her dress, and another of them nudged her elbow. In the midst of this little babel of confusion the door opened softly, and Dr. Dennis came in. Marion turned toward him and laughed—a perplexed laugh that might mean something besides amusement.

"What is it?" he asked, answering the look instead of the laugh.

"It is everything," she said quickly. "You mustn't stay a minute, Dr. Dennis; we are not in company trim today at all. Unless you will do the work, we can't have you."

"I came to hear, not to work," he said smiling, and at the same time looking troubled.

"You will hear very little that will interest you for the next ten minutes at least; though I don't know but you would better stay; it would be a good introduction to the talk that I want to have with you early in the week. I am coming tomorrow after school, if I may."

Dr. Dennis gave the assent promptly, named the hour that he would be at leisure, and went away wondering what they were accomplishing in the primary class.

This was the introduction to Marion's talk in the study with Dr. Dennis. She wasted no time in preliminaries, but had hardly seated herself before the subject on her mind was brought forward.

"It is all about that class, Dr. Dennis. I am going to prove a failure."

"Don't," he said, smiling at her words but looking his disturbance; "we have had failures enough in that class to shipwreck it; it is quite time we had a change for the better. What is the trouble?"

"The trouble is, we do nothing. Two-thirds of our time is occupied in getting ready to do; and even then we can't half accomplish it. Then we don't stay ready and have to begin the work all over again. Yesterday, for instance, there were three absences among the teachers; that means confusion, for each of those teachers have seven children who are thus thrown loose on the world. Think how much time we must consume in getting them seated somewhere and under someone's care; and then imagine, if you can, the amount of time that they consume in saying, 'Our teacher doesn't do so, she does *so.*'"

"What is the reason that the teachers in that room are so very irregular?"

"Why, they are not irregular; that is, as Sunday

school teachers rate regularly. To be sure, it would never do to be teaching a graded school, for instance, and be as careless as some of them are about regularity. But that is a different matter, of course; this is only a Sunday school! But for all that, I think they do as well as the average. You see, Dr. Dennis, there are twenty of them, and if each one of them is present every Sunday in the year save three, that makes a good deal of regularity on their part and yet averages absences every Sabbath to be looked after. Don't you see?"

"I see," he said, smiling; "that is a mathematical way of putting it. There is reason in it, too. How in the world do you manage when there are vacancies?"

"Which is always," Marion said quickly. "There has not been a Sabbath since I have had charge when all the teachers were present; and I have taken pains to inquire of the former superintendent, who reports very much the same. Isn't it so in all schools, Dr. Dennis?"

"Of course there must of necessity be some detentions; but not so many, probably, as there actually are, if we were in the habit of being very conscientious about these matters; still, I don't know that we are worse than others. But you haven't told me how you manage."

"I manage every way; there is no set way to do it. I stand around in much the same state of perplexity in which you found me yesterday. The children each have their special friends who have been put in other classes, and they are on the *qui vive* to be with them, which adds not a little to the general confusion. Sometimes we have a regular whirl about seats, enlarge two or three classes, and crowd some seats most uncomfortably, leaving others empty; sometimes we go out to the Bible classes for volunteers—and, by the way, it is nearly impossible to find any. I wish you would preach a sermon on that subject. It is so easy to say, 'Oh, please excuse me,' it requires so little courage to do it; and is such a comfortable and unanswerable way of disposing of the whole matter. At the same time, there is some degree of excuses for the refusals. Think of the folly of setting a young girl who knows nothing about little children and has made no preparation to teach them, beside half a dozen little restless mortals and bidding her interest them in the lesson for ten minutes. She doesn't know how to interest them, and she knows she doesn't, and the fact embarrasses her. Before she has fairly found out what she is expected to do, her time is gone; for it takes a wonderful amount of time to get ready to work."

"But these young girls have only to teach certain Scripture verses and a prayer or a hymn, or something of that sort have they not? One would think they might be equal to that without preparation."

"Do you think so?" Marion asked, a gleam of fun in her keen eyes. "I should like to see you try it, provided you have no better mental caliber to assist you than some of the volunteers have. Why, there is a right and wrong way of teaching even a Bible verse. Do you know, sir, that you may repeat words to children like a list from a spelling lesson, and they will get no more idea from it than if it were a French sentence and will be able to commit it about as readily? If I had children, I should rebel at their being taught even Bible verses by novices. Why, it isn't allowed in public schools! The days have gone by when anybody is supposed to be smart enough to teach children to drawl through the alphabet. We have the best of trained teachers even for that work, why should the Sunday school not need them even more, infinitely more?

"Now that reminds me of a difficulty which is present, even when the teachers are all there. They are not the right sort of teachers, many of them; they do just such work as would not be tolerated on weekdays by any board of trustees; they whisper to each other; sometimes about the music which they are practicing, sometimes about the party that is to come off tomorrow. These are the exceptions, I know; but there are such exceptions in our school, and human nature is much the same the world over. I presume they are everywhere; at any rate, we have to deal just now with *our* school, and I know they are there.

"Dr. Dennis, there are at least seven of those twenty teachers in my room who ought to be in good, solid, earnest-working Bible classes, getting faith for help every Sunday; getting ideas that shall make them of use in the world, instead of frittering their time away on what at best seems to them but a very mechanical work, teaching some little children to repeat the Twenty-Third Psalm or to say the Lord's Prayer. The very fact that they do not recognize the dignity of such work unfits them for it; and the fact that they have no lesson to teach, I mean no lesson which they have to prepare carefully, excuses them from any attempt at Bible study."

"I believe you would make an excellent lecturer, if you were to take the field on a subject that interested you." This was Dr. Dennis's most irrelevant answer to Marion's eager words. She was not to be thrown off her theme.

"Then I shall try it, perhaps, on this very subject, for it certainly interests me wonderfully. Indeed, I am practicing now, with you for my audience."

"Don't think I am not interested, for I am," he said, returning to gravity and anxiety on the instant. "I see the subject to be full of perplexities; the class has seemed a bewildering one; the idea of putting the babies away alone in their own room fitted up for the purpose, and feeding them with milk until they are old enough to bear strong meat has been something of a hobby with me. I like it theoretically, but I confess to you that I have never been able to enjoy its practical workings in our school."

"I don't wonder," Marion said with energy. "It works most distressingly. I am coming to the very pith of my lecture now, which is this: I have been teaching school for more than seven years. I have taught all sorts and sizes of pupils. I had a fancy that I could manage almost anything in that line, believing that I had been through experiences varied enough to serve me in whatever line I could need, but I have found myself mistaken; I have found a work now that I can't accomplish. Mind you, I don't say that no one can do it; I am not quite so egotistic as that. If I do lecture, I have only to say that my teaching in that room is a failure. I can't do it, and I mean to give it up."

"Don't," Dr. Dennis said nervously. "You will be the third one in a year's time."

"I don't wonder. I wonder that they are alive."

"But, Miss Wilbur, you are a dark and gloomy lecturer. When you demolish air castles, have you nothing to build up in their places? Would you send the babies back into the main room again, to be worn out with quiet and lack of motion?"

"Not a bit of it. I like the baby-room plan as well as any mortal; and I have a remedy which it seems to me would arrange the whole thing. Of course it seems so to me; we always like our own ways. The truth is,

Dr. Dennis, I like nurseries, and think they ought to be maintained; but I don't like the idea of too many mothers there."

"Just what, in plain English, would you do, my friend, if you were commander in chief of the whole matter, and all we had to do was to obey you?"

"It isn't at all modest to tell," Marion said, laughing, "but it is true. I would banish every one of those twenty teachers and reign alone in my glory. No, I wouldn't, either. I would pick out the very best one among them and train her for an assistant."

"And manage the whole number yourself!"

"Why not? There are only a hundred of them, and I have managed that number for six hours a day, five days a week, without difficulty."

"Well, now, let me see just what you think you gain."

"It would take too long to tell. In my own opinion, I gain almost everything. But, in the first place, let me suppose a case. We have one good teacher, we will say, in that class, who knows just what she is about, and comes prepared to be about it. She has, say, two assistants, each carefully trained to a certain work; each understanding that in the event of the detention of the leader, one of them will be called on to teach the class, each pledging herself to notify the other of necessary absences. Don't you see that it will rarely, if ever, happen that one of the three cannot be at her post? The very sense of importance and responsibility attached to their office will lessen the chance of absence, while one teacher in twenty is almost sure to be away. Then we have those young girls in their places in the Bible class learning to be teachers indeed."

"But, Miss Wilbur, would not such a work be very hard for the leader?"

"Why harder than the present system in our school? I think, mind you, that it wouldn't be nearly so hard. But, for the sake of the argument, I will say, Why any harder? Why cannot her one assistant relieve her in just the same way that the other twenty are supposed to do now? Is there any known reason why a hundred children cannot repeat the Lord's Prayer together as well as have a lesson taught them together? Children like it, I assure you; there is an enthusiasm in numbers; they would much rather speak aloud and in beautiful unison, as they can be trained to do, than speak so low that the recitation loses half its beauty, because they must not disturb others.

"Then, I don't know how it is with other teachers, but, theoretically, you may plan out the work of these young teachers as much as you please, and, practically, they will do very much as they please; and it is a great deal harder for me to sit listening to a sort of teaching that I don't like and know that I am obliged to be still and endure it, than it is to do it myself.

"The idea that one hour of work on the Sabbath is so fearfully wearing is in my humble opinion all nonsense; those who think so have never been teachers of graded schools six hours a day, five days in the week, I don't believe. However, that is my opinion, you know. I may be quite mistaken as to theory; but I know as much as this: I am sure I could do the teaching alone, and I am sure that I can't do it with twenty helpers, so I just want to give it up."

"Don't give up the subject yet, please; I am interested. There is an argument on the other side that is very strong, I think. You haven't touched upon it. I have heard a good deal said, and thought it a point well taken, about the personal influence of each teacher. A sense of ownership that teachers of large classes can hardly call out because of their inability to visit their scholars and to be intimate with their little plans and with their home life."

Marion did a very rude thing at this point—she sat back in her rocking chair and laughed. Then she said:

"We are dealing, you remember, with our school. Now, you know the young ladies in that class. What proportion of them, should you imagine, without knowing anything about the facts, do really visit their pupils during the week and keep themselves posted as to the family life of any of them?"

A faint attempt at a smile hovered over Dr. Dennis's face as he said:

"Not many I am afraid. Indeed, to be very truthful, I don't believe there are five."

"I know there are not," Marion said decidedly. "And my supposition is that our school will average as well as others. There are exceptions, of course, but we are talking about the average. Now, that item sounds real well in a lecture, or on paper, but when you come to the practical part, they simply *don't* do it. Some of them know no more how to do it than kittens would, or than Ruth Erskine knows how to call on the second stratum of society in her own church."

Whereupon both pastor and visitor laughed. Dr. Dennis had heard of Ruth's attempt in that line.

"We have to deal with very commonplace human beings, instead of with angels. I think that is the trouble," Marion said, returning to the charge. "We can make nice rules, and they look well and sound beautifully; then if we can carry them out they are delightful, no doubt. But if we can't, why, what are we going to do about it? If the ladies in question were salaried teachers in the day school, a board of trustees could come together and dismiss them if they did not obey the laws. Who thinks of such a thing in the Sunday school? It is like calling all these teachers together for a teachers' meeting. You can *call* them to your heart's content; I know you can, for I have tried it; and if there is not a concert or a tea party or a lecture or a toothache on the evening in question, some of them will come, and others *won't*."

16

THEORY VERSUS PRACTICE

DR. DENNIS sat regarding his caller with a thoughtful air, while she sat back in the rocker and fanned herself, trying to cool off her eagerness somewhat and feeling that she was exhibiting herself as a very eager person indeed, and this calm man probably thought her impetuous. She resolved that the next remark he called forth should be made very quietly, and in as indifferent a manner as possible.

"Why should not the primary room be classified as well as the main department?" he asked at last.

To Marion there was so much that was absurd involved in the question that it put her indifference to flight at once.

"Why should there be a separate room at all if they are to be so classified? Why not keep them in the regular department, under the superintendent's eye, and where they can have the benefit of the pastor's remarks?"

"Because, while they are so young, they need more freedom than can be given them in the main room. They need to be allowed to talk aloud and to sing frequently and to repeat in concert."

"Precisely; and they do not need to be set down in corners, to be whispered at for a few minutes. Besides, Dr. Dennis, don't you think that if in the school proper, the scholars were all of nearly the same age and the same mental abilities—I mean if they averaged in that way—it would be wiser to have very large classes and very few teachers?"

"There are reasons in favor of that, and reasons against it," he said thoughtfully. "I am inclined, however, to think that the arguments in favor overbalance the objections; still, the serious objection is, that a faithful teacher wants little personal talks with her pupils and will contrive to be personal in a way that she cannot do so well in a large class."

"That is true," Marion said, as one yields a point that is new to her and that strikes her as being sensible. "But the same objection cannot be made in the primary classes, because little children are innocent and full of faith and frankness. There is no need of special privacy when you talk with them on religious topics; they would just as soon have all the world know that they want to love and serve Jesus as not; they are not a bit ashamed of it; it is not until they grow older, and the influences of silent tongues on that subject all around them have had their effect, that they need to be approached with such caution."

"How is it that you are so much at home in these matters, Miss Wilbur? For one who has been a Christian but a few weeks, you amaze me."

Marion laughed and flushed and felt the first tinge of embarrassment that had troubled her since the talk began.

"Why," she said hesitatingly, "I suppose, perhaps, I have common sense, and see no reason why it should be smothered when one is talking about such matters.

People's brains are not made over when they are converted. The same class of rules applies to them, I suppose, that applied before."

"I shouldn't wonder if a majority of people thought that common sense had nothing to do with religion," he said, laughing; "and that is what makes us silly and sentimental when we try to talk about it. In our effort to be solemn, and suit our words to the theme, we are unnatural. But your statement with regard to the little children is true; I have often observed it."

"That other point, about visiting, was the one that troubled me," Marion said. "It doesn't annihilate it to say that teachers don't visit; they don't, to be sure, with here and there a delightful exception. My experience on the matter, as well as on several other matters connected with the subject, reaches beyond these few weeks of personal experience. I have had my eyes very wide open; I was alive to inconsistencies wherever I found them; the world and the church, and especially the Sunday school, seemed to me to be full of professions without any practice. I rather enjoyed finding such flaws. Why I thought the thin spots in other people's garments would keep me any warmer, I am sure I don't know; but I was fond of bringing them to the surface.

"Still, because a duty isn't done is no sign that it cannot be. Of course, a teacher with six pupils could visit them frequently, while one with a hundred could do it but rarely; and yet, systematic effort would accomplish a great deal in that direction, it seems to me. I don't know why we should have more than fifty people in our churches; certainly the pastor could visit them much more frequently, and keep a better oversight, than when he had eight hundred, as you have; yet we don't think it the best way after all. We recognize the enthusiasm of numbers and the necessity for economizing good workers, so long as the field for work is so large.

"But I know a way in which a strong personal influence could be kept over even a hundred children; by keeping watch for the sick and sorrowing in their homes, and establishing an intimacy there, and by making a gathering of some sort, say twice a year, or oftener, if a person could, and giving the day to them; and, well, in a hundred different ways that I will not take your time to speak of; only we teachers of day schools know that we can make our influence far reaching, even when our numbers are large; and we know that there is such an influence in numbers and in disciplined action, that, other things being equal, we can teach mathematics to a class of fifty better than we can to a class of five; and if mathematics, why not the Lord's Prayer?

"Now I have relieved my mind on this subject," she added, laughing, as she arose, "and I feel a good deal better. Mind, I haven't said at all that the present system cannot be carried out successfully; I only say that I can't do it. I have tried it and failed; it is not according to my way of working."

"But the remedy, my dear friend, in our class, for instance. Suppose we wanted to reorganize, what would we do with the teachers in rule at present?"

Marion dropped back again into her chair with a dismayed little laugh and an expressive shrug of her shapely shoulders.

"Now you have touched a vital difficulty," she said. "I don't pretend to be able to help people out of a scrape like that. Having gotten themselves in, they must get out the best way they can, if there is any way."

"I am surprised that you do not suggest that they be unceremoniously informed that their services are not needed, and advise them to join a Bible class," Dr. Dennis said dryly. "That is the practical and helpful way that the subject is often disposed of in our conventions. I often wonder if those who so suggest would like to be the pastor of the church where such advice was adopted, and undertake to heal all the sores that would be the result."

"So long as human nature is made of the queer stuff that it is, I offer no such remedy," Marion said decidedly. "It is very odd that the people who do the least work in this world are the most sensitive as to position, etc. No, I see the trouble in the way. It could be partly disposed of in time, by sending all these subclasses out into the other school and organizing a new primary class out of the babies who have not yet come in."

"But there would be an injustice there. It would send out many babies who ought to have the privileges of the primary room for some time yet."

"And there is another difficulty; it would send out those young girls as teachers of the children, and they are not fit to teach; they should be studying."

"After all," he said, going back to his own thoughts instead of answering her last remark, "wouldn't the style of teaching that you suggest for this one woman and her assistant involve an unusual degree of talent and consecration and abnegation?"

"Yes," Marion said, quickly and earnestly, "I think it would; and I believe that there is no teaching done in our Sabbath school that is worthy of the name that does not involve all of these requirements; especially is it the case in teaching little children divine truths; one might teach them the alphabet without positive mental injury if they were not fully in sympathy, yet I doubt that; but one cannot teach the Sermon on the Mount in a way to reach the child heart unless one is thoroughly and solemnly in earnest and loves the souls of the little children so much that she can give up her very self for them.

"This is my theory; I want to work toward it. That is one of the strong reasons why I think two or three teachers are better for a primary class than twenty; because a church can generally furnish that number of really consecrated workers that she can spare for the primary class, while to find twenty who can be spared for that room one would need to go to paradise, I am afraid. Now I know, Dr. Dennis, that such talk sounds as if I were insufferably conceited; but I don't believe I am; I simply know what I am willing to try to do; and, to a certain extent, I know what I *can* do. Why should I not? I have tried it a long time."

"If you are conceited," Dr. Dennis said, smiling, "it is a real refreshing form for it to appear in. I am almost a convert to your theory; at least, so far as I need converting. If I should tell you that something like your idea has always been mine, you would not consider me a hypocrite, would you?"

"If you think so, why have we the present system in our school?"

"My dear friend, I did not manufacture the school; it is as I found it; and there are those young ladies, who, however unfaithful they are—and a few of them are just that—do not reach the only point where they could give positive help, that of resigning, and giving us a chance to do better. Besides, they are, as you say, sensitive; they do not like to be called to account for occasional absences; in fact, they do not like being controlled in any way."

"That is one of the marked difficulties," Marion

said eagerly. "Now I have heard people talk, who led you to infer that it was the easiest thing in life to mold these young teachers into the required shape and form; that you had only to sweetly suggest and advise and direct, and they sweetly succumbed. Now, don't their mothers know that young ladies naturally do no such thing? It is very difficult for them to yield their opinions to one whose authority they do not recognize; and they are not fond of admitting authority even where family life sanctions it. Oh, the whole subject is just teeming with difficulties; put it in any form you will, it seems to me to be a mistake.

"Where you give these young ladies the lesson to teach, the diverse minds that are brought to bear on it make it almost impossible for the leader to give an intelligent summing up. Now is she to discover what special point has been taken up by each teacher? As a bit of private experience, I think she will be a fortunate woman if she finds that *any* point at all has been reached in many of the classes.

"There is only now and then a teacher who believes that little children are capable of understanding the application of a story. I can't understand why, if that is the best method of managing a primary class, people take the trouble to have a separate room and another superintendent. Why don't they stay in the main department? I always thought that one of the special values of a separate room was that the lesson may be given in a distinct and natural tone of voice, and with illustrations and accompaniments that cannot be used, where many classes are together, without disturbing some of them.

"If, on the other hand, the subteachers are not expected to give the lesson, but only to teach certain opening recitations, then you have the spectacle of employing a dozen or twenty persons to do the work of one. Then there's another thing; our room is not suited to the plan of subdivision, and there is only occasionally a room that has been built to order, which is—"

"On the whole, you do not at all believe in the plan of subdivision," Dr. Dennis said, laughing.

And then callers came, and Marion took her leave.

"I am not quite sure whether I like him or dislike him, or whether I am afraid of him just a trifle." This she said to the girls as they went home from prayer meeting. "He has a queer way of branching off from the subject entirely, just when you suppose that you have interested him. Sometimes he interrupts with a sentence that sounds wonderfully as if he might be quizzing you. He is a trifle queer anyway. I don't believe I love him with all the zeal that a person should bestow on a pastor. I am loyal on that subject theoretically, but practically I stand in awe."

"I don't see how you can think him sarcastic," Flossy said. "There is not the least tinge of that element in his nature, I think; at least I have never seen it. I don't feel afraid of him, either; once I thought I should; but he is so gentle and pleasant and meets one halfway and understands what one wants to tell better than one understands oneself. Oh, I like him ever so much. He is not sarcastic to me."

Marion looked down upon the fair little girl at her side with a smile that had a sort of almost motherly tenderness in it, as she said gently:

"One would be a very bear to think of quizzing a hummingbird, you know. It would be very silly in him to be sarcastic to you."

Eurie interrupted the talk:

"What is the matter with the prayer meetings?" she

asked. "Do any of you know? I do wish we could do something to make them less forlorn. I am almost homesick every time I go. If there were more people there, the room wouldn't look so desolate. Why on earth don't the people come?"

"Constitutionally opposed to prayer meetings; or it is too warm, or too damp, or too something, for most of them to go out," Marion said.

And Ruth added:

"It is not wonderful that you find sarcastic people in the world, Marion. The habit grows on you."

"Does it," Marion asked, speaking with sadness. "I am sorry to hear that. I really thought I was improving."

"The question is, can we do anything to improve matters?" Eurie said. "Can't we manage to smuggle some more people into that chapel on Wednesday evenings?"

"Invite them to go, do you mean?" Flossy said, and her eyes brightened. "I never thought of that. We might get our friends to go. Who knows what good might be done in that way? What if we try it?"

Ruth looked gloomy. This way of working was wonderfully distasteful to her. She specially disliked what she called thrusting unpopular subjects on people's attention. But she reflected that she had never yet found a way to work which she did like; so she was silent.

Flossy, according to her usual custom, persistently followed up the new idea.

"Let us try it," she said. "Suppose we pledge ourselves each to bring another to the meeting next week."

"If we can," Marion said significantly.

"Well, of course, some of us can," Eurie answered.

"You ought to be able to, anyway. There you are in a schoolroom, surrounded by hundreds of people who ought to go; and in a boardinghouse, coming in contact with dozens of another stamp, who are in equal need. I should think you had opportunities enough."

"I know it," Marion said promptly. "If I were only situated as you are, with nobody but a father and mother and a brother and a couple of sisters to ask—people who are of no special consequence to you, and about whom it will make no personal difference to you whether they go to church or not—it would be some excuse for not bringing anybody; but a boardinghouse full of men and women and a room full of schoolgirls!—consider your privileges, Marion Wilbur."

Eurie laughed.

"Oh, I can get Nell to go," she said. "He nearly always does what I want him to. But I was thinking how many you have to work among."

"Six people are as good to work among as sixty, until you get them all," Marion answered quickly.

As for Ruth, it was only the darkness that hid her curling lip. She someway could not help disliking people who, like Nellis Mitchell, always did what they were asked to do, just to oblige. Also, she dreaded this new plan. She had no one to ask, no one to influence. So she said to herself, gloomily, although (knowing that it was untrue) she did not venture to say it aloud. She gave consent, of course, to the proposition to try by personal effort to increase the number at prayer meeting. It would be absurd to object to it. She did not care to own that she shrank from personal effort of this sort; it was a grief to her very soul that she did so shrink.

"Remember, we stand pledged to try for one new face at the prayer meeting," Eurie said as she bade them good-night. "Pledged to try, you understand, Marion; we can at least do that, even if we don't succeed."

"In the meantime, remember that we have our Bible evening tomorrow," Marion returned. "You are to come bristling with texts from your standpoint; it will not do to forget that."

17

The Discussion

MARION went about her dingy room, brushing off a bit of dust here, setting a chair straight there, trying in what ways she might to brighten its homeliness. She was a trifle sore sometimes over the contrast between that room and the homes of her three friends. Sometimes she thought it a wonder that they could endure to leave the brightness and cheer that surrounded their home lives and seek her out.

There were times when she was very much tempted to spend a large portion of her not-too-large salary in bestowing little home-looking things on this corner of the second-rate boardinghouse; a rocking chair; a cozy-looking, bright-covered, old-fashioned lounge; a tiny center table, instead of the square, boxy-looking thing that she had; not very extravagant her notions were, just a suggestion of comfort and a touch of brightness for her beauty-loving eyes to dwell on; but these home things, and these bright things, cost money, more money than she felt at liberty to spend.

When her necessary expenses of books and dress and a dozen apparently trifling incidentals were met, there was little enough left to send to that faraway, struggling uncle and aunt, who needed her help sadly enough, and who had shared their little with her in earlier days.

There was no special love about this offering of hers; it was just a matter of hard duty; they had taken care of her in her orphanhood, a grave, preoccupied sort of care, bestowing little time and no love on her that she could discover; at the same time, they had never either of them been unkind, and they had fed and clothed her and never said in her presence that they grudged it; they had never asked her for any return, never seemed to expect any; and they were regularly surprised every half year when the remittance came.

But so far as that was concerned, Marion did not know it; they were a very undemonstrative people. Uncle Reuben had told her once that she need not do it, that they had not expected it of her; and Aunt Hannah had added, "No more they didn't." But Marion had hushed them both by a decided sentence, to the effect that it was nothing more than ordinary justice and decency. And she did not know even now that the gratitude they might have expressed was hushed back by her cold, businesslike words.

Still, the remittance always went; it had required some special scrimping to make the check the same as usual and yet bring in Chautauqua; it had been delayed beyond its usual time by these new departures, and it was on this particular evening that she was getting it ready for the mail. For seven years, twice a year, she had regularly written her note:

AUNT HANNAH:——I enclose in this letter a check for _____. I hope you are as well, as usual.

In haste,
M. J. WILBUR.

This, or a kindred sentence as brief and as much to the point. Tonight her fingers had played with the pen instead of writing, and at last, with a curious smile hovering around her lip, she wrote the unaccustomed words "Dear Aunt." It would have taken very little to have made the smile into a quiver; it seemed just then so strange that she should have no one to write that word "dear" to; that she should use it so rarely that it actually looked like a stranger to her. Then the writing went on thus:

"I hope I have not caused you discomfort by being somewhat later than usual with your check. Matters shaped themselves in such a way that I could not send it before. I hope it will be of a little help and comfort to you. I wish it were larger. Give my re-love to Uncle Reuben."

The "re" was the beginning of the word "regards," but she thought better of it and wrote "love." He was her father's brother, and the only relative she had. Then the pen paused again, and the writer gnawed at the painted holder, and mused, and looked sober first, then bright faced, and finally she dashed down this line:

Dear Aunt Hannah, I have found my father's Friend, even the Lord Jesus Christ. He is indeed mighty to save, as Father used to say that he was. I have proved it, for he has saved me. I wish you and Uncle Reuben knew him.

Yours truly,
MARION

I suppose Marion would have been very much surprised had she known what I know, that Aunt Hannah and Uncle Reuben shed tears over that letter and put it in the family Bible. And, someway, they felt more thankful for the check than they had ever done before.

Marion did not know this, but she knew that her own heart felt lighter than usual as she hurried about her room. The girls came before she was fairly through with her preparations—a bright trio, with enough of beauty and grace and elegance about them to fairly make her room glow.

"Here we are," said Eurie. "We have run the gauntlet of five calls and a concert, and I don't know how many other things in prospective, for the sake of getting to you."

"Did you come alone?"

"No; my blessed Nell came with us to the door, and most dreadfully did he want to come in. I should have let him in, only I knew by Ruth's face she thought it awful; but he would have enjoyed the evening. Nell does enjoy new things."

"There is no special sensation about Bible verses. I presume they would have palled on him before the evening was over." This was said in Ruth's coldest tone.

"You are mistaken in that, my lady Ruth. I have found several verses in my search that have given me a real sensation. Besides which, I have proved my side beyond the shadow of a reasonable doubt, and I am very anxious to begin."

Marion laughed.

"I daresay we have each proved our sides to our entire satisfaction," she said. "The question is, which side will bear the test of our combined intellects being brought to bear on it? Did you bring your Bibles, girls? Oh yes, you are armed. Flossy, your Bible is splendid; when the Millennium dawns I am going to have just such a one. By the way, won't that be a blissful time? Don't you want to live to see it? Eurie, inasmuch as you are so anxious to begin, you may do so. Let us 'carry on our investigations in a scientific way,' as Professor Easton says. Give us your 'unanswerable argument,' and I will answer it with my unanswerable one on the other side; then if Ruth can prove to us that we are both mistaken, and each can follow her own judgment in the matter, we will be quenched, you see, unless Flossy can give a balancing vote."

"Well, in the first place," Eurie said, "I found to my infinite astonishment, and, of course, to my delight, that the Bible actually stated that there was a time to dance. Now, if there is a time for it, of course it is the proper thing to do; that just settled the whole question. How absurd it would be to put in the Bible a statement that there was a time to dance, and then to tell us that it was wrong to dance!"

"Eurie, are you in earnest or in sport?" Marion asked at last, looking at her with a puzzled air, and not sure whether to laugh or be disgusted.

"A little of both," Eurie said, breaking into a laugh. "But now, to be serious, there really is such a verse; did you know it? I am sure I didn't. I was very much astonished; and I think it does prove something. It indicates that dancing is a legitimate amusement, and one that was indulged in during those times."

"Do you advocate its use under the same circumstances in which it was used in those times?"

"I'm sure I don't know. Was there anything peculiar in its use?"

"Didn't you follow out the references as to dancing?"

"No, indeed, I didn't. I wish I had. Does it give an account of it? That would have been better yet."

"It would have enlightened you somewhat," Marion said, laughing. "If you had been on the other side now, you would have been sure to have followed out the connection as I did; then you would have found that to be true to your Bible you must dance in prayer meeting, or in church on the Sabbath, or at some time when you desired to express religious joy."

"Pooh!" said Eurie. "Now is that so?"

"Of course it's so. Just amuse yourself by looking up the references to the word in the concordance, and I will read them for our enlightenment."

"Well," said Eurie, after several readings, "I admit that I am rather glad that form of worship is done away with. I am fond of dancing, but I don't care to indulge when I go to prayer meeting. But, after all, that doesn't prove that dancing is wrong."

"Nor right?" Ruth said questioningly. "Doesn't it simply prove nothing at all? That is just as I said; we have to decide these questions for ourselves."

"But, Eurie, did you content yourself with just one text? I thought you were to have an army of them."

"What is the use in that?" Ruth asked. "One text is as good as a dozen if it proves one's position."

"A multitude of witnesses," Marion said significantly; and added, "girls, Ruth has but one text in support of her position; see if she has."

"Well, I have another," said Eurie. "The wisest man who ever lived said, 'A merry heart doeth good like a medicine.' Now I am sure that advocates bright, cheerful, merry times, just such as one has in dancing; and there are dozens of such verses, indicating that it is a duty we owe to society to have happy and merry times together; and a simpler way of doing it than any I know is to dance. We are not gossiping, nor saying censorious things, when we are dancing; and we are having a very pleasant time for our friends."

"'Is any merry? let him sing psalms,'" quoted Marion. "Would you like to indulge in that entertainment at the same time you were dancing; or do you think the same state of mind could be expressed as well by either dancing, or psalm singing, as one chose?"

"Eurie Mitchell, you are just being nonsensical!" Ruth said, speaking in a half-annoyed tone. "You are not absurd enough to suppose that either of those verses are arguments in favor of dancing, or against dancing, or indeed have anything to do with the subject? What is the use in trying to make people think you are a simpleton when you aren't."

"Dreadful!" said Eurie. "Is that what I'm doing? Now, I thought I was proving the subtle nature of my argumentive powers. See here, I will be as sober as a judge. No, I don't think those verses have to do with it; at least, the latter hasn't. I admit that I thought the fact that a time to dance was mentioned in the Bible was an item in its favor as far as it went; but it seems I should rather have said as far as *I* went, for it went farther, as Marion has made me prove with that dreadful concordance of hers. We don't own such a terrible book as that, and I have to go skimming over the whole Bible in a distracting manner. I just happened on the verse that says 'there is a time to dance,' and I didn't know but there might be a special providence in it. But now, frankly, I am on the side that Ruth has taken. It seems to be a question that is left to individual judgment. There is no 'thus saith the Lord' about it, any more than there is about having company, and going out to tea, and a dozen other things. We are to do in these matters what we think is right; and that in my opinion, is all there is about it."

"Then you retire from the lists?" Marion asked.

"Not a bit of it. I am just as emphatically of the opinion that there is no harm in dancing as I ever was. What I say is that the Bible is silent on that subject, leaving each to judge for herself."

"'As he thinketh in his heart, so is he,'" quoted Ruth. "That is my verse, one of them; and I think it is unanswerable. If you, Marion, think it is wicked to dance, then you would be doing a wrong thing to dance; but, Eurie, believing it to be right and proper, has a right to dance. Each person as he thinks in his heart."

"Then, if I think in my heart that it is right to go skating on Sunday, it will be quite right for me to go? Is that the reasoning, Ruth?"

"No, of course; because in that instance you have the direct command 'Remember the sabbath day, to keep it holy.'"

"But who is going to prove to me in what way I should keep it holy? I may skate with very good thoughts in my heart and feel that I am keeping the spirit of the command; and, if I think so in my heart, why, isn't it so?"

"You know it isn't a parallel case," Ruth said, slightly nettled.

"Flossy, would you speak for a dollar?" Eurie asked, suddenly turning to her. She had been utterly grave and silent during all this war of words, but, to judge from her face, by no means uninterested. She shook her head now with a quiet smile.

"I know what I think," she said, "but I don't want to speak yet; only I want to know, Ruth, about that verse; I found that and thought about it. I couldn't see that it means what you think it does. I used to think in my very heart that joining the church and trying to do about right was all there was of religion; but I have found that I was wonderfully mistaken. Can't persons be honest and yet be very much in the dark because they have not informed themselves?"

"Why, dear me!" said Marion, "only see, Ruth, where your doctrine would lead you! What about the heathen women who think in their hearts that they do a good deed when they give their babies to the crocodiles?"

"I found that verse about Paul persecuting all who called on the name of Jesus, and he says he verily thought he was doing God's service." This was Flossy's added word.

"See here," said Eurie, "we are not getting at it at all. I haven't any verses, and you have demolished Ruth's. The way is for you and Flossy to open your batteries on us and let us prove to you that they don't any of them mean a single word they say, or *you* say; or *something, anything,* so that we win the argument. What I want to know is, what earthly harm do people see in dancing? I don't mean, of course, going to balls and mingling with all sorts of people and dancing indecent figures. I mean the way we girls have been in the habit of it, Ruth and Flossy and I. We never went to a ball in our lives, and we were never injured by dancing, so far as I can discover, and yet we have done a good deal of it. Now I love to dance; it is the very pleasantest amusement I can think of; and yet I honestly want to get at the truth of this matter; I want to leave; I don't in the least know why churches and Christians think such dancing is wrong. I couldn't find a thing in the Bible that showed me the reason. To be sure, I had very little time to look, and a very ignorant brain to do it with, and no helps. But I am ready to be convinced, if anybody has anything that will convince me."

"Just let me ask you a question," Marion said: "Why did you think, before you were converted, that it was wrong for Christian people to dance?"

"How do you know I did?" asked Eurie, flushing and laughing.

"Never mind how I know; though you must have forgotten some of the remarks I have heard you make about others, to ask me. But please tell me."

"Honestly, then, I don't know; and it is that thought, or rather that remembrance, which disturbs me now. I had a feeling that someway it was an inconsistent thing to do, and that if I was converted I should have to give it up, and it was a real stumbling block in my way for some days. But I don't this minute know a single definite reason why I, in common with the rest of the girls and the young men in our set, felt amused whenever we saw dancing church members. I have thought perhaps it was prejudice, or a misunderstanding of the Christian life."

18

THE RESULT

"NOW, what I want," said Marion, "is to have you people who are posted answer a few questions. You know I am not a dancer; I have only stood aside and looked on; but I have as high a respect for common sense as any of you *can* have, and I want to use some of it in this matter; so just tell me, is it true or not that there is a style of dancing that is considered improper in the extreme?"

"Why, yes, of course there is," Eurie said quickly.

"Is it the style that is indulged in at our ordinary balls, where all sorts of characters are admitted, where, in fact, anyone who can buy a ticket and dress is welcome? You know you were particular to state that none of you went to balls; are these some of the reasons?"

"*My* principal reason is," Ruth said with an upward curve of her haughty lip, "that I do not care to associate with all sorts of people, either in the ball-room or anywhere else."

"Besides which, you are reasonably particular who of your acquaintances has the privilege of frequently clasping your hand and placing an arm caressingly around your waist, to say nothing of almost carrying you through the room, are you not?"

Ruth turned toward the questioner, flashing eyes, while she said:

"That is very unusual language to address to us, Marion. Possibly we are quite as high toned in our feelings as yourself."

"Oh, but now, I appeal to your reason and common sense; you say, yourself, that these should be our guide. Isn't it true that you, as a dancer, allow familiarity that you would consider positively insulting under other circumstances? Am I mistaken in your opinion as to the proper treatment that ladies should receive from gentlemen at all other times save when they are dancing?"

"It's a solemn fact," said Eurie, laughing at the folly of her position, "that the man with whom I dance has a privilege that if he should undertake to assume at any other time would endanger his being knocked down if my brother Nell was within sight."

"And it is true that there are lengths to which dancers go that you would not permit under any circumstances?"

"Undeniable," Eurie said again. "Yet I don't see what that proves. There are lengths to which you can carry almost any amusement. The point is, we don't carry them to any such lengths."

"That isn't the whole point, Eurie. There are many amusements which no one carries to improper lengths. We do not hear of their being so perverted; but we do not hear of them in the ballroom. The question is, has dancing such a tendency? Do impure people have dancehouses which it is a shame for a person to enter? Are young men and young women, our brothers and sisters, led astray in them? We mustn't be too delicate to speak on these things, for they exist; and they are found among people for whom the Lord died, and many of them will be reclaimed and be in heaven with us. They are our brethren; *can* they be led away by the influences of the dance? If we are all really in earnest in this matter, will you each give your opinion on this one point?"

"I suppose it is unquestionable," Ruth said, "that dancehouses are in existence, and that they are patronized by the lowest and vilest of human beings; but the sort of dance indulged in has no more likeness to the dances of cultivated society than—"

"Than the drunkard lying in the gutter bears likeness to the elegant young man of fashion who has taken his social sips from a silver goblet lined with gold at his mother's refreshment table," Marion said, interrupting her, and speaking with energy. "Yet you will admit that the one may be, and awfully often is, the stepping-stone to the other."

"It is true," Eurie said; "both are true. I never thought of it before, but there is no denying it."

As for Flossy, she simply bowed her head, as one interested but not excited.

"Then may I bring in one of my verses, 'Pure religion and undefiled before God and the Father is this, To visit the fatherless and widows in their affliction, and to keep himself *unspotted* from the world.' Does that apply? If the world can carry this amusement to such depths of degradation, and if the elegant parlor dance is or *can* be, in the remotest degree, the first step thereto, *are* we keeping ourselves unspotted if we have anything to do with it, countenance it in any way? Don't you see that the question, after all, is the same in many respects as the cardplaying one? We have been over this ground before.

"Suppose we grant, for argument's sake, that not one of you is in danger of being led away to any sort of excess, and I should hardly dare to admit it in my own case, because of a verse in this same old book, 'Let him that thinketh he standeth take heed lest he fall'; but if it *should* be so, let me give you another of my selections—rather, let me read the entire argument."

Whereupon she turned to the tenth chapter of First Corinthians and read St. Paul's argument about eating meat offered to idols, pausing with special emphasis over the words, " 'Conscience, I say, not thine own, but of the other.' Did I understand you to say, Eurie, that it is a very general belief among dancers that Christians are inconsistent who indulge in this amusement?"

"It is a provoking truth that there is. Don't you know, Ruth, how we used to be merry over the Symonds girls and that young Winters who were church members? Well, they made rather greater pretensions with their religion than some others did, and that made us specially amused over them."

"Then, Eurie, wasn't their influence unfortunate on you?"

"I am not on your side, Mistress Wilbur. You should have more conscience than to keep me all the time condemning myself!"

"That is answer enough," Marion said, smiling. "I am only asking for information, you know. I never danced. But in the light of that confession, hear this: 'But if thy brother be grieved with thy meat, now walkest thou not charitably. Destroy not him with thy meat, for whom Christ died. Let not *then your good be evil spoken of.*' Isn't that precisely what you were doing of the good in those church members, Eurie? Now a sophist would possibly say that the argument of Paul had reference to food offered to idols, and not to dancing; but I think here is a chance for us to exercise that judgment and common sense which we are so fond of talking about.

"The main point seems to be not to destroy those for whom Christ died. Does it make any difference whether we do it with our digestive organs or with our feet? But what is the sophist going to do with this: 'It is good neither to eat flesh, nor to drink wine, nor any thing whereby thy brother stumbleth, or is offended, or is made weak.' You see, he may, or may not, be a fool for allowing himself to be led astray. St. Paul says nothing about that. He simply directs as to the Christian's duty in the matter."

Ruth made a movement of impatience.

"You are arguing, Marion, on the supposition that a great many people are led astray by dancing; whereas I don't believe that to be the case."

"Do you suppose one soul ever was?"

"Why, yes, I suppose so."

"We even know one," Eurie said, speaking low and looking very grave.

"Do you believe it is possible that another soul may in the next million years?"

"Of course it is possible."

"Then the question is, how much is one soul worth? I don't feel prepared to estimate it, do you?" To which question Ruth made no reply. "There is another point," Marion said. "You young ladies talk about being careful with whom you dance. Don't you accept the attentions of strange young gentlemen who have been introduced to you by your fashionable friends? Take Mr. Townsend, the young man who came here a stranger and was introduced in society by the Wagners, because they met him when abroad. Didn't you dance with him, Eurie Mitchell?"

"Dozens of times," said Eurie promptly.

"And Flossy, didn't you?"

Flossy nodded her golden head.

"Well, now you know, I suppose, that he has proved to be a perfect libertine. Honestly, wouldn't you both feel better if he had never had his arm around you?"

"Marion, your way of saying that thing is simply disgusting!" Ruth said in great heat.

"Is it my way of saying it, or is it the thing itself?" Marion asked coolly. "I tell you, it is impossible to know whether the man who dresses well and calls on you at stated intervals, looking and talking like a gentleman, is not a very Satan, who will lead away the pretty, guileless, unsuspecting young girl who is worth his trouble; and the leading often and often commences with a dance; and the young girl may never have been allowed to dance with him at all had not stately and entirely unexceptionable leaders of society, like our Ruth here, allowed it first.

"It is the same question after all, and it narrows down to a fine point. A thing that can possibly lead one to eternal death, a Christian has no business to meddle with, even if he knows of but one soul in a million years who has been so wrecked. In all this we have not even glanced at the endless directions to 'redeem the time,' to be 'instant in season' and 'out of season,' to 'work while the day lasts,' to 'watch and be sober.' What do all these verses mean? Are we obeying them when we spend half the night in a whirl of wild pleasure?

"The fact remains that a majority of people are not temperate in their dancing; they do it night after night;

they long after it, and are miserable if the weather or the cough keeps them away. I know dozens of such young ladies; I have them as my pupils; my heart trembles for them; they are just intoxicated with dancing; and they quote you, Ruth Erskine, as an example when I try to talk with them; I have heard them. Whether it is wrong for other people or not, as true as I sit here, I can tell you this: I have two girls in my class who are killing themselves with this amusement, carried to its least damaging extreme, for they still think they are very careful with whom they dance; and you are in a measure, at least, responsible for their folly. You needn't say they are simpletons; I think they are, but what of it? 'Shall the *weak* brother perish, for whom Christ died?'"

"Nell made a remark that startled me a little, it was so queer." Eurie said this after the startled hush that fell over them at the close of Marion's eager sentence had in part subsided. "We were speaking of a party where we had been one evening and some of the girls had danced every set, till they were completely worn out. Some of them had been dancing with rather questionable young men, too; for I shall have to own that all the gentlemen who get admitted into fashionable parlors are not angels by any means. I know there are several who are supposed to be of the first society that Father has forbidden me ever to dance with.

"We were talking about some of these, and about the extreme manner in which the dancing was carried on, when Nell said: 'I'll tell you what, Eurie, I hope my wife wasn't there tonight.' 'Dear me!' I said, 'I didn't know she was in existence. Where do you keep her?' He was as sober as a judge. 'She is on the earth somewhere, of course, if I am to have her,' he said; 'and what I say is, I hope she wasn't there. If I thought she was among those dancers, I would go and knock the fellow down who insulted her by swinging her around in that fashion. I want my wife's hand to be kept for me to hold; I don't thank anybody else for doing that part for me.'"

"Precisely!" Marion said. "It is considered unlady-like, I believe, for people to talk about love and marriage. I never could see why; I'm sure neither of them is wicked. But I suppose each of us occasionally thinks of the possibility of having a friend as dear even as a husband. How would you like it, girls, to have him spend his evenings dancing with first one young lady and then another, offering them attentions that, under any other circumstances, would stamp him as a liber-tine?

"Whichever way you look at this question, it is a disagreeable one to me. I may never be married; it is not at all likely that I ever shall; I ought to have been thinking about it long ago, if I was ever going to indulge in that sort of life; but if I *should,* I'm heartily glad of one thing—and, mind, I mean it—that no man but my husband shall ever put his arm around me, nor hold my hand, unless it is to keep me from actual danger; falling over a precipice, you know, or some such unusual matter as that."

"Flossy hasn't opened her lips this evening. Why don't you talk, child? Does Marion overwhelm you? I don't wonder. Such a tornado as she has poured out upon us! I never heard the like in my life. It isn't all in the Bible; that is one comfort. Though, dear me! I don't know but the spirit of it is. What do you think about it all?"

"Sure enough," Marion said, turning to Flossy, as Eurie paused. "Little Flossy, where are your verses? You were going to give us whatever you found in the

Bible. You were the best witness of all, because you brought such an unprejudiced determination to the search. What did you find?"

"My search didn't take the form I meant it should," Flossy said. "I didn't look far nor long, and I did not decide the question for anybody else, only for myself. I found only two verses, two pieces of verses; I mean, I stopped at those and thought about them all the rest of the week. These are the ones," and Flossy's soft sweet voice repeated them without turning to the Bible:

"'Whatsoever ye do in word or deed, do all in the name of the Lord Jesus'; *'Whatsoever* ye do, do it heartily, as to the Lord, and not unto men.' Those verses just held me; I thought about dancing, about all the times in which I had danced, and the people with whom I had danced, and the words we had said to each other, and I could not see that in any possible way it could be done in the name of the Lord Jesus, or that it could be done heartily, as unto the Lord. I settled my own heart with those words; that for me to dance after I knew that whatever in word or deed I did, I was pledged to do *heartily* for the *Lord,* would be an impossibility."

An absolute hush fell upon them all. Marion looked from one to the other of the flushed and eager faces, and then at the sweet drooping face of their little Flossy.

"We have spent our strength vainly," she said at last. "It is our privilege to get up higher; to look at all these things from the mount whereon God will let us stand, if we want to climb. I think little Flossy has got there."

"After all," Eurie said, "that verse would cut off a great many things that are considered harmless."

"What does that prove, my beloved Eureka?" Marion said quickly. "'If thy right hand offend thee, cut it off, and cast it from thee,' is another Bible verse. These verses of Flossy's mean something, surely. What *do* they mean is the question left for us to decide. After all, Ruth, I agree with you; it is a question that must be left to our judgment and common sense; only we are bound to strengthen our common sense and confirm our judgments in the light of the lamp that is promised as a guide to our feet."

Almost nothing was said among them after that, except the commonplaces of good-nights. The next afternoon, as Marion was working out a refractory example in algebra for Gracie Dennis, she bent lower over her slate and said:

"Miss Wilbur, did you know that your friends Miss Erskine, Miss Shipley, and Miss Mitchell had all declined Mrs. Garland's invitation and sent her an informal little note signed by them all, to the effect that they had decided not to dance anymore?"

"No," said Marion, the rich blood mounting to her temples, and her face breaking into a smile. "How did you hear?"

"Mrs. Garland told my father; she said she honored them for their consistency and thought more highly of their new departure than she ever had before. It *is* rather remarkable so early in their Christian life, don't you think?"

"Rather," Marion said with a smile, and she followed it with a soft little sigh. *She* had not been invited to Mrs. Garland's. There was no opportunity for her to show whether she was consistent or not.

19

KEEPING THE PROMISE

IT WAS curious how our four girls set about enlarging the prayer meeting. That idea had taken hold of them as the next thing to be done.

"The wonder was," Eurie said, "that Christian people had not worked at it before. I am sure," she added, "that if anyone had invited me to attend, I should have gone long ago, just to please, if it was one that I cared to please."

And Marion answered with a smile:

"I am sure you would, too, with your present feelings."

Still none of them doubted but that they would have success. They saw little of each other during the days that intervened, and their plan necessarily involved their going alone, or with what company they could gather, instead of meeting and keeping each other company, as they had done in the first days of their prayer-meeting life.

Marion came first, and alone. She went forward to their usual seat with a very forlorn and desolate air. She had entered upon the work with enthusiasm and with eager desire and expectation of success. To be sure, she was a long time deciding whom to ask, and several times changed her plans.

At last her heart settled on Miss Banks, the friend with whom she had almost been intimate before these new intimacies gathered around her. Latterly they had said little to each other. Miss Banks had seemed to avoid Marion since that rainy Monday when they came in contact so sharply. She was not exactly rude, not in the least unkind; she simply seemed to feel that the points of congeniality between them were broken, and so avoided her.

She did this so successfully that, even after Marion's thought to invite her to the meeting had taken decided shape, it was difficult to find the opportunity. Having gotten the idea, however, she was persistent in it; and at last, during recess, on the very day of the meeting, she came across her in the library, looking aimlessly over the rows of books.

"In search of wisdom or recreation?" Marion asked, stopping beside her and speaking with the familiarity of former days.

"In search of some tiresome references for my class in philosophy. Some of the scholars are provokingly in earnest in the study and will not be satisfied with the platitudes of the textbook."

"That is a refreshing departure from the ordinary state of things, isn't it?" Marion asked, laughing at the way in which the progress of her pupils was put. Then, without waiting for an answer, and already feeling her resolution beginning to cool, she plunged into the subject that interested her. "I have been in search of you all the morning."

"That's surprising," Miss Banks said coolly.

"Couldn't I be found? I have been no further away than my schoolroom."

"Well, I mean looking for you at a time when you were not engaged, or perhaps looking forward to seeing you at such a time, would be a more proper way of putting it," said Marion, trying to smile and yet feeling a trifle annoyed.

"One is apt to be somewhat engaged in a schoolroom during school hours, especially if one is a teacher."

They were not getting on at all. Marion decided to speak without trying to bring herself gracefully to the point.

"I want to ask a favor of you. Will you go to meeting with me tonight?"

"To meeting," Miss Banks repeated without turning from the bookcase. "What meeting is there tonight?"

"Why, the prayer meeting at the First Church. There is always a meeting there on Wednesday nights."

Miss Banks turned herself slowly away from the book she was examining and fixed her clear, cold gray eyes on Marion:

"And so there has been every Wednesday evening during the five years that we have been in school together, I presume. To what can I be indebted for such an invitation at this late day?"

It was very hard for Marion not to get angry. She knew this cold composure was intended as a rebuke to herself for presuming to have withdrawn from the clique that had hitherto spent much time together.

"What is the use of this?" she asked; a shade of impatience in her voice, although she tried to control it. "You know, Miss Banks, that I profess to have made a discovery during the last few weeks; that I try to arrange all my actions with a view to the new revelations in life and duty which I have certainly had; in simple language you know that, whereas, I not long ago presumed to scoff at conversion and at the idea of life abiding in Christ, I believe now that I have been converted, and that the Lord Jesus is my Friend and Brother; I want to tell you that I have found rest and peace in him. Is it any wonder that I should desire it for my friends? I do honestly crave for you the same experience that I have enjoyed, and to that end I have asked you to attend the meeting with me tonight."

It is impossible to describe the changes on Miss Banks's face during this sentence. There was a touch of embarrassment, and more than a touch of incredulity, and over all a look of great amazement. She continued to survey Marion from head to foot with those cold, gray eyes, for as much as a minute after she had ceased speaking. Then she said, speaking slowly, as if she were measuring every word:

"I am sure I ought to be grateful for the trouble you have taken; the more so as I had not presumed to think that you had any interest in either my body or my soul. But as I have had no new and surprising revelations, and know nothing about the Friend and Brother of whom you speak, I may be excused from coveting the like experience with yourself, however delightful you may have found it. As to the meeting, I went once to that church to attend a prayer meeting, too, and if there can be a more refined and long drawn-out exhibition of dullness than was presented to us there, I don't know where to look for it. I wonder why the school bell doesn't ring? It is three minutes past the time by my watch."

Marion, without an attempt at a reply, turned and

went swiftly down the hall. She was glad that just then the tardy bell pealed forth, and that she was obliged to go at once to the recitation room and involve herself in the intricacies of algebra.

Without the incentive to self-control, she felt that she would have given way to the hot, disappointed tears that were choking in her throat. How sad her heart was as she sat there alone in the prayer room. It was early and but few were present. She had never felt so much alone. The companionship which had been so close and so constant during the few weeks past seemed suddenly to have been removed from her, and when she essayed to go back to the old friend, she had stood coldly and heartlessly—aye, worse than that— mockingly aloof.

She had overheard her that very afternoon, detailing to one of the under teachers, fragments of the conversation in the library. Marion's heart was wounded to its very depths. Perhaps it is little wonder that she had made no other attempt to secure company for the evening. There were schoolgirls by the score that she might have asked; doubtless some one of the number would accept her invitation, but she had not thought so. She had shrunken from any other effort, in mortal terror.

"I am not fitted for such work," she said in bitterness of soul; "not even for *such* work; what *can* I do?" and then, despite the class, she had brushed away a tear. So there she sat alone, till suddenly the door opened with more force than usual, and closed with a little bang, and Eurie Mitchell, with a face on which there glowed traces of excitement, came like a whiff of wind and rustled into a seat beside her, alone like herself.

"You here?" she said, and there was surprise in her whisper. "Thought you would be late, and not be alone. I am glad of it—I mean I am almost glad. Don't you think, Nell wouldn't come with me! I counted on him as a matter of course, he is so obliging—always willing to take me wherever I want to go, and often disarranging his own engagements so that I need not be disappointed. I was just as sure of him I thought as I was of myself, and then I coaxed him harder than I ever did before in my life, and he wouldn't come in. He came to the door with me and said I needn't be afraid but that he would be on hand to see me home, and he would see safely home any number of girls that I chose to drum up, but as for sitting in here a whole hour waiting for it to be time to go home, that was beyond him—too much for mortal patience!

"Wasn't it just too bad! I was so sure of it, too. I told him about our plans—about our promise, indeed, and how I had counted on him, and all he said was: 'Don't you know the old proverb, Sis: "Never count your chickens before they are hatched"; or, a more elegant, phrasing of it, "Never eat your fish till you catch him"? Now, I'm not caught yet; someway the right sort of bait hasn't reached me yet.' I was never so disappointed in my life! Didn't you try to get someone to come?"

"Yes," said Marion, "and failed." She forced herself to say that much. How *could* Eurie go through with all these details? "If her heart had ached as mine does, she couldn't," Marion told herself. She might have known if she had used her judgment that Eurie's heart was not of the sort that would ever ache over anything as hers could; and yet Eurie was bitterly disappointed.

She had counted on Nell and expected him, had high hopes for him; and here they were dashed into nothingness! Who knew that he could be so obstinate over a trifle? Surely it was a trifle just to come to prayer meeting once! She knew she would have done it for him, even in the days when it would have been a bore. She did not understand it at all.

Meantime, Ruth had been having her experiences. This promise of hers troubled her. Perhaps you cannot imagine what an exceedingly disagreeable thing it seemed to her to go hunting up somebody to go to prayer meeting with her. Where could she turn? There were so few people with whom she came in contact that it would not be absurd to ask.

Her father she put aside at once as entirely out of the question. It was simply an absurdity to think of asking him to go to prayer meeting! He rarely went to church even on the Sabbath; less often now than he used to do. It would simply be annoying him and exposing religion to his contempt, so his daughter reasoned. She sighed over it while she reasoned; she wished most earnestly that it were not so; she prayed, and she thought it was with all her heart, that God would speak to her father in some way, by some voice that he would heed; and yet she allowed herself to be sure that his only and cherished daughter had the one voice that could not hope to influence him in the least.

Well, there was her friend, Mr. Wayne. I wonder if I can describe to you how impossible it seemed to her to ask him to go? Not that he would not have accompanied her; he would in a minute; he would do almost anything she asked; she felt as sure that she could get him to occupy a seat in the First Church prayer room that evening as she felt sure of going there herself; but she asked herself, of what earthly use would it be?

He would go simply to please what he would suppose was a whim of hers; he would listen with an amused smile, slightly tinged with sarcasm, to all the words that would be spoken that evening, and he would have ready a hundred mildly funny things to say about them when the meeting closed; for weeks afterward he would be apt to bring in nicely fitting quotations gleaned from that evening of watchfulness, fitting them into absurd places and making them seem the veriest folly—that would be the fruit.

Ruth shrank with all her soul from such a result; these things were sacred to her; she did not see how it would be possible to endure the quizzical turn that would be given to them. I want you to notice that in all this reasoning she did not see that she had undertaken not only her own work but the Lord's. When one attempts not only to drop the seed but to *make* the fruit that shall spring up, no wonder one stands back appalled!

Yet was she not busying her heart with the results? The end of it was that she decided whatever else she did, to say nothing to Mr. Wayne about the meeting. No, I am mistaken, that was not the end; there suddenly came in with these musings a startling thought:

"If I cannot endure the foolishness that will result from one evening, how am I to endure companionship for a lifetime?"

That was a thought that would not slumber again. But she must find someone whom she was willing to ask to go to prayer meeting; there was her miserable promise hedging her in.

Who was she willing to ask? She ran over her list of acquaintances; there wasn't one. How strange it was! She could think of those whom Flossy might ask, and there was Eurie surrounded by a large family; and as for Marion, her opportunities were unlimited; but for her forlorn self, in all the large circle of her acquaintances, there seemed no one to ask. The truth was, Ruth was shiveringly afraid of casting pearls before swine—not that she put it in that way; but she would rather have been struck than to have been made an object of ridicule. And yet there were times when she wished she had lived in the days of martyrdom! The church of today is full of just such martyr spirits!

The result was precisely what might have been expected: She dallied with her miserable cowardice, which she did not call by that name at all, until there really was no person within reach to invite to the meeting. Who would have supposed all this of Ruth Erskine! No one would have been less likely to have done so than herself.

She went alone to the meeting at a late hour, and with a very miserable, sore, sad heart, to which Marion's was nothing in comparison. Yet there was something accomplished, if she had but known it. She was beginning to understand herself; she had a much lower opinion of Ruth Erskine as she sat there meeting the wondering gaze of Eurie, and the quick, inquiring glance of Marion than she ever had felt in her life.

I said she was late, but Flossy was later. Somebody else must have been at work about that meeting and have been more successful than our girls, for the room was fuller than usual. Marion had begun to grow anxious for the little Flossy that had crept so near to their hearts, and to make frequent turnings of the head to see if she were not coming.

When at last she shimmered down the aisle, a soft, bright rainbow, for she hadn't given over wearing her favorite colors, and she could no more help getting them on becomingly than a bird can help looking graceful in its plumage. (Why should either of them try to help it?) But Flossy was not alone; there was a tall, portly form, and a splendidly balanced head resting on firm shoulders that followed her down to the seat, where the girls were waiting for her.

20

HOW IT WAS DONE

FLOSSY came quite down the broad aisle to the seat which the girls had, by tacit understanding, chosen for their own, her face just radiant with a sort of surprised satisfaction, and the gentleman who followed her with an assured and measured step was none other than Judge Erskine himself. He may have been surprised at his own appearance in that place for prayer, but no surprise of his could compare with the amazement of his daughter, Ruth. For once in her life her well-bred composure forsook her, and her look could be called nothing less than an absolute stare.

Of the four, Flossy only had succeeded. The way of it was this:

Having become a realist, in the most emphatic sense of that word, to have promised to bring some-one with her to meeting if she possibly could, meant to her just that, and nothing less than that. Of course, such an understanding of a promise made it impossible to stop with the asking of one person, or two, or three, provided her invitations met with only refusals.

She had started out as confident of success as Eurie;

she felt nearly certain of Col. Baker; not because he was any more likely of his own will to choose the prayer meeting than he had been all his life thus far, but because he was growing every day more anxious to give pleasure to Flossy.

Having some dim sense of this in her heart, Flossy reasoned that it would be right to put this power of hers to the good use of winning him to the meeting, for who could tell what words from God's Spirit might reach him while there? So she asked him to go.

To her surprise, and to Col. Baker's real annoyance, he was obliged to refuse her. He was more than willing to go, even to a prayer meeting, if thereby he could take one step forward toward the place in her life that he desired to fill. Therefore his regrets were profuse and sincere.

It was club night, and, most unluckily, they were to meet with him, and he was to provide the entertainment. Under almost any other circumstances he could have been excused. Had he even had the remotest idea that Flossy would have liked his company that evening, he could have made arrangements for a change of evening for the club; that is, had he known of it earlier. But, as it was, she would see how impossible it would be for him to get away. Quick-witted Flossy took him at his word.

"Would he remember, then," she asked with her most winning smile, "that of all places where she could possibly like to see him regularly, the Wednesday evening prayer meeting at the First Church was the place."

What a bitter pill an evening prayer meeting would be to Col. Baker! But he did not tell her so. He was even growing to think that he could do that, for a while at least.

From him Flossy turned to her brother; but it was club night to him, too, and while he had not the excuse that the entertainer of the club certainly had, it served very well as an excuse, though he was frank enough to add, "As for that, I don't believe I should go if I hadn't an engagement; I won't be hypocrite enough to go to the prayer meeting." Such strange ideas have some otherwise sensible people on this subject of hypocrisy!

It required a good deal of courage for Flossy to ask her mother, but she accomplished it and received in reply an astonished stare, a half-embarrassed laugh, and the expression:

"What an absurd little fanatic you are getting to be, Flossy! I am sure one wouldn't have looked for it in a child like you! Me? Oh, dear, no! I can't go; I never walk so far you know; at least very rarely, and Kitty will have the carriage in use for Mrs. Waterman's reception. Why don't you go there, child? It really isn't treating Mrs. Waterman well; she is such an old friend."

These were a few of the many efforts which Flossy made. They met with like results, until at last the evening in question found her somewhat belated and alone, ringing at Judge Erskine's mansion. That important personage being in the hall, in the act of going out to the post office, he opened the door and met her hurried, almost breathless, question:

"Judge Erskine, is Ruth gone? Oh, excuse me. Good evening. I am in such haste that I forgot courtesy. Do you think Ruth is gone?"

Yes, Judge Erskine knew that his daughter was out, for she stepped into the library to leave a message a few moments ago, and she was then dressed for the street and had passed out a moment afterward.

Then did he know whether Katie Flinn, the chambermaid, was in? "Of course you won't know," she added, blushing and smiling at the absurdity of her question. "I mean could you find out for me whether she is in and can I speak to her just a minute?"

He was fortunately wiser tonight than she gave him credit for being, Judge Erskine said, with a courtly bow and smile.

It so happened that just after his daughter departed, Katie had sought him, asking permission to be out that evening until nine o'clock, a permission that she had forgotten to secure of his daughter; therefore, as a most unusual circumstance which must have occurred for Flossy's special benefit, he was posted even as to Katie's whereabouts. He was unprepared for the sudden flushing of Flossy's cheeks and quiver of her almost baby chin.

"Oh, I am so sorry!" she said, and there were actual tears in her blue eyes.

Judge Erskine saw them, and felt as if he were in some way a monster. He hastened to be sympathetic. If she was alone and timid, it would afford him nothing but pleasure to see her safely to any part of the city she chose to mention. He was going out simply for a stroll with no business whatever.

"Oh, it isn't that," Flossy said hastily. "I am such a little way from the chapel, and it is so early I shall not be afraid; but I am so disappointed. You see, Judge Erskine, we girls were each to bring one with us to the meeting tonight, and I have tried so hard; I have asked almost a dozen people, and none of them could go. At last I happened to think of your Katie Flinn; I knew she was in our Sunday school, and I thought perhaps if I asked her, she would go with me, if Ruth had not done it before me. She was my last chance, and I am more disappointed than I can tell you."

Shall I try to describe to you what a strange sensation Judge Erskine felt in the region of his heart as he stood there in the hall with that pretty blushing girl, who seemed to him only a child, and found that her quivering chin and swimming eyes meant simply that she had failed in securing even his chambermaid to attend the prayer meeting? He never remembered to have had such an astonishing feeling, nor such a queer choking sensation in his throat.

His own daughter was dignified and stately; the very picture of her father, everyone said; he had no idea that she could shed a tear any more than he could himself; but this timid, flushing, trembling little girl seemed made of some other material than just the clay that he supposed himself to be composed of.

He stood regarding her with a sort of pleased wonder. In common with many other stately gentlemen, he very much admired real, unaffected, artless childhood. It seemed to him that a grieved child stood before him. How could he comfort her? If a doll, now, with curling hair and blue eyes could do it, how promptly should it be bought and given to this flesh-and-blood doll before him.

But no, nothing short of someone to accompany her to prayer meeting would appease this little troubled bit of humanity. In the magnanimity of his haughty heart the learned judge took a sudden and almost overpowering resolution.

Could he go? he asked her. To be sure, he was not Katie Flinn, but he would do his best to take the place of that personage if she would kindly let him go to the said meeting with her.

It was worth a dozen sittings, even in prayer meet-

ing, Judge Erskine thought, to see the sudden clearing
of that tearful face; the sudden radiant outlook from
those wet eyes.

Would he go? Would he *really* go? Could anything
be more *splendid?*

And, verily, Judge Erskine thought, as he beheld her
shining face, that there hardly could. He felt precisely
as you do when you have been unselfish toward a
pretty child, who, some way, has won a warm spot in
your heart.

He went to the First Church prayer meeting for the
first time with no higher motive than that—never
mind, he went. Flossy Shipley certainly was not responsible for the motive of his going; neither did it in
any degree affect the honest, earnest, persistent effort
she had made that day. Her account of it was simple
enough, when the girls met afterward to talk over
their efforts.

"Why, you know," she said, "I actually *promised* to
bring someone with me if I possibly could; so there
was nothing for it but to try in every possible way up
to the very last minute of the time I had. But, after all,
I brought the one whom I had not the least idea of
asking; he asked himself."

"Well," Marion said after a period of amazed silence, "I have made two discoveries. One is that
people may possibly have tried before this to enlarge
the prayer meeting; possibly we may not, after all, be
the originators of that brilliant idea; they may have
tried and failed, even as we did; for I have learned that
it is not so easy a matter as it at first appears; it needs
a power behind the wills of people to get them to do
even so simple a thing as that. The other important
thought is, there are two ways of keeping a promise;
one is to make an attempt and fail, saying to our

contented consciences, 'There! I've done my duty, and it is no use, you see'; and the other is to persist in attempt after attempt, until the very pertinacity of our faith accomplishes the work for us. What if we follow the example of our little Flossy after this, and let a promise mean something?"

"My example!" Flossy said with wide, open eyes. "Why, I only *asked* people, just as I said I would; but they wouldn't come."

There was one young lady who walked home from that eventful prayer meeting with a very unsatisfied conscience. Ruth Erskine could not get away from the feeling that she was a shirker; all the more so, because the person who had sat very near her was her father! Not brought there by any invitation from her; it was not that she had tried and failed; that form of it would have been an infinite relief; she simply had not tried, and she made herself honestly confess to herself that the trouble was, she could not be satisfied with one who was within the reach of her asking.

Yet conscience, working all alone, is a very uncomfortable and disagreeable companion, and often accomplishes for the time being nothing beyond making his victim disagreeable. This was Ruth to the fullest extent of her power; she realized it, and in a measure felt ashamed of herself and struggled a little for a better state of mind.

It seemed ill payment for the courtesy which had made Harold Wayne forsake the club before supper for the purpose of walking home with her from church. He was unusually kind, too, and patient. Part of her trouble, be it known, was her determination in her heart not to be driven by that dreadful conscience into saying a single personal word to Harold Wayne. Not that she put it in that way; bless you, no! Satan rarely blunders enough to speak out plainly; he has a dozen smooth-sounding phrases that mean the same thing.

"People need to be approached very carefully on very special occasions, which are not apt to occur; they need to be approached by just such persons, and in just such well-chosen words," etc.

Though why it should require such infinite tact and care and skill to say to a friend, "I wish you were going to heaven with me," when the person would say without the slightest hesitation, "I wish you were going to Europe with me," and be accounted an idiot if he made talk about tact and skill and caution, I am sure I don't know.

Yet all these things Ruth said to herself. The reason the thought ruffled her was because her honest conscience knew they were false and that she had a right to say, "Harold, I *wish* you were a Christian"; and had no right at all with the results.

She simply could not bring herself to say it; she did not really know why, herself; probably Satan did.

Mr. Wayne was unusually quiet and grave; he seemed to be doing what he could to lead Ruth into serious talk; he asked about the meeting, whether there were many out, and whether she enjoyed it.

"I sort of like Dr. Dennis," he said. "He is tremendously in earnest; but why shouldn't a man be in earnest if he believes what he is talking about. Do you suppose he does, Ruth?"

"Of course," Ruth said shortly, almost crossly; "you know he does. Why do you ask such a foolish question?"

"Oh, I don't know; half the time it seems to me as if the religious people were trying to humbug this world; because, you see, they don't act as if they were in dead earnest—very few of them do, at least."

"That is a very easy thing to say, and people seem to be fond of saying it," Ruth said, and then she simply would not talk on that subject or any other; she was miserably unhappy; an awakened conscience, toyed with, is a very fruitful source of misery. She was glad when the walk was concluded.

"Shall I come in?" Mr. Wayne asked, lingering on the step, half smiling, half wistful. "What do you advise, shall I go back to the club or call on you?"

Now, Ruth hated that club; she was much afraid of its influence over her friend; she had determined, as soon as she could plan a line of operation, to set systematically at work to withdraw him from its influence; but she was not ready for it yet. And among other things that she was not ready for was a call from Mr. Wayne; it seemed to her that in her present miserable, unsettled state it would be simply impossible to carry on a conversation with him. True to her usually frank nature, she answered promptly:

"I have certainly no desire for you to go to the club, either on this evening or any other; but, to be frank, I would rather be alone this evening; I want to think over some matters of importance and to decide them. You will not think strangely of me for saying that, will you?"

"Oh no," he said, and he smiled kindly on her; yet he was very much disappointed; he showed it in his face.

Many a time afterward, as Ruth sat thinking over this conversation, recalling every little detail of it, recalling the look on his face and the peculiar sadness in his eyes, she thought within herself, "If I had said, 'Harold, I want you to come in; I want to talk with you; I want you to decide now to live for Christ,' I wonder what he *would* have answered."

But she did not say it. Instead, she turned from him and went into the house; and—he went directly to his club: an unaccountable gloom hung over him; he must have companionship; if not with his chosen and promised wife, then with the club. That was just what Ruth was to him; and it was one of the questions that tormented her.

There were reasons why thought about it had forced itself upon her during the last few days. She was pledged to him long before she found this new experience. The question was, Could she fulfil those pledges? Had they a thought in common now? Could she live with him the sort of life that she solemnly meant to live? If she *could,* was it right to do so? You see she had enough to torment her; only she set about thinking of it in so strange a manner; not at all as she would have thought about it if the pledges she had given him had meant to her all that they mean to some, all that they ought to mean to anyone who makes them. This phase of it also troubled her.

21

RUTH AND HAROLD

THERE had been in Judge Erskine's mind a slight
sense of wonderment as to how he should meet his
daughter the morning after his astounding appearance
at prayer meeting. Such a new and singular departure
was it that he even felt a slight shade of embarrassment.

But, before the hour of meeting had arrived, his
thoughts were turned into an entirely new channel.
He met her, looking very grave, and with a touch of
tenderness about his manner that was new to her. She,
on her part, was not much more at rest than she had
been the evening before. She realized that her heart
was in an actual state of rebellion against any form of
decided Christian work that she could plan. Clearly,
something was wrong with her. If she had been
familiar with a certain old Christian, she might have
borrowed his language to express in part her feeling.

"To will is present with me; but how to perform
that which is good I find not." Not quite that, either,
for while she said, "I *can't* do this thing, or that thing,"
she was clear-minded enough to see that it simply

meant, after all, "I will not." The will was at fault, and she knew it. She did not fully comprehend yet that she had set out to be a Christian, and at the same time to have her own way in the least little thing; but she had a glimmering sense that such was the trouble.

Her father, after taking surreptitious glances at her pale face and troubled eyes, decided finally that what was to be said must be said and asked abruptly:

"When did you see Harold, my daughter?"

Ruth started, and the question made the blood rush to her face, she did not know why.

"I saw him last evening, after prayer meeting, I believe," she answered, speaking in her usual quiet tone but fixing an inquiring look on her father.

"Did he speak of not feeling well?"

"No, sir; not at all. Why?"

"I hear that he is quite sick this morning; was taken in the night. Something like a flu, I should judge; may be nothing but a slight attack, brought on by late suppers. He was at the club last night. I thought I would call after breakfast and learn the extent of the illness. If you want to send a message or note, I can deliver it."

That was the beginning of dreary days. Ruth prepared her note—a tender, comforting one; but it was brought back to her; and as her father handed it to her he said;

"He can't read it now, Daughter. I daresay it would comfort him if he could; but he is delirious; didn't know me; hasn't known anyone since he was taken in the night. Keep the letter till this passes off, then he will be ready for it."

Very kind and sympathetic were Ruth's friends. The girls came to see her and kissed her wistfully with tears in their eyes, but they had little to say. They knew just how sick her friend was, and they felt as though there was nothing left to say. Her father neglected his business to stay at home with her, and in many a little, thoughtful way touched her heavy heart as the hours dragged by.

Not many hours to wait. It was in the early dawn of the third morning after the news had reached her that the doorbell pealed sharply through the house. There was but one servant up; she answered the bell.

Ruth was up and dressed and stood in the hall above, listening for what that bell might bring to her. She heard the hurried voice at the door, heard the peremptory order:

"I want to see Judge Erskine right away." She knew the voice belonged to Nellis Mitchell, and she went down to him in the library. He turned swiftly at the opening of the door, then stood still, and a look of blank dismay swept over his face.

"It was your father that I wanted to see," he said quickly.

"I know," she answered, speaking in her usual tone. "I heard your message. My father has not yet risen. He will be down presently. Meantime, I thought you might possibly have news of Mr. Wayne's condition. Can you tell me what your father thinks of him this morning?"

How very quiet and composed she was! It seemed impossible to realize that she was the promised wife of the man for whom she was asking. Nellis Mitchell was distressed; he did not know what to say or do. His distress showed itself plainly on his face.

"You need not be afraid to tell me," she said, half smiling and speaking more gently than she was apt to speak to this young man. It almost seemed that she was trying to sustain him and help him to tell his story. "I am not a child, you know," she added, still with a smile.

"You do not know what you are talking about," he said hoarsely. "Ruth, won't you please go upstairs and tell your father I want him as soon as possible?"

She turned from him half impatiently.

"My father will be down as soon as possible," she said coldly. "He is not accustomed to keep gentlemen waiting beyond what is necessary. Meantime, if you know, will you be kind enough to give me news of Mr. Wayne? I beg you, Mr. Mitchell, to remember that I am not a silly child, to whom you need be afraid to give a message, if you have one."

He must answer her now; there was no escape.

"He is," he began, and then he stopped. And her clear, cold, grave eyes looked right at him and waited. His next sentence commenced almost in a moan. "Oh, Ruth, you *will* make me tell you! It is all over. He has gone."

"Gone!" she repeated, incredulously, still staring at him. "Where is he gone?"

What an awful question! She realized it herself almost the instant it passed her lips. It made her shudder visibly. But she neither screamed nor fainted, nor in any way, except that strange one, betrayed emotion. Instead, she said:

"Be seated, Mr. Mitchell, and excuse me; Father is coming." Then she turned and went back upstairs.

He heard her firm steps on the stairs as she went slowly up; and this poor bearer of faithful tidings shut his face into both his hands and groaned aloud for such misery as could not vent itself in any natural way. He understood that there was something more than ordinary sorrow in Ruth's face. It was as if she had been petrified.

Through the days that followed, Ruth passed as one in a dream. Everyone was very kind. Her father showed a talent for patience and gentleness that no one had known he possessed.

The girls came to see her, but she would not be seen. She shrank from them. They did not wonder at that; they were half relieved that it was so. Such a pall seemed to them to have settled suddenly over her life that they felt at a loss what to say, how to meet her. So when she went to them, from her darkened and gloomy room, kind messages of thanks for their kindness, and asked them to further show their sympathy by allowing her to stay utterly alone for a while, they drew relieved sighs and went away. This much they understood. It was not a time for words.

As for Flossy, she should not have been numbered among them. She did not call at all; she sent by Nellis Mitchell a tiny bouquet of lilies of the valley, lying inside of a cool, broad green lily leaf, and on a slip of paper twisted in with it was written:

"Yea, though I walk through the valley of the shadow of death, I will fear no evil." How Ruth blessed her for that word! Verily she felt that she was walking through the very blackest of the shadows! It reminded her that she had a friend.

Slowly the hours dragged on. The grand and solemn funeral was planned, and the plans carried out. Mr. Wayne was among the very wealthy of the city. His father's mansion was shrouded in its appropriate crape, the rooms and the halls and the rich, dark, solemn coffin glittering with its solid silver screws and handles were almost hidden in rare and costly flowers. Ruth, in the deepest of mourning robes, accompanied by her father, from whose shoulder swept long streamers of crape, sat in the Erskine carriage and followed directly after the hearse, chief mourner in the long and solemn train.

In every conceivable way that love could devise and wealth could carry out, were the last tokens of respect paid to the quiet clay that understood not what was passing around it.

The music was by the quartet choir of the First Church and was like a wail of angel voices in its wonderful pathos and tenderness.

The pastor spoke a few words, tenderly, solemnly pointing the mourners to One who alone could sustain, earnestly urging those who knew nothing of the love of Christ to take refuge *now* in his open arms and find rest there.

But alas, alas! not a single word could he say about the soul that had gone out from that silent body before them; gone to live forever. Was it possible for those holding such belief as theirs to have a shadow of hope that the end of such a life as his had been could be bright?

Not one of those who understood anything about this matter dared for an instant to hope it. They understood the awful solemn silence of the minister. There was nothing for that grave but silence. Hope for the living, and he pointed them earnestly to the source of all hope; but for the dead, silence.

What an awfully solemn task to conduct such funeral services. The pastor may not read the comforting words: "Blessed are the dead which die in the Lord," because before them lies one who did not die in the Lord, and common sense tells the most thoughtless that if those are blessed who die in the Lord there must be a reverse side to the picture, else no sense to the statement. So the verse must be passed by. It is too late to help the dead, and it need not tear the hearts of the living. He cannot read, "I shall go to him, but he shall not return to me."

God forbid, prays the sad pastor in his heart, that mother or father or friend shall so die as to go to this one, who did not die in the Lord. We cannot even hope for that. All the long line of tender, helpful verses, glowing with light for the coming morning, shining with immortality and unending union must be passed by; for each and every one of them has a clause which shows unmistakably that the immortality is glorious only under certain conditions, and in this case, they have not been met.

There must in these verses, too, be a reverse side, or else they mean nothing. What shall the pastor do? Clearly he can only say, "In the midst of life we are in death." That is true; his audience feels it; and he can only pray: "So teach *us* to number our days, that we may apply our hearts unto wisdom."

But, oh, how *can* the mothers stand by open graves wherein are laid their sons or daughters, and endure the thought that it is a separation that shall stretch through eternity! How wonderful that any of us are careless or thoughtless for a moment so long as we have a child or a friend unsafe!

During all this time of trial Ruth's three friends were hovering around her, trying by every possible attention and thoughtfulness to help or comfort her, and yet feeling their powerlessness in such a way that it almost made them shrink from trying.

"Words are such a mockery," Marion said to her one evening, as they sat together. "Sometimes I almost hate myself for trying to speak to you at all. What can any human being say to one who is shrouded in an awful sorrow?"

Ruth shuddered visibly.

"It *is* an 'awful' sorrow," she said; "you have used the right word with which to express it; but there is a shade to it that you do not understand. I don't believe that by experience you ever will; I pray God that you may not. Think of burying a friend in the grave without the slightest hope of ever meeting him in peace again!"

"You have nothing to do with that, Ruth; God is the judge. I don't think you ought to allow yourself to think of it."

"There I think you are mistaken; I believe I ought to think of it. Marion, you know and *I* know that there is simply nothing at all on which to build a hope of meeting in peace the man we buried last week. You think it almost shocking that I can speak of him in that way; I know you do. People are apt to hide behind the very flimsiest veil of fancied hopes when they talk of such things.

"Perhaps a merciful God permits some to hug a worthless hope when they think of their dead treasures, since it can do no harm to those who are gone; but I am not one of that class of people. Besides, I am appearing to you, and everybody, in a false light. I am tired of it. Marion, Mr. Wayne was not to me what he ought to have been, since I was his promised wife. You know how I have changed of late; you know there was hardly a thought or feeling of mine in which he could sympathize; but the worst of it is, he never did sympathize with me in the true sense; he never filled my heart.

"My promise to him was one of those false steps that people like me, who are ruled by society, take because it seems to be the proper thing to do next, or because we feel it might as well be that as anything; perhaps because it will please one's father in a business point of view, or please one's own sense of importance; satisfy one's desire to be foremost in the fashionable world. I am humiliating myself to tell you plainly that my promise meant not much more than that. I did not realize how empty it was till I found that all my plans and aims and hopes in life were changed. That, in short, life had come to seem more to me than a glittering weariness that was to be borne with the best grace I could assume. This was nearly all I had found in society, or hoped to find.

"I followed Mr. Wayne to the grave in the position of chief mourner, because I felt that it was a token of respect that I owed to the memory of the man whom I had wronged, and because I felt that the world had no business with our private affairs; but he was not to me what people think he was, and I feel as though I wanted you to know it, even though it humiliates me beyond measure to make the confession. At the same time I have an awful sorrow, too awful to be expressed in words.

"Marion, I think you will understand what I mean when I say that I believe I have the blood of a lost soul clinging to my garments. I know, as well as I sit here tonight, that I might have influenced Harold Wayne into the right way. I know his love for me was so sincere and so strong that he would have been willing to try to do almost anything that I had asked. I believe in my soul that had I urged the matter of personal salvation on his immediate attention, he would have given it thought. But I *never* did—*never.*

"Marion, even on that last evening of his life—I mean, before he was sick—when he himself invited the words, I was silent. I did not mean to continue so; I meant, when I got ready, to speak to him about this matter; I meant to do everything right; but I was determined to take my own time for it, and I took it, and now he is *gone!* Marion, you know nothing about such a sorrow as that! Now, why did I act in this insane way?

"I know the reason, one of them at least; and the awful selfishness and cowardice of it only brands me deeper. It was because I was afraid to have him become a Christian man! I knew if he did I should have no excuse for breaking the pledges that had passed between us; in plain words, I would have no excuse for not marrying him; and I did not want to do it! I felt that marriage vows would mean to me in the future what they never meant in the past, and that there was really nothing in common between Mr. Wayne and myself; that I could not assent to the marriage service with him and be guiltless before God. So to spare myself, to have what looked like a conscientious excuse for breaking vows that ought never to have been made, I deliberately sacrificed his *soul!* Marion Wilbur, think of that!"

"You didn't mean to do that!" Marion said in an awe-stricken voice; she was astonished and shocked, and bewildered as to what to say.

Ruth answered her almost fiercely:

"No, I didn't mean to; and as to that, I never meant to do anything that was not just right in my life; but I meant to have just exactly my own way of doing things, and I tell you I took it. Now, Marion, while I blame myself as no other person ever can, I still blame others. I was never taught as I should have been about the sacredness of human loves and the awfulness of human vows and pledges. I was never taught that for girls to dally with such pledges, to flirt with them, before they knew anything about life or about their own hearts was a sin in the sight of God. I ought to have been so taught.

"Perhaps if I had had a mother to teach me I should have been different; but I am not even sure of that. Mothers seem to me to allow strange trifling with these subjects, even if they do not actually prepare the way. But all this does not relieve me. I have sinned; no one but myself understands how deeply, and no one but me knows the bitterness of it.

"Now I feel as though the whole of the rest of my life must be given to atone for this horrible fatal mistake. I wasted the last hour I ever had with a soul, and I have before me the awful consciousness that I might have saved it.

"It is all done now and can never be undone; that is the saddest part of it. But there is one thing I can do; I need never live through a like experience again; I will give the rest of my life to atone for the past; I will never again be guilty of coming in contact with a soul unprepared for death without urging upon that soul, as often as I have opportunity, the necessity for preparation; I see plainly that it is the important thing in life."

There hovered over Marion's mind, while these last sentences were being spoken, words something like these:

"The blood of Jesus Christ his Son cleanseth us from all sin."

She almost said to Ruth that even for this sin the atonement had been made; she must not try to make another. But the error that only faintly glimmered in Ruth's sentence was so mixed with solemn and helpful truth that she felt at a loss as to whether there was error at all, and so held her peace.

22

◆━━═◆═━━◆

REVIVAL

AS THE early autumn months slipped away, and
touches of winter began to show around them, it
became evident that a new feeling was stirring in the
First Church.

No need now to work for increased numbers at the
prayer meeting; at least there was not the need that
formerly existed; the room was full, and the meetings
solemn and earnest. The Spirit of God was hovering
over the place. Drops of the coming shower were
already beginning to fall.

What was the cause of the quickened hearts? Who
knew, save the Watcher on the tower in the eternal
city? Was it because of the sudden and solemn and
hopeless death occurring in the very center of what
was called "the first circles"? Was it the spirit developed apparently by this death, showing itself in eager,
indefatigable effort wherever Ruth Erskine went,
with whomsoever she came in contact?

Was it Marion Wilbur's new way of teaching, that
included not only the intellect of her pupils, but
looked beyond that, with loving word, for the empty

soul? Was it Eurie Mitchell's patient way of taking up home work and care that had been distasteful to her, and that she had shunned in days gone by? Was it Flossy Shipley's way of teaching the Sabbath-school lessons to "those boys" of hers?

Was it the quickened sense which throbbed in the almost discouraged heart of the pastor whenever he came in contact with any of these four? Was it the patient, persistent, unassuming work of John Warden, as he went about in the shop among his fellow workmen, dropping an earnest word here, a pressing invitation there?

Who shall tell whether either or all of these influences, combined with hundreds of others, set in motion by like causes, were the beginnings of the solemn and blessed harvesttime that dawned at last on those who had been sowing in tears?

The fact was apparent. Even in the First Church, that model of propriety and respectability, that church which had so feared excitement or unusual efforts of *any* sort, there was a revival!

Among those who were coming, and who were growing willing to let others know that they were awakening to a sense of the importance of these things, were Dr. and Mrs. Mitchell, Eurie's father and mother. To themselves they did not hesitate to say that the change in Eurie was so marked and so increasing in its power over her life that it obliged them to think seriously of this thing.

Among the interested also were a score or more of girls from Marion's room in the great school; and more came every day. Marion's face was shining, and she gathered her brood about her as a mother would the children of her love and longing.

Among them were four of Flossy's boys; and half a

dozen boys, friends of theirs, who were not Flossy's, and who yet, someway, joined her train and managed to be "counted in." Among them was Judge Erskine—I mean among those who continued to come to the meetings—coming alone, being reverent and thoughtful during the services but going away with bowed head and making no sign; there was something in the way with Judge Erskine that no one understood.

As for Ruth—how she worked during these days! Not with a glad light in her eyes, such as Marion and Flossy had; not with a satisfied face, as if the question of something to do that was worth doing, and that helped her, had been settled, such as Eurie Mitchell wore; rather, with a sad feverish impatience to accomplish *results;* shrinking from nothing, willing to do anything, go anywhere, yet meeting with far less encouragement, and seeing far less fruits, than any of the others. She did not realize that she was working with a sort of desperate intention of overbalancing the mischief of her mistakes by so much work now that there would be a sort of even balance at the scales. She would have been shocked had she understood her own heart.

Meantime, where was Satan? Content to let this reaping time alone? Oh, bless you, no! Never busier, never more alert, and watchful, and cautious, and *skillful* than now! It was wonderful, too, how many helpers he found whose names were actually on the roll of the First Church!

There were those who had had in mind all the fall having little entertainments, "just a few friends, you know, nothing like a party; they were sorry to be obliged to have them just now while there were meetings; but Miss Gilmore was in town and would be here so short a time, they *must* invite her; it would not be treating her well to take no notice of her visit; and, really, the people whom they proposed to invite were those who did not attend church, so no harm could be done."

These were some of Satan's helpers. There were others who were more outspoken. They "did not believe in special efforts; seasons of excitement; religious dissipations—nothing else. People should be religious at all times, not put it on for special occasions."

It was well enough to have a special season for parties, and a special season for going to the seaside, and a special season for doing one's dressmaking, and a special season for cleaning house, and a special season for everything under the sun but religious meetings; these should be conducted—at all times. Was that what they meant? Oh, dear, no! They should not be conducted at all. Was *that* what they meant? Who should tell what they *did* mean? One lady said:

"The idea of the bell ringing every evening for prayer meeting! It was too absurd! People must have a little time for recreation; these weeks just before the holidays were always by common consent the time for festivities of all sorts; it was downright folly to expect young people to give up their pleasures and go every evening to meeting."

So she issued her cards for a party, and gathered as many of the young people about her as she could. And this woman was a member of the First Church! And this woman professed to believe in the verse that read, "Whether therefore ye eat, or drink, or whatsoever ye do, do all to the glory of God!"

There were others who went to these parties, hushing their consciences meantime by the explanation that the social duties were important ones, and that one whose heart was right could serve God as well having religious conversation at a party, as she could occupying a seat at a prayer meeting. Perhaps they really believed it. What marvel? Satan himself is transformed into an angel of light.

The trouble about the sincerity was that those same persons were not unaware of certain sneering remarks that were being made, to the effect that if church members could go to parties when there were meetings at their own church, *they* could surely be excused from the meetings; and they could not have been utterly ignorant of the verse that read plainly, "Let not your good be evil spoken of."

There were still others who compromised matters, taking the meetings for the first hour of the evening and a party for the next three; and the lookers-on said sneeringly that there was a strife going on between the soul, the flesh, and the devil, and they wondered which would conquer!

So all these classes flourished and worked in their different ways in the First Church; just as they always *will* work, until that day when the wheat shall be forever separated from the tares. The wonder is why so many blinded eyes *must* insist that because there are tares, there is therefore no wheat. The Lord said, "Let both grow together until the harvest."

"I don't understand it," Ruth said one day to Marion, as they talked the work over and tried to lay plans for future helpfulness. "Why do you suppose it is that I seem able to do nothing at all? I try with all my might; my heart is surely in it, and I long with a desire that seems almost as if it would consume me to see some fruit of my work, and yet I don't. What *can* be the difficulty?"

"I don't know," Marion said, speaking hesitatingly, as one who would like to say more if she dared. "I don't feel competent to answer that question, and yet, sometimes, I have feared that you might be trying to compromise with the Lord."

"I don't understand you; in what way do you mean? I try to do my duty in every place that I can think of. I am not compromising on any subject, so far as I know. If I am, I will certainly be grateful to anyone who will point out to me."

"I am not sure that it is sufficiently clear to my own mind to be able to point it out," Marion said, still visibly embarrassed. "But, Ruth, it sometimes seems to me as if you had said to yourself, 'Now I will work so much and pray so much, and then I ought to have rest from the pain that is goading me on, and I ought to be able to feel that I have atoned for past mistakes, and the account against me is squared.'"

Ruth turned from her impatiently.

"You are a strange comforter," she said, almost indignantly. "Do you mean by that to intimate that you think I ought *never* to look or hope for rest of mind again because I have made one fearful mistake? Do you mean that I ought always to carry with me the sense of the burden?"

"I mean no such thing. You cannot think I so estimate the power of the sacrifice for sin, Ruth, I mean simply this: Nothing that you or I can do can possibly make one sin white, one mistake as though it had not been, give one moment of rest to a troubled heart. But the blood of Jesus Christ can do all this, and it does seem to me that you are ignoring it and trying to work out your own rest."

Ruth was thoughtful; the look of vexation passed from her face.

"It may be so," she said after a long silence. "I begin dimly to understand your meaning; but I don't know how to help it, how to feel differently. I surely ought to work, and surely I have a right to expect results."

"In one sense, yes, and in another I don't believe we have. I begin to feel more and more that you and I have *got* in some way to be made to understand that it is not our way, but the Lord's, that we must be willing to do, or, what is harder, to leave undone, exactly what he said, *do* or *not* do. I can't help feeling that you are planning in your own heart just what ought to be done, and then allowing yourself to feel almost indignant and ill-used because the work is not accomplished."

"I don't know how you have succeeded in seeing so deeply into my heart," Ruth said with a wan smile. "I believe it is so, though I am not sure that I ever saw it before."

"I know why I see it; because it is my temptation as well as yours. You and I are both strong willed; we have both been used to having our own way; we want to continue to have it; we want to do the right things, provided we can have the choosing of them. Flossy, now, with her yielding nature, is willing to *be led,* as you and I are not. I have to fight against this tendency to carry out my plans and look for *my* results all the time. The fact is, Ruth, we must learn to work for *Christ,* and not set up business for ourselves and still expect him to give the wages."

"Still," said Ruth, "I don't know. There seems to me to be nothing that I am not willing to do. I can't think of anything so hard that I would not unhesitatingly do it. I have changed wonderfully in that respect. A little while ago I was not willing to do anything. Now I am ready for anything that can be done."

"Are you?" Marion asked with a visible shiver. "Ruth, are you *sure?* I can't say that; I want to say it, and I pray that I may be able; yet I can think of so many things that I might be called on to do that I shrink from. I have given up trying to do them, and fallen back on the promise, 'My grace is sufficient,' only praying, 'Lord, give me the needed grace for today; I will not reach out for tomorrow.' And, Ruth, I feel sure that neither you nor I must try to cover our past errors with present usefulness. Nothing but the blood of Christ can cover *any* wrong; we *must* rest on that, and on that alone."

"I believe I only understand in part what you mean. I don't see how you ever reached so far ahead of me in faith and in understanding. But I believe you *are* farther. Still, I can't think of anything that I am not willing and ready to do. I wish I might be tried; I wish he would give me some work, not of my own planning, that he might see how willing I am to do anything."

This was Ruth's last remark to her friend that evening. Flossy and Eurie both came in, and they went out to the meeting together, Ruth thinking still of the talk they had, and feeling sure that she could do whatever she found, and yet the Master was planning a way for her that very evening, the entrance to which she had never seen, never dreamed of as possible. So many ways he has for leading us! Blessed are those who have come to the experience that makes them willing to be led, even in darkness and blindness, trusting to the Sun of Righteousness for light.

23

━━━◆━━━

THE STRANGE STORY

JUDGE Erskine was in his library, slowly pacing back and forth, his forehead lined with heavy wrinkles and his face wearing the expression of one involved in deep and troubled thought. He had just come home from the evening meeting, the last meeting of the series that had held the attention of so many hearts during four weeks of harvesttime.

Judge Erskine had been a silent and attentive listener. All through the solemnities of the sermon, that seemed written for his sake and to point right at him, he had never moved his keen, steady eyes away from the preacher's face. The text of that sermon he was not likely to forget. He had looked it up and read it, with its connections, the moment he reached the privacy of his library.

"The harvest is past, the summer is ended, and we are not saved." That was the text. Judge Erskine said it over and over to his own soul. It was true; it fitted his condition as precisely as though it had been written for him. The harvest that would tell for eternity had been reaped all around him. He had looked and listened and resolved; and still he stood outside, un-garnered.

Moreover, one portion of the solemn sermon fitted him, also. When Dr. Dennis spoke of those who had let this season pass, unhelped, because they had an inner life that would not bear the gaze of the public, because they were not willing to drag out their past and cast it away from them, Judge Erskine had started and fixed a stern glance on the preacher.

Did he know his secret that had been hidden away with such persistent care? What scoundrel could have enlightened him? This, only for a moment; then he settled back and realized his folly. Dr. Dennis knew nothing of himself or his past. Then came that other awfully solemn thought—there was One who did. Could it be that his voice had instructed the pastor what special point to make in that sermon with such emphasis and power? Was the keen eye of the eternal God pointing his finger, now, at him, and saying: "Thou art the man"?

He *knew* all this was true; he knew that the work of the past month had greatly moved him; he knew on the evening when the text had been, "Almost thou persuadest *me* to be a Christian," that he had felt himself *almost* persuaded; he knew then, as he did now, that but one thing stood in the way of his entire persuasion.

As he walked up and down his library on this evening, he felt folly persuaded in his own mind that the time had arrived when he was being called on persistently for a decision. More than that, he felt that the decision was to be not only for time, but for eternity; that he *must* settle the question of his future then and there. He had locked the door after him as he came into the library, with a sort of grim determination to settle the question before he stepped into the outside world again. How would it be settled? He did not know himself. He did not dare to think how it would end; he simply felt that the conflict must end.

Meantime, Ruth was upstairs on her knees, praying for her father. Her heart felt very heavy. She had prayed for this father with all her soul; prayed, with what she felt was a degree of faith, that this evening, at the meeting, he might settle the question at issue and settle it forever. She had felt a bitter, and almost an overwhelming, disappointment that the meeting closed and left him just where he had stood for a month.

There seemed nothing left to do. She had not spared her words, her entreaties. She had gotten bravely over her fears of approaching her father. But now it seemed to her that there was nothing left to say. She could still pray, and it was with a half-despairing cry that she fell on her knees, realizing in her very soul that only the power of God could convert her father. Into the midst of this longing, clinging cry for help there came a knock.

"Judge Erskine would like to have you come to the library for a few minutes, if you have not retired."

This was Katie Flinn's message. And Ruth, as she swiftly set about obeying the summons, said:

"Oh, Katie, pray for Father!" For among those who, during the last few weeks, had learned to pray was Katie Flinn. Poor Katie, with the simple childlike faith and loving heart which she brought to the service, was destined to be a shining light in a dark world; and the glory thereof would sparkle forever in Flossy Shipley's crown.

Judge Erskine turned as his daughter opened the door, and motioned her to a seat. Then he continued his walk. Something in his face hushed into silence the words that were on her lips; but presently he stopped before her, and his voice startled her with its strangeness.

"My daughter, I have something to tell you, and something to ask you. I shall have to cause you great grief and shame, and I want to begin first by asking you to forgive your father."

Ruth felt her face growing pale. What *could* he mean? Had she not always looked up to him as above most men, even Christian men?—faultless in his business transactions, blameless in his life? She attempted to speak, and yet felt that she did not know what to say. Apparently he expected no word from her; for he went on hurriedly:

"You have, during these few weeks past, shown a sort of interest in me that I never saw manifested before. I have reason to think that you have concluded, lately, that the most earnest desire you can have concerning your father, is to see him a Christian man. I can conscientiously tell you that I have felt the necessity for this experience as I never did before; that I realize its importance, and that I want it; yet there is something in the way, something that I must do and confess and abide by for the future, that I shrink from more on your account than my own. My child, do you want this thing enough to endure disgrace and humiliation, and a cross, heavy and hopeless, all your life?"

"Father," she said, half rising, and looking at him with a bewildered air, a vague doubt of his sanity, and a half fear of his presence, creeping into her heart, "what can you possibly mean? How can disgrace, or crossbearing, or trouble of any sort, be connected with *you*? I cannot understand you."

"I know you cannot. You think I am talking wildly,

and you are half afraid of me; but I am perfectly sane. I wish, with all my soul, that a certain portion of my life could be called a wild dream of a disordered brain; but it is solemnly true. Ruth, if I come out before the world and avow myself a Christian man with the determination to abide by the teachings of the Lord Jesus Christ, it involves my bringing to this house a woman who will have to be recognized as my wife, and a girl who will have to share with you as my daughter; a woman whom you will have to call Mother, and a girl who is your sister. Are you equal to that?"

Every trace of blood left Ruth Erskine's face. Her father watched her narrowly with his hand touching the bell rope; it seemed as if she must faint; but she motioned his hand away.

"Don't ring," were the first words she said; "I am not going to faint. Father, tell me what you mean."

The actual avowal made, and the fact established that his daughter was able to bear it and to still keep the story between themselves seemed to quiet Judge Erskine. His intense and almost uncontrollable excitement subsided; the wild look in his eyes calmed, and, drawing a chair beside his daughter, he began in a low steady voice to tell her the strange story:

"Acts that involve a lifetime of trouble can be told in a few words, Ruth. When your mother died I was almost insane with grief; I can't tell you about that time; I was young and gay, and full of plans and aims and intentions, in all of which she had been involved. Then came the sudden blank, and it almost unsettled my reason. There was a young woman boarding at the same house where I went who was kind to me, who befriended me in various ways and tried to help me to endure my sorrow. She grew to be almost necessary to my endurance of myself. After a little I married her. I did not take this step till I found that my friendship with her, or, rather hers with me, was compromising her in the eyes of others. Let me hurry over it, Ruth. We lived together but a few weeks; then I was obliged to go abroad. Away from old scenes and associations and plunged into business cares, I gradually recovered my usual tone of mind. But it was not till I came home again that I discovered what a fatal blunder I had made. That young woman had not a single idea in common with my plans and aims in life; she was ignorant, uncultured, and, it seemed to me, unendurable. How I ever allowed myself to be such a fool I do not know. But up to this time, I had at least, not been a villain. I didn't desert her, Ruth; I made a deliberate compromise with her; she was to take her child and go away, hundreds of miles away, where I would not be likely ever to come in contact with her again, and I was to take your mother's child and go where I pleased. Of course I was to support her, and I have done so ever since; that was eighteen years ago; she is still living, and the daughter is living. I have always been careful to keep them supplied with money; I have tried to have done for the girl what money could do; but I have never seen their faces since that time. Now, Ruth, you know the miserable story. There are a hundred details that I could give you that perhaps would lead you to have more pity for your father, if it did not lead you to despise him more for his weakness. It is hard to be despised by one's child. I tell you truly, Ruth, that the bitterest of this bitterness is the thought of you."

The proud man's lip quivered and his voice trembled, just here.

Poor Ruth Erskine! "I am willing to do *anything*,"

she had said to Marion, not two hours before; and here was a thing, the possibility of which she had never dreamed, staring her in the face, waiting to be done, and she felt that she could not do it. Oh, why was it necessary? "Why not let everything be as it has been?" said that wily villain Satan, whispering in her ears. "They were false vows; they are better broken than kept. He does not love her, though he said he did. And how can we ever endure it, the shame, the disgrace, the horrid explanations, our name, the *Erskine* name, on everybody's lips, common loafers sneering at us? And then to have the family changed; myself to be only a back figure; a mother who is not, and never *was* my mother, taking my place; and the other one—Oh, it cannot be possible that we must endure this! There must be some other way. They are doubtless contented, why could it not remain as it is?"

As if to answer her unspoken thoughts, Judge Erskine suddenly said:

"I have canvassed the entire subject in all its bearings, you may be sure of that. I am living a lie. I am saying my wife is dead, when a woman to whom before God I gave that name is living; I am saying that I have but one child, when there is another to whom I am as certainly father as I am to you. I am leaving them, nay, obliging them, to live a daily lie. I have assured myself to a certainty that one sin can never be atoned for by another sin; there is but one atonement; and the Source of all help says, 'If we *confess* our sins, he is faithful and just to forgive us our sins, and to cleanse us from *all* unrighteousness.' I know there is only one way of cleansing, Daughter."

"Get thee behind me, Satan." The only perfect life gave that sentence once, not alone for himself; thank God he has many a time since enabled his weak children of the flesh to repeat it in triumph. The grace came then and there to Ruth Erskine. She rose up from her chair, and going over to her father did what she had never remembered doing in her life before. She bent down and wound both arms around his neck and kissed him. Her voice was low and steady:

"Father, don't let this, or anything earthly, stand between you and Christ. You are not a sinner above all others. It is only the interposing hand of God that has kept me from taking sinful vows upon my lips. Let us do just what is right. Send for them to come home, and I will try to be a daughter and a sister; and I will stand by you and help you in every possible way. There are harder trials than ours will be, after all."

It was his daughter who finally and utterly broke the proud, haughty heart. Judge Erskine bowed himself before her and sobbed like a child in the bitterness and the humiliation of his soul.

"God bless you," he said at last, in broken utterance. "There is an almighty Savior; I need nothing more than your words to convince me of the truth of that. If love to him can lead your heart to such forgiveness as this, what must his forgiveness be? Ruth, you have saved my soul; I will give up the struggle; I have tried to fight it out; I have tried to say that I could not; for my own sake, and for my own name, it seemed impossible. Then when I got beyond that, and felt that for myself, if I could have rest in the love of Christ, and could feel that he forgave me, I cared for nothing else. Then I said, 'I cannot do this, for my child's sake; I can never plunge her into this depth of sin and shame.' Then, my daughter, there came to me a message from God, and of all those that *could* come to a miserable man like me, it was this: 'He that loveth son or daughter more than me is not worthy of me.' Then

I saw that I must be willing even to lose your love, to make you despise me; and that was the bitterest cup of all. But, thank God, he has spared me this. God bless you, my daughter."

There was something almost terrible to Ruth, in seeing her cold, calm father so moved. She had never realized what awfully solemn things *tears* were till she saw them on her father's cheeks, and felt them falling hot on her head, from eyes so unused to weeping. The kisses she gave him were very soft and clinging—full of tender, soothing touches. Then father and daughter knelt together, and the long, long struggle with sin and pride and *silence* was concluded.

Do you think this was a lasting victory for Ruth Erskine? You do not understand the power of "that old serpent, the devil," if you cannot think how he came to her again and again in the silence of her own room, even into the midst of her rejoicings over the newly washed soul, even while the joy in heaven among the angels was still ringing out over her father, came whispering to her heart to say:

"Oh, I can't, I can't. Think of it! The Erskines! How *can* we endure it? Is it *possible* that we must? Perhaps the woman would rather live as she is."

As if *that* had anything to do with the question of right and wrong! The very next instant Ruth curled her lip sneeringly over her own folly. She never forgot that night, nor how the conflict waged. She tried to imagine herself saying *Mother* to one who really had a nominal right to the title. Not that it was an unfamiliar word to her. The old aunt who had occupied the mother's place in the household since Ruth was a wee creature of two years, she had learned almost from the instincts of childhood to call "Mamma." And as she grew older and was unused to any other name for Mrs. Wheeler, the widowed aunt, she toned it into the familiar and comfortable word *Mother* and had always spoken to and of her in that name.

Yet she knew very well how little the title meant to her. She had loved this old lady with a sort of pitying, patronizing love, realizing even very early in her life that she, herself, had more self-reliance, more executive ability, in her little finger than was spread all over the placid lady who early learned that "Ruthie" was to do precisely as she pleased.

Such a cipher was this same old lady in the household that when a long-lost son appeared on the surface, during Ruth's absence at Chautauqua, proving, sturdy old Californian as he was, to have a home and place for his mother, and a heart to take her with him, her departure caused scarcely a ripple in the well-ordered household of the Erskines.

She had been its nominal head for eighteen years, but the real head who was absent at Chautauqua, had three or four perfectly trained servants, who knew their young mistress's will so well that they could execute it in her absence as well as when she was present.

So when Ruth took, in the eyes of everybody, the position that had really been hers so long, it made no sort of change in her plans or ways. And beyond a certain lingering tenderness when she spoke of her by that familiar title *Mother,* there was no indication that the woman who had had so constant and intimate a connection with her life was remembered.

But this name applied to another, and that other, one whom she had never seen in her life, and who yet was actually to occupy the position of head of the household—her father's wife, in the eyes of society her mother, spoken of as such, herself asked, "How is your mother?" or "What does your mother think of this?" Would anyone dare to use that name to her? No one had so spoken of her aunt. They all knew she was only her aunt, though she chose to pet her by the use of that tender name. Could she bear all these things and a hundred others that would come up?

"Marion," she said the next day as she chanced to meet that young lady on the street, "I have something to tell you. I want to call on you to witness that I shall never again be guilty of that vainglorious absurdity of saying that I am ready for anything. One can never know whether this is true or not; at least I am sure I never can. What I am to say in the future is simply, 'Lord, make me willing to do what there is for me to do this day.' Remember that in a few days you will understand what I mean."

Then she went on. Marion pondered over it. She did not understand it at all. What trial could have come to Ruth that had brought her the knowledge of the weakness of her own heart? She wondered if it had also brought her peace.

24

LONELINESS

I SUPPOSE there has never been an earnest worker, an enthusiast on any subject, in this changeful world but has been a victim at some time to the dismalness of a reaction. The most forlorn little victim that could be imagined was Flossy Shipley on that evening after the meetings, on which her soul had fed so long, were closed.

Everything in nature and in circumstances conspired to sink her into her desolate mood. In the first place, it was raining. Now a rain closing in upon a warm and dusty summer day is a positive delight; one can listen to the pattering drops with a sense of eager satisfaction; but a rain in midwinter, after a day of sunless mist and fog, almost amounting to rain, when the streets are that mixture of snow and water that can be known only as slush, when every opening of a door sends in gusts of damp air that chill to one's very bones, this weather is a trial; at least it seemed such to poor little Flossy.

She shivered over the fire in the coal grate. It glowed brightly, and the room was warm and bright, yet to Flossy there was a sense of chill in everything. She was all alone; and the circumstances connected with that loneliness were not calculated to brighten the evening for her. The entire family had gone out to a party, not one of those quiet little entertainments which people had been so careful to explain and apologize for during the meetings, but a grand display of toilet and supper and expenditure of all kinds.

Mrs. Westervelt, the hostess, being at all times noted for the display of her entertainments, had lavished more than the usual amount of time and money on the present ones, and waited for the meetings to close with the most exemplary patience, in order that she might gain a very few among her guests from those who felt the impropriety of mixing things too much.

To be sure, the society in general which was admitted to Mrs. Westervelt's parlors was not from that class who had any scruples as to what time they attended parties, but there were two or three notable exceptions, and those the lady had been anxious to claim.

Prominent among them had been the Erskines, it never seeming to occur to Mrs. Westervelt's brain that there could be other excuse found for not accepting her invitation save the meetings that Ruth had taken to attending in such a frantic manner. Let me say, in passing, that neither Ruth Erskine nor her father honored the invitation; they had other matters to attend to.

Meantime, Flossy Shipley had utterly disgusted her mother, and almost offended her father, by giving a peremptory and persistent refusal. Such a storm of talk as there had been over this matter almost exhausted the strength of poor little Flossy, who did not like argument, and who yet could persist in a most unaccountable firm manner when occasion required.

"Such an absurd idea!" her sister Kitty said, flashing contemptuous eyes on her. "I wonder what you think is going to become of you, Flossy? Do you mean to mope at home all the rest of the winter? I assure you that Mrs. Westervelt is not the only one who intends to give a party. We are going to have an unusually gay season to revive us after so much bell tolling. Don't you mean to appear anywhere? You might as well retire to a convent at once, if that is the case."

"People will be saying of me, as they do of Mrs. Treslam, soon, that I do not allow you to appear in society while Kitty is still a young lady." This Mrs. Shipley said, and her tone, if not as sharp as Kitty's, had a note of grievance in it that was hard to bear.

Then Charlie had taken up the theme: "What is the use in turning mope, Sis? I'm sure you can be as good as you like and go to a party occasionally."

"I don't mean to mope, Charlie," Flossy said, trying to speak cheerfully, but there were tears in her eyes and a tremulous sound in her voice. "I am truly happier at home than I am at those places; I don't like to go. It is not entirely because I feel I ought not; it is because I don't want to."

"She has risen above such follies," Kitty said, and it is impossible to tell you what a disagreeable inflection there was in her voice. "Mother, I am sorry that the poor child has to associate with such volatile creatures as you and I. She ought to have some kindred spirit."

"I am sure I don't know where she will find any," Mrs. Shipley said with a sigh, "outside of that trio of girls, who among them have contrived to make a perfect little slave of you. I am sure I don't know who has any influence over you. I used to think you regarded your mother's wishes a trifle, but I find I am mistaken."

"Oh, Mother!" Flossy said, and this time the tears began to fall, "why *will* you talk so? I am sure I try to please you in every way that I can. I did not know that you cared to have me go to parties, unless I wanted to go."

Either the tears or something else made her brother indignant. "What a scene about nothing," he said irritably. "Why can't you let Flossy go to parties or not, as she pleases? Parties are not such delightful institutions that she need be expected to be in love with them. I should be delighted if I never had to appear at another. Why not let people have their fun in this world where they choose to find it? If Flossy has lately discovered that hers can only be found in prayer meeting, I am sure it is a harmless enough diversion while the fit lasts."

Mrs. Shipley laughed. Her son could nearly always put her into good humor. Besides, she didn't like to see tears on her baby's face; that was her pet name for Flossy.

"Oh, I don't know that it makes any serious difference," she said; "not enough to spoil your eyes over, Flossy. I don't want you to go out with us unless you want to; only it is rather embarrassing to be constantly arranging regrets for you. Besides, I don't see what it is all coming to. You will be a moping, forsaken creature; old before your time, if this continues."

As for Mr. Shipley, he maintained a haughty silence, neither expressing an opinion on that subject nor on any other, which would involve him in a conversation with Flossy. She knew that he was more seriously displeased with her than were any of the others; not so much about the parties as about other and graver matters.

Col. Baker was the son of Mr. Shipley's old friend.

For this reason, and for several others, Mr. Shipley was very fond of him. It had long been in accordance with his plans that Flossy should become, at some future time, Mrs. Col. Baker, and that the estates of the two families should be thus united.

While he was not at all the sort of man who would have interfered to push such an arrangement against the preferences of the parties concerned, he had looked on with great and increasing satisfaction while the plans of the young people evidently tended strongly in that direction.

That his daughter, after an absence from home of only two weeks, should have come in contact with that which seemed to change all her tastes and views and plans, in regard to other matters, but which had actually caused her to turn with a steady and increasing determination away from the friend who had been her acknowledged protector and attendant ever since she was a child, was a matter that he did not understand nor approve.

"I am not a tyrant," he would say sullenly when Mrs. Shipley and himself talked the matter over; when she, with the characteristics of a mother, even while her child annoyed and vexed her, yet struggled to speak a word for her when a third person came in to blame. "I never ordered Flossy to be so exceedingly intimate with Col. Baker that their names have been coupled together ever since she was a baby. I never insisted on her accepting his attentions on all occasions. It was her own free will. I own that I was pleased with the inclination she displayed and did what I could to make the way pleasant for her, but the thing is not of my planning. What I am displeased with is this sudden change. There is no reason for it and no sense in it. It is just a mere baby performance, a girlish freak, very unpleasant for him and very disagreeable for us. The child ought not to be upheld in it."

So they did their best not to uphold her and succeeded among them in making her life very disagreeable to her.

The matter had culminated on the evening before the party in question. Col. Baker, despite the persistent and patient efforts on Flossy's part to show him the folly of his course, had insisted on obliging her to speak a decided negative to his earnestly pressed question. The result was an unusually unpleasant domestic scene and a general air of gloom and unhappiness.

Mr. Shipley had not ordered his daughter to marry Col. Baker. He would have been shocked beyond measure at such a proceeding on the part of a father. But he made her so unhappy with a sense of his disappointment and disapproval, that more than once she sighed wearily and wished in her sad little heart that all this living was over.

Finally, they all went off to Mrs. Westervelt's party and left her alone. She had never felt so much alone in her life. The blessed meetings, which had been such a wealth of delight and helpfulness to her heart, were closed. The sweet and holy and elevating influences that had surrounded her outer life for so long were withdrawn. She missed them bitterly.

It almost seemed to her as if everything were withdrawn from her. Father, mother, sister, and even her warmhearted brother, were all more or less annoyed at her course. Charlie had been betrayed into more positive sharpness than this favorite sister had ever felt from him before. He felt that his friend Col. Baker had been ill treated.

There was a very sore spot about this matter for

Flossy. The truth was, she could not help seeing that in a sense her father was right; she had brought it on herself; not lately, not since her utter change of views and aims, but long before that. With what satisfaction had she allowed her name to be coupled familiarly with that of Col. Baker; how much she had enjoyed his exclusive attentions; not that she really and heartily liked him with a liking that made her willing to think of him as belonging to her forever; she had chosen, rather, not to allow herself to think of any such time; she had contented herself with saying that she was too young to think of such things; that she was not obliged to settle that question till the time came.

But, mind you, all the time she chose to allow, and enjoy, and encourage by her smiles and her evident pleasure in them, very special attentions, that gave other people liberty to speak of them almost as one. To call it by a very plain name, which Flossy hated and which made her cheek glow as she forced herself to say it of herself, she had been flirting with Col. Baker. It isn't a nice word; I don't wonder that she hated it. Yet so long as young ladies continue to be guilty of the sort of conduct that can only be described by that unpleasant and coarse-sounding word, I am afraid it will be used.

All that was over now, at least it was over as much as Flossy could make it; but there remained an uncomfortable sense that she had wronged a man who honestly loved her; not intentionally—no decent woman does that—but thoughtlessly; so many silly girls do that. She had lost her influence over him now; rather, she had been obliged to put herself in a position to lose all influence. She might have been his true, faithful friend now, and helped him up to a higher manhood, only by her former folly she had put it out of her power. These were not pleasant reflections. Then there was no denying that she felt very desolate.

"A forlorn, friendless creature," her mother had said she would become, or words to that effect. The thought lingered with her. She looked over her list of friends; there was always those three girls, growing dearer by every day of association; yet their lives necessarily ran much apart; it would naturally grow more and more so as the future came to them. Then, too, she was equally intimate with each of them; they were all equally dear to her.

Now a woman cannot have three friends who shall all fill that one place in her heart which she finds. She thought of her home ties; strong they certainly were; growing stronger every day. There were few things that she did not feel willing to do for her father; but the one thing that he wanted just now was that she should marry Col. Baker; she could not do that, even to please him.

He would recover from that state of feeling, of course; but would not other kindred states of feeling constantly arise, both with him and with her mother? Could she not foresee a constant difference of opinion on almost every imaginable topic? Then there was her sister, Kitty. Could any two lives run more widely apart than hers and Kitty's were likely to? Had they a single taste in common?

As for Charlie, Flossy turned from that subject; it was too sore and too tender a spot to be probed. She trembled for Charlie; he was walking in slippery places; the descent was growing easier; she felt that rather than saw it; and she felt, too, that his friend Col. Baker was the leader; and she felt, too, that her intimacy with Col. Baker had greatly strengthened his.

No wonder that the spot was a sore one. Grouping

all these things together and brooding over them, with no sound breaking the silence save the ceaseless *drip, drip* of the rain and the whirls of defiant wind, she sat there in her loneliness, the large armchair in which she crouched being drawn up before that glowing fire, is it any wonder that the firelight revealed the fact that great silent tears were slowly following each other down Flossy's round, smooth cheek? She felt like a pitiful, lonely, forsaken baby.

It was not that she was utterly miserable; she recognized even then the thought that she had an almighty, everlasting, unchanging Friend. She rejoiced even then at the thought, not as she might have rejoiced, not as it was her privilege to do, but I mean she knew that all these trials and mistakes and burdens were but for a moment. She knew that tomorrow, when the sun shone again, she would be able to come out from behind these clouds and grasp some of the brightness of her life and endure with patience the little annoyances that were to be borne; remembering that she was still very young, and that there was a chance for a great deal of brightness for her, even on this side.

But, in the meantime, her intensely human heart craved human companionship and sympathy; craved it to such a degree that if it had not been for the rain and the darkness and the growing lateness of the hour, she would have gone out then after one of those three girls to share her mood with her.

Into the midst of this state of dismal journeying into the valley of gloom there pealed the sound of the bell. It did not startle her; the callers in their circle would be sure to be engaged at the party and to suppose that she was. Besides, it was hardly an evening for ordinary callers—something as important as a party was would be expected to call out people tonight. It was someone with a business message for Father, she presumed; and she did not arouse from her curled-up position among the cushions of that great chair.

Half listening, half giving attention to her own thoughts, she was conscious that a servant came to answer the bell, that the front door opened and shut, that there was a question asked and answered in the hall. Then she gave over attending to the matter. If she were needed, the girl knew she was in the library. Yes, she was to be summoned for something, to receive the message probably, for the library door quietly unclosed.

"What is it, Katie?" she asked in a sort of muffled undertone, to hide the traces of disturbance in her voice, and not turning her head in that direction; she knew there were tears on her cheeks.

"Suppose it should not be Katie, may anyone else come in and tell you what it is?" This was the sentence wherewith she was answered. What a sudden springing up there was from that chair! Even the tears were forgotten; and what a singular ring there was to Flossy's voice as she whirled round to full view of the intruder and said, "Oh, Mr. Roberts!"

Now, dear friends of this little lonely Flossy, are you so stupid that you need to be told that in less than half an hour from that moment she believed that there could never again come to her an absolutely lonely hour? That whatever might come between them, whether of life or of death, there would be that for each to remember that would make it impossible ever to be desolate again. For there is no desolation of heart to those who part at night to meet again in the morning; there may be loneliness and a reaching out after, and sometimes an unutterable longing for the morning, but to those who are sure, *sure* beyond the possibility of a doubt, that the eternal morning *will* dawn, and dawn for them, there is never again a desolation.

25

THE ADDED NAME

THAT same evening was fraught with memorable associations to others beside Flossy Shipley. It began in gloom and unusual depression even to bright-faced Marion. Those of the scholars who had been constant attendants at the meetings felt the inevitable sense of loneliness and loss that must follow the close of such unusual means of help.

I have actually heard some Christian people advance this fact, that there was a reaction of loneliness after such meetings closed, as a good reason why they were unwise efforts, demoralizing in their results. It is a curious fact that such reasoners are never found to advocate the entire separation of family friends on the plea that a reunion followed by a separation is demoralizing in its results because it leaves an added sense of loneliness.

It is, perhaps, to be questioned whether loneliness is, after all, demoralizing in its effects. Be that as it may, many of the scholars felt it. Then there were some among their number who had persistently shunned the meetings and their influences, who, now that the opportunity was passed, felt those stings of conscience that are sure to follow enlightened minds who have persisted in going a wrong road.

Also there were those who had been almost persuaded, and who yet, so far as their salvation was concerned, were no nearer it that day than though they had never thought of the matter, for *almost* never saves a soul. All these influences combined served to make depression the predominant feeling. Marion struggled with it and tried to be cheerful before her pupils, but sank into gravity and unusual sadness at every interval between the busy hours of the day.

Late in the afternoon she had a conversation with one of the girls which did not serve to encourage her heart. It was the drawing hour. Large numbers of the young ladies in her room had gone to the studio with the drawing master; those few who remained were engaged in copying their exercises for the next morning's class. Marion was at leisure, her only duty being to render assistance in the matter of copying wherever a raised hand indicated that help was needed.

Answering one of these calls she found herself at the extreme end of the large room, quite near to Grace Dennis's desk, and in passing she noticed that Gracie, while her book was before her and her pen in hand, was not writing at all, but that her left hand was shading a face that looked sad and pale, and covering eyes that might have tears in them. After fulfilling her duty to the needy scholar, she turned back to Grace.

"What is it?" she said softly, taking the vacant seat by Grace's side and touching tenderly the crown of hair that covered the drooping head. Grace looked up quickly with a gleam of sunshine, through which shone a tear.

"It is a fit of the blues, I am almost afraid. I am very

much ashamed of myself; I don't feel so very often, Miss Wilbur. I think the feeling must be what the girls call blues; I am not sure."

"Do you feel in any degree sure what has caused such a remarkable disease to attack you?" Marion asked in a low, tender, yet cheery and a half-amused tone.

The words made Gracie laugh, but the tenderness in the tone seemed to start another tear.

"You will be amused at me, Miss Wilbur, or ashamed of me, I don't know which. I am ashamed of myself, but I do feel so forlorn and lonely."

"Lonely!" Marion echoed with a little start. She realized that she herself knew in its fullness what that feeling was, but for Gracie Dennis, treasured as she was in an atmosphere of fatherly love, it was hard to understand it. "If I had my dear father, I don't think I should feel lonely," she said gently.

"I know," Grace answered; "he is the dearest father a girl ever had, but there is only a little bit of him mine, Miss Wilbur. I don't mean that, either; I am not selfish. I know he loves me with all his heart, but I mean his time is so very much occupied that he can only give me very little bits now and then. It has to be so; it is not his fault. I would not have him any different, even in this; but then if I had a sister, don't you see how different it would be? Or even a brother, or," and here Gracie's head dropped low and her voice quivered. "Miss Wilbur, if I had a mother, one who loved me and would sympathize with me and help me, I think I would be the happiest girl in all the world."

There was every appearance that, with a few more words of tender sympathy, this young girl would lose all her self-control and be that which she so much shrank from, an object of general wonderment and conversation. Marion felt that she must bestow her sympathy sparingly.

"I daresay you would give yourself over to a hearty struggle not to hate her outright," she said in a quiet, matter-of-fact tone. The sobs which were shaking the young girl beside her were suddenly checked. Presently Gracie looked up, a gleam half of mirth, half of defiance, in her handsome eyes. "I mean a *real* mother," she said.

"Haven't you one? Doesn't she love her darling and watch over and wait for her coming?" The voice had taken on its tenderness again. Then, after a moment, Marion added:

"It is hard to realize, I know, but I believe it, and I look toward that thought with all my soul. You remember, Gracie, that I have nothing but that to feed on, no earthly friend to help me realize it."

Grace stole a soft hand into her teacher's. "I wish you would love me very much," she said brightly. "I wish you would let me love you. Do you know you help me every time you speak to me? And you do it in such strange ways, not at all in the direction that I am looking for help. I do thank you so much."

"Then suppose you prove it to me by showing what an immaculate copy of your exercise you can hand in tomorrow. Don't you know it is by just such commonplace matters as that that people are permitted to show their love and gratitude and all those delightful things? That is what glorifies work."

Another clinging pressure of hands, and teacher and pupil went about their duties. But though Marion had helped Gracie, she had not helped herself, except that in a tired sort of way she realized that it was a great pleasure to be able to help anybody—most of all, this favorite pupil. Still the dreariness did not lessen. It went home with her to her dingy boardinghouse, followed her to the gloomy dining room and the uninviting suppertable.

The most that was the trouble with Marion Wilbur was that she was tired in body and brain. If people only realized it, a great many mental troubles and trials result from overworked bodies and nerves. Still, it must be confessed that there were few, if any, outside influences that were calculated to cheer Marion Wilbur's life.

You are to remember how very much alone she was. There were no letters to be watched for in the daily mails, no hopeful looking forward if one failed to come, no cheery saying to one's heart, "Never mind, it will surely come tomorrow." This state is infinitely better than the hopeless glance one bestows upon the postman, realizing he is nothing to them.

No friends—father and mother gone so long ago! That of one there was no recollection at all, of the other, tender childhood memories, sweet and lasting and incomparably precious, but only memories. No sister, no brother, no cousins that had taken the place to her of sisters; only that old uncle and aunt, who were such staid and common and plodding people that sometimes the very thought of them tired this girl so full of life and energy.

Girl I call her, but she had passed the days of her girlhood. Few knew it; it was wonderful how young and fresh her heart had kept. That being the case, of course, her face had taken the same impress. It was hard for Ruth Erskine to realize that her friend Marion was really thirteen years older than herself. There were times when Marion herself felt younger than Ruth did.

But the years were there, and in her times of

depression, Marion realized it. So many of them recorded, and yet no friends to whom she had a right, feeling sure that nothing in human experience this side of death would be likely to come in and take her away from them. The very suppertable at that board-inghouse was sufficient to add to her sense of desolation.

It is a pitiful fact that we are such dependent creatures that even the crooked laying of a cloth, and the coffee stains and milk stains and gravy stains thereon, can add to our sense of friendlessness. Then, what is there particularly consoling or cheering in a cup of weak tea and a bit of bread a trifle sour, spread over by butter more than a trifle strong; even though it is helped down by some very dry bits of chipped beef? This was Marion's supper.

The boarders were, some of them, cross, some of them simply silent and hurried, all of them damp, for they were, every one, workers out in the damp, dreary world; the most of them, in fact, I may say all of them, were very tired; yet many of them had work to do that very evening. Marion ate her supper in silence, too; at least she bit at her bread and tried to swallow her simpering tea.

When her heart was bright and her plans for the evening definite and satisfactory, she could manage the sour bread and strong butter even, with something like relish, but there was no use in trying them tonight. She even tormented herself with the planning of a dainty supper, accompanied by exquisite table arrangements such as she would manage for a sister, say, if she had one—a sister who had been in school all day and was wet and hungry and tired, if she had the room and the table and the china and the materials out of which to construct the supper. She was reasonable enough to see that there were many *ifs* in the way, but the picture did not make the present supper relish.

She struggled to rally her weary powers. She asked the clerk next her if it had been a busy day, and she told the sewing girl at her left about a lovely bouquet of flowers that one of the girls brought to school, and that she had meant to bring home to her, if presented. To be sure, it was not. But the intention was the same, and the heart of the sewing girl was cheered.

Finally Marion gave over trying to swallow the supper, and assuring herself with the determination to go early to bed and so escape faintness, she went up three flights of stairs to her room.

"When I am rich and a woman of leisure, I will build a house that shall have pleasant rooms and good bread and butter, and I will board schoolteachers and sewing girls and clerks for a song." This she said aloud.

Then she set about making a bit of blaze, or a great deal of smoke in the little imp of a stove. The stove was small and cracked and rusty and could smoke like a furnace. What a contrast to the glowing coal grate where Flossy at this hour toasted her pretty cheeks. Yet Marion, in her way, was less dismal than Flossy in hers.

It was not in Marion's nature to shed any tears; instead, she hummed a few notes of a glorious old tune triumphant in every note, trying thus to rob herself of gloom and cheat herself into the belief that she was not very lonely and that her life did not stretch out before her as a desolate thing. She did not mean to give herself up to glooming, though she did hover over the little stove and lean her cheek on her hand and look at nothing in particular for a few minutes. What she said when she rallied from the silence was simply:

"What an abominable smoke you can make to be

sure, Marion Wilbur, when you try. Hardly anyone can compete with you in that line, at least."

Then she drew her school reports toward her, intending to make them out for the week thus far, but she scribbled on the flyleaf with her pencil instead. She wrote her own name, "Marion J. Wilbur," a pretty enough name. She smiled tenderly over the initial of *J*—nobody knew what that was for.

Suppose the girls knew that it stood for *Josiah,* her father's name; that he had named her, after the mother was buried, *Marion*—that after the mother, *Josiah*—that after the father, *Wilbur*—the dear name that belonged to them both; in this way fancying in her gentle heart that he linked this child to them both in a way that would be dear to her to remember.

It was dear; she loved him for it; she thoroughly understood the feeling, but hardly anyone else would. So she thought she had never given them a chance to smile over the queer name her father had given. She could smile herself, but she wanted no one else to do so.

Then she wrote *Grace L. Dennis.* What a pretty name that was. She knew what the *L* was for—Lawrence, the family name—Grace's mother's name. Her mother, too, had died when she was a wee baby. Gracie remembered her, though, and by that memory so much more did she miss her.

Marion knew how that was by her remembrance of her father. All the same she would not have that blotted out, by so much richer was Gracie than herself, and then that living, loving father. Marion smiled over the folly of Grace Dennis considering her life a lonely one. "Yet, I presume she feels it, poor darling," she said aloud, and with a sigh. It was true that every heart knew its own bitterness.

Then she said, "I really must go to work at these reports. I wonder what the girls are doing this evening? Eurie is nursing her mother, I suppose. Blessed Eurie! Mother and Father both within the fold, brought there by Eurie's faithful life. Mrs. Mitchell told me so, herself. What a sparkle that will make in Eurie's crown. I wonder what Ruth meant this morning? Poor child! She has trouble too; different from mine. Why, as to that, I really haven't any. Ruth ought to 'count her marcies,' though, as old Dinah says. She has a great deal that I haven't. Yes, indeed, she has! I suppose little Flossy is going through tribulation over that tiresome party. I wonder why one half of the world have to exist by tormenting the other half? Now, Marion Wilbur, stop scribbling names and go to work."

Steady scratching from the old steel pen a few minutes, then a knock and a message: Dr. Dennis wanted to see her a few minutes, if she had leisure.

"Dr. Dennis!" she said, rising quickly and pushing away her papers. "Oh, dear me! Where is that classbook of mine? He wants those names, I daresay, and I haven't them ready. I might have been copying them while I was mooning my time away here."

The first words she said to him as she went down to the stuffy boardinghouse parlor were, "I haven't them ready, Dr. Dennis; I'm real sorry, and it's my fault, too. I had time to copy them, and I just didn't do it."

"I haven't come for them," he said, smiling and holding out his hand. "How do you do?"

"Oh, quite well. Didn't you come for them? I am glad, for I felt ashamed. Dr. Dennis, don't you see how well one woman can do the work of twenty? Don't you like the way the primary class is changed? Oh, by the way, you want that book, don't you? I meant to send it home by Gracie."

"I don't want it," he said, laughing this time. "Are you resolved that I may not call on you without a good and tangible reason? If that be the case, I certainly have one. I want you to sit down here while I tell you about it."

"I'm not in the mood for a scolding," she said, trying to speak gaily, though there was a curious little tremble to her voice. "I have been away down in the valley of gloom today. I believe I am a little demoralized. Dr. Dennis, I think I need a prayer meeting every evening; I could be happier then, I know."

"A Christian ought to be able to have one," he said quickly. "Two souls ought to be able to come together in communion with the Master every evening. There is a great deal of wasted happiness in the world. I want to talk to you about that very thing."

Dr. Dennis was not given to making long calls on his parishioners; there were too many of them, and he had too little time; but he made an unprecedentedly long one on Marion Wilbur.

When she went back to her room that night, the fire was gone out utterly; not even smoke remained. She lit her smoky little lamp—there was no gas in the third story—and looked at her watch with an amazed air; she had not imagined that it could be nearly eleven o'clock! Then she pushed the reports into a drawer and turned the key; no use to attempt reports for that evening. As she picked up her classbook, the scribbling on the flyleaf caught her eye again. She smiled a rare, rich, happy smile; then swiftly she drew her pencil and added one more name to the line. "Marion Wilbur—Marion J. Wilbur," it read. There was just room on the line for another word; then it read—"Marion J. Wilbur Dennis!" To be sure, she took her rubber quickly from her pocket and obliterated every trace of that last. But what of it? There are words and deeds that cannot so easily be obliterated; and Marion, as she laid her grateful head on her fluffy little pillow that night, was thankful it was so and felt no desire to erase them.

Desolate? Not she; God was very gracious. The brightness that she felt sure she could throw around some lives, she knew would have a reflex brightness for her. Then, queerly enough, the very next thing she thought of was that dainty supper she planned for herself that she could have prepared for a school-teacher, wet, hungry, and tired. Why not for a school-girl? If she had no sister to do it for, why not for a daughter? "Dear little Gracie!" she said. Then she went to sleep.

Meantime, during that eventful evening, Ruth sat in her room alone, busy with grave and solemn thoughts. Her father was already many miles away. He had gone to see his wife and daughter. Eurie, at that same hour, was bending anxiously over a sick mother, trying to catch the feebly whispered direction, with such a heavy, heavy pain at her heart. But the same patient, wise, all-powerful Father was watching over and directing the ways of each of his four girls.

26

━━◆◇◆━━

LEARNERS

ALTHOUGH the sense of desolation was gone from Flossy Shipley, she was not without something to be troubled over. As to that, when one sets out to be troubled, one can nearly always find an excuse.

Flossy lay awake over hers for hours that night. Mr. Roberts was given to keeping more proper hours than those in which partygoers indulge. So it happened that the library was vacant when the family returned, the gas turned low, and the grate carefully supplied with coal to give them a warm greeting. But the easy chairs before the bright fire told no tales of all the pleasant and helpful words that had been spoken there that evening.

So far as the family knew, Flossy had spent her evening in solitude. But they would come to know it; would have to be introduced to Mr. Roberts; there would have to be a prompt explanation of their interest in each other. Flossy meant to have no delays, nor chances for mistakes, this time.

The momentous question was, how would her father receive the message, what word would he have for the stranger? She could almost have wished that his coming had been delayed for a few weeks more, until the sore sullen feeling ever-disappointed plans had had time to quiet. But, as it was, since Mr. Roberts was to be in the city and she was to see him, she would have no pretense of his being merely a chance acquaintance of her Chautauqua life, making friendly calls; at least her father should know that they both meant more than that. Whether he would ignore the claims they made and choose to treat Mr. Roberts as a stranger, Flossy did not know; it seemed more than likely that he would.

As to that, she could not help owning to herself that he would have very plausible reasons for so doing. What was she supposed to know about Mr. Evan Roberts? Closely questioned, she would have to admit that she had never heard of his existence till those golden Chautauqua days; that although she walked and talked much with him during those two weeks, there had been so much to talk about, such vital interests that pressed upon them, so many things for her to learn that they had spent no time at all in talking about each other's past.

She remembered now that, strangely enough, she had no idea even at this moment what his business was, except that from some casual remark she judged that he was familiar with mercantile life; he might have some money or he might be very poor, she had not the least idea which it was; he might be of an old and honored family, or his father might have been a blacksmith and his mother, even now, a washerwoman. She admitted to herself that she knew nothing at all about it; and she was obliged also to admit that, so far as she herself was concerned, she did not care.

But Mr. Shipley was very different. Most assuredly

he would care. How could he understand why she should be able to feel such perfect trust in this stranger? If she should try to tell him of those wonderful prayers she had heard from Mr. Robert's lips, what would such evidence be to him? If she should try to tell him how, by this man, she had been led into the light of love and trust that glowed brighter and stronger with every day, how little information it would give him! What an utter mystery would such language be to him!

As she thought of all these puzzling things, what wonder that she turned her pillow many times in search of a spot to rest and gave a great many long-drawn sighs?

It so happened that Mr. Roberts, while he had not troubled himself to enlighten Flossy as to his position and prospects, had by no means supposed that her father would be as indifferent to these small matters as she was; he had come armed with credentials and introductions. Overwhelming ones they were to Mr. Shipley. He waited for no introductions nor explanations to come from Flossy.

Instead, the very next morning, at the earliest hour that business etiquette would allow, he sought Mr. Shipley at his business office, presented his card and letters, and made known his desire to transact mercantile business with him in the name of his firm. And the rich man, Mr. Shipley, arose and bowed before him.

Was he not a representative? Nay, a junior partner of the firm of Bostwick, Smythe, Roberts & Co.? Names world renowned among mercantile men. Could human ambition reach higher than to have flattering offers of business from that great house? Than to be actually sought out by this young partner, singled from

among all the merchant princes of the city, as the one
to be taken into business confidence!

Mr. Shipley's ambitious dreams reached no more
dizzy height than this.

Mr. Roberts was invited, urged to accept the hos-
pitalities of his home, to make the acquaintance of his
family, to command his horses, his carriage, his servants, in short, to become one of their family so long
as he could be prevailed upon to remain in the city.

But Mr. Roberts had more communications to
make; he frankly announced that he was already
acquainted with his family, at least with that portion
of it, which was of enough importance to include all
the rest; of course, he did not say this to the father, and
yet his manner implied it, as he meant it should. Mr.
Roberts was frank by nature; he no more believed in
concealments of any sort than did Flossy.

Then and there, he told the story that the two easy
chairs in the library knew about. He even apologized
earnestly for seeking the daughter first. It had not
been his intention; he had meant to call on the family;
but they were absent, and he found Miss Flossy alone.
And—well, if Mr. Shipley had been particular, as
assuredly he would have been, if Mr. Roberts had not
been of the firm of Bostwick, Smythe, Roberts & Co.
it might have been embarrassing to have explained the
very precipitate result of his call.

But, as it was, Mr. Shipley was so amazed and so
bewildered and so overwhelmed with delighted pride,
that he would almost have forgiven the announcement that Mr. Roberts was already his son-in-
law, without leave or license from him. As it was, all
the caution had to be on Mr. Robert's side. He asked
that letters might be sent to his brother-in-law, Mr.
Smythe, and to his father, Mr. James Roberts, proving,

not his financial standing, the unmistakable knowledge of the private affairs of the firm that had established him there, but of his moral character and his standing in the Christian world.

Do you believe that Mr. Shipley felt the necessity? Not he! Had he not been willing more than that, anxious that his daughter's fortune should be linked with Col. Baker's? Did he now know what was Col. Baker's standing in the moral and Christian world? After all, is it any wonder, when there are such fathers, that many daughters make shipwreck of their lives? As for Mr. Roberts, he was almost indignant:

"The man would actually sell her, if by that means he could be recognized in business by our house."

If it had been any other young man than himself who was in question, how his indignation would have blazed at such proceedings! But since it *was* himself, he decided to accept the situation.

As for Flossy, she did not look at the matter in that light; when she found that all the perplexities and clouds had been so suddenly and so strangely smoothed and cleared from before her way, she thought of those hours of wakeful anxiety that she had wasted the night before; and of how, finally, she had *made* her heart settle back onto the watchful care and love of the Father, who was so wise and so powerful, and in the quiet of her own room, she smiled, as she said aloud:

"'Commit thy way unto the Lord; trust also in him; and he shall bring it to pass.' How much pleasanter it would have been to have committed it in the first place, before I wearied my heart with worrying over what I could not lift my finger to make different!"

So, in less time than it has taken me to tell it, the rough places smoothed suddenly before Flossy Shipley's feet. She was free now, to go to parties or to prayer meetings or to stay at home, according to her own fancy, for was she not the promised wife of a partner of the firm of Bostwick, Smythe, Roberts & Co.?

It transpired that Mr. Roberts had come to make a somewhat extended stay in the city to look after certain business affairs connected with the firm, and also to look after certain business interests of the great Master, whose work he labored at with untiring persistence, always placing it above all other plans, and working at it with a zeal that showed his heart was there.

Flossy, during those days, took great strides as a learner in Christian work. Among other things, she was let into the mysteries of some of the great and systematic charities of the city, and found what wonderful things God's wealth could do, placed in the hands of careful and conscientious stewards. She had thought at first that it made no difference at all to her whether Mr. Roberts had to work for his daily bread or whether he had means at his disposal; but very early in her acquaintance with him she learned to thank God that great wealth had been placed in his hands, and so, was to be at her disposal, and that she was learning how to use it.

Some of her new experiences had their embarrassing side. Mr. Roberts had been but a few days in the city when he had certain protégés which circumstance had thrown in his way, in whom he became deeply interested. One of these, he engaged to take Flossy to visit.

"They are very poor," he had said to her, supposing that thereby he enlightened her.

Now Flossy had small knowledge in that direction. There was a certain old lady living at the extreme east end who had once been a servant in their family, and Flossy's nurse. In her, Flossy was much interested, and had been often to see her. She kept house in a bit of a room that was always shining with cleanliness; her floor was covered with bright rag carpeting; her bed was spread with a gay covered quilt, and her little cook-stove glistened, and the bright teakettle sputtered cheerily. This was Flossy's idea of poverty.

Therefore, when she arrayed herself for a wintry walk with Mr. Roberts, there was to her mind no incongruity between the rich black silk, the velvet cloak, the elegant laces, and costly furs, and the "very poor family" she was about to visit. Why should there be? She had trailed that same silk over old Auntie Green's bright-colored rag carpet a good many times without experiencing any discomfort therefrom.

As for Mr. Roberts, he regarded her with a half-amused smile which she did not observe, and said nothing. Probably he had an idea that she would soon be wiser than she was then.

"It is too far to walk," he said as they reached a point where streetcars diverged in many directions; so he hailed a passing car and, during the talk that followed, Flossy was conveyed to a portion of the city she not only had never seen before, but that she did not know existed.

She looked about her in dismay as she stepped down from the car, and during the short rapid walk that followed, had all she could do to rescue her silken robes from contact with awful filth and to keep her dainty handkerchief applied to her poor little nose. Rapidly and silently they made their way to a long, high building, whose filthy outside stairs they descended and found themselves in a cellar the like of which Flossy had never dreamed of.

A dreadful pile of straw covered over by a tattered and horribly dirty rag that had once been a quilt; on this bed lay a child not yet ten years old, whose deathly pale face and glassy eyes told the story of hopeless sickness. No pillow on which to lay the poor little head with its tangled masses of yellow hair, nothing anywhere that told of care bestowed or necessary wants attended to. Over in another corner on another filthy heap of straw and rags lay the mother, sick, too, with the same absence of anything like decency in everything that pertained to her.

Utter dismay seized upon Flossy. Could it be possible that human beings, beings with souls, for whose souls her blessed Savior died, were left to such awful desolation of poverty as this! Mr. Roberts promptly turned upside down an old tub that was used to doing duty as a chair, and seated her thereon, while he went forward to the woman.

"Have you had your dinner today?" was the first question he asked.

"Yes, I have; and thank you kindly, too," she added gratefully. "The woman took the money and bought meat as you told her and made a broth, and I and the little girl had some; it was good. The little girl took quite a few spoonfuls of it and said it tasted good; it did me more good to hear her say that than it did to eat mine," the poor mother said, and a wistful motherly look went over to the heap of rags in the corner.

"I am glad that she could eat it," he said simply. Then he further told that he had been arranging for some things to be brought to make both of them more comfortable; they would be here soon, could the woman who made the broth come in and attend to them?

The sick woman shook her head. She was gone for

the day; would not be back till dark, then would have to get her children's supper and do her washing that very night. "She's *awful* poor," the woman added with a heavy sigh. "We are all of us that; if I could get up again, I could do something for my little girl. I most know I could, but, as it is—" And then there was that hopeless sigh.

Meantime Flossy, after sitting with a distressed and irresolute face for a few minutes, had suddenly risen from her tub and gone over to the little girl. Bending beside her they had talked together in a low voice, and as Mr. Roberts turned to see if she had endured the scene as long as her nerves would admit, she turned toward him and there was more decision in her voice than he had ever heard before.

"Mr. Roberts, can you find some clean water for this basin, and haven't you a large handkerchief with you? This poor child must have her face washed. She says her head aches very badly; that will help it. And Mr. Roberts, can't you go out immediately to the store and get some clothes for this bed, and a pillow, don't they have such things in stores?"

"I have seen to that," he said; "there will be some bedclothing here, and other necessities very soon; but how can we manage to have the beds made up? I have ordered bedsteads and mattresses, and bedclothing has been prepared; but I have failed thus far in getting anyone to help arrange them."

"Can't you set up a bedstead?" asked Miss Flossy.

"Why, I think I could," he answered her meekly.

"Very well, then, I can make the beds. As for the child, she must have a bath and a clean dress before she is ready for any bed. I can tell you just what to do, Mr. Roberts; you must go down to the east end, No. 217 South Benedict Street and find my old Auntie Green, and tell her that she is needed here just as soon as she can get here; tell her I want her; it will be all right then. In the meantime, this child's face must be washed and her hair combed. I see there is a kettle behind that stove; could you manage to fill it with water, and then could you make a better fire? Then, I can stay here and do a good many things while you are gone."

While our little Flossy was talking, she was removing her lavender kid gloves and pinning up out of sight her lace ruffles. Then she produced from some one of the bewildering and dainty pockets that trimmed her dress a plain, hemstitched handkerchief, which she unceremoniously dropped into the tin basin, and announced herself all ready for the water.

"But, Flossy," said her embarrassed attendant in dismay, "you can't do these things, you know; wouldn't it be better to come with me, and we will go after this Auntie Green and tell her just what to do and furnish the means to do it with. You know you are not used to anything of this kind."

"I know it," she said quietly. "I never knew there was anything like this in the world; I am bowed in the very dust with shame and dismay. There is very little that I know how to do, but I can wash this poor, neglected child's face. Go right away, please; there is no time to lose, I am sure."

What swift, deft fingers she had, to be sure. He could not help stopping for a moment in his bewilderment to watch her; then he went, and meekly and swiftly did her bidding. There was much done during that afternoon. Mr. Roberts quietly sinking into the errand man who was useful, chiefly because he could promptly do as he was told; and he felt with every additional direction and with every passing moment an increased respect for the executive abilities of the little girl whom he had looked forward to rousing by degrees to a sense of the importance of this work and gradually to a participation in other than the money charities of the day.

When they went away from that door, as they ascended the filthy stairs again, she said:

"What an awful thought that human beings exist in such places as this, and that I did not know it and have done nothing for them!" She was certainly not exhausted, not overcome with the stench and the filth, though there was water dripping at that moment from her rich, silk dress. She noticed it, and as she brushed off the drops she said:

"Evan, if you knew, I wonder that you did not tell me to wear my Chautauqua dress. I shall know better next time. I must have that poor little girl cured; there are ever so many things to do; oh, Evan, you must teach me how."

"You need no teacher," he said softly, almost reverently, "other than the divine Teacher whom you have had. I am become a learner."

27

FLOSSY'S PARTY

MARION, on her way from school, had stopped in to learn, if she could, what shadow had fallen over Ruth. But before anything like confidence had been reached, Flossy Shipley came, full of life and eagerness.

"I am so glad to find two of you together," she said, "it expedites matters so much. Who do you think can be going to give a party next?"

"A party!" said Marion, "I am sure I don't know. I am prepared for any sort of news on that subject; one would think there had been a party famine for years, and lost time was to be made up, to see the manner in which one entertainment crowds after another since the meetings closed. It is a mercy that I am never invited; it would take all my leisure, and a great deal of notepaper, to prepare regrets. Who is it?"

"I haven't the least idea that you could guess, so I am going to tell you; it's just myself."

Both of her listeners looked incredulous.

"I am," she said gleefully. "I am at work on the arrangements now as hard as I can be; and Marion Wilbur, you needn't go to talking about notepaper and regrets; you are to come. I shall have to give up Eurie, and I am sorry too, she would have helped along so much; but of course she cannot leave her mother."

"How is her mother?" asked both girls at once.

"Oh, better; Nellis says the doctor feels very hopeful, now; but of course, Eurie doesn't leave her, and cannot for a long time. Nellis Mitchell is a splendid fellow. How strange it is that his interest in religious matters should have commenced with that letter which Eurie sent him from Chautauqua, before she had much interest herself."

"Nobody supposed that he had, I am sure," Ruth said; "I thought him the most indifferent of mortals."

"So did I, and would never have thought to pray for him at all, if Eurie had not asked me to, specially. Did you know he led the young people's meeting last evening? Did splendidly, Grace Dennis said. By the way, isn't Grace Dennis lovely? Marion, don't you think she is the most interesting young lady in your room?"

"I think you don't enlighten us much in regard to the party," Marion said, her cheeks growing red under that last question.

"I ought to be on my way; my tea will be colder than usual if I don't hasten; what scheme have you now, Flossy, and what do you want to do with it?"

"Ever so many things; you know my boys? Well, they are really young men; and anyone can see how they have improved. Some of them have real good homes, to be sure; but the most of them are friendless sort of boys. Now, I want to get them acquainted; not with the frippery people who would have nothing to do with them, but with some of our real splendid boys and girls who will enjoy helping them. I'm going to

have the nicest little party I ever had in my life; I mean
to have some of the very best people there; then I shall
have some of the silly ones, of course; partly because
I can't help it, and partly because I want to show them
what a nice time reasonable beings can have together,
if they choose. Nellis Mitchell is enlisted to help me
in ever so many ways, and Mr. Roberts will do what
he can, but you know he is a stranger. My great
dependence is on you two. I want you to see to it that
my boys don't feel lonely or out of place one single
minute during the entire evening."

"But I am afraid I shall feel lonely and out of place,"
Marion said; "you know I am never invited to parties."

Flossy laughed.

"Wouldn't it be a strange sight to see you feeling
out of place?" she asked gaily. "Marion, I can't conceive of a place to which you wouldn't do credit."

Whereupon Marion arose and made a low curtsy.

"Thank you," she said in mock gravity. "I never had
a compliment before in my life; I shall certainly come;
there is nothing like a little flattery to win people."

"Don't be nonsensical," pleaded Flossy; "I am really
in earnest. Ruth, I may depend upon you? I know you
are not going to entertainments this winter, but mine
is to be a small one, compared with the others; and
you know it will be unlike any that we have had at
our house."

Ruth hesitated.

"When is it to be?" she asked, her cheeks glowing
over her own thoughts. "I shall be engaged on Friday
evening of next week."

"It is to be on Wednesday."

"Then I will come. And if I play, Marion, will you
sing to entertain the unusual guests?"

"Of course," Marion said promptly. "I never sang in company in my life; but do you suppose there is anything I will not do for Flossy's guests, after what she has just said? Only, Flossy, I shall have to wear my black cashmere."

"Wear your brown calico, if you choose; you look royal in it," Flossy said, turning a beaming face on Marion. She had heard her sing, she knew what a rare musical treat it would be to those boys of hers. So this was Flossy's last departure from the beaten track.

Those who are familiar with the imperative laws and lines which circumscribe the fashionable world will realize just how marked a departure it was. It was a remarkable party. The very highest and most sought after of the fashionable world were there, a few of them, and John Warden was there in his new business suit of gray, looking and feeling like a man.

Flossy's boys were all present, and those who knew of them and their associations and advantages, marvelled much at their ease of manner and perfect propriety of behavior. How could they have learned so much? Flossy did not know, herself, but the boys did.

Her exquisite grace of manner, her perfect observance of all the rules and courtesies of polite society in her intercourse with them, had produced its legitimate fruit; had instinctively inclined them to be able to treat her with the same sort of grace which she freely and everywhere bestowed on them.

Had she not met them on the street, in the very heart of Broadway when she was walking with some of her fashionable friends? Had she not taken pains to recognize them with a specially cordial bow, and if near enough, with a deliberate speaking of their names, being sure to slightly emphasize the unusual prefix *Mr.*

These and a hundred other kindred trifles, so small that they are not noted among the qualifications for Sabbath-school teachers, so powerful for good that they often turn the current of a human life, had been carefully regarded by Flossy, and tonight she was triumphant over her success. She had not only helped her boys to be true to their convictions of right and dignity, not only to take on true manliness of decision in regard to the all-important question of personal religion, she had helped them to be gentlemen. There is many a faithful teacher to whom, thinking of these minor matters, it might be said:

"These ought ye to have done, and not to leave the other undone."

From first to last, Flossy's party was a success. To Ruth and Marion it was a study, developing certain curious features which they never forgot. Marion had her own private bit of interest that not another present, save Gracie Dennis knew about. She was not a partygoer. Even so small a gathering as this was new to her. She looked upon all these people with a keen interest; many of them she was meeting for the first time. That is, she was being introduced to them and receiving their kindly greetings; for Flossy had succeeded in gathering only those, who whatever they might think of her choice of guests, were much too well bred to exhibit other than pleasure while they were her guests.

But only Marion knew that she was destined to meet these people again, and probably often, under different circumstances; the probability was that many of them would be her own guests, would receive and return her calls, would fall into the habit of consulting her in regard to this or that matter of church interest that would come up; not one of them dreamed of such a thing; and when she tried to lead them into conversation on matters pertaining to the church interests, they looked their surprise that she should have such intelligent knowledge concerning these matters.

Altogether it was an evening full of private fun on her part. There was to be such a curious turnabout of position, she realized so fully that it would be such unutterable surprise to the people that it was impossible not to feel amused and to treasure up certain words and phrases that would sound very queerly to the speakers thereof, if they remembered them when those said changes became manifest to the eyes of the world.

There was more than fun to be gotten out of the evening; she watched the young people with eager interest. She was to be a great deal to these young people; she must try to understand them, to win them. She wanted to be a help, a comfort, a guide. She had wonderful plans and aims. She blessed Flossy in her heart for this opportunity to study her lesson before it should be time to practice it.

That same Flossy afforded her help in another direction. There was no hiding the hold that she had gotten, not only on those young men of her class, but those of their friends that they had brought within her influence. There was no disguising the fact that among the young ladies she was a favorite; one whom they liked to have among them, whom they liked to please. How had she done it all?

"I can never be Flossy," Marion said to herself, an amused smile hovering around her lips at the thought that she should have a shadow of desire to become their little Flossy. "But it is worthwhile to steal her secret of success, if I can, and practice it."

Close watching revealed a good deal of the secret; as much of it at least as could be put into words. Evidently the little lady had the power of making other people's interests her own for the time being; of impressing the one with whom she came in contact with a sense of his own importance, in her eyes; at least she was interested in what he said and did, and in what interested him. She could enter into the minute details of a matter which did not concern her in the least with such apparent interest and desire to know all that was to be known about it that one could hardly help the feeling that certainly the subject was worthy of attention.

Then her face spoke for her; it could cloud in an instant in sympathy with any sort of trouble or anxiety and sparkle with happy smiles in the very next second over some bit of brightness that was mentioned.

"She is a blessed little hypocrite, and that is the whole of it," was Marion's mental comment. "That sort of hypocrisy is worth studying. It is as natural to Flossy as that lovely pink on her cheek; but I am afraid I should have to acquire it; I don't feel interested in other people's affairs; now that is a fact. Why should she? In the first place, I know it is natural for her to like to please people; that is the beginning of it; she has that advantage over me, for she was always so, and I always *wasn't* so. But she has something else; she did not care once to please such as these rough boys of hers, at least they were rough when she started the refining process; how she had worked for them; I never realized it so much as tonight. It is just this: She has sanctified her power of pleasing and put it to a grand use in fishing for souls. Meantime, I have some degree of power of that kind, though it doesn't show in the same way. But I am not sure I have thought of it with a view to using it for such work; also, I daresay one can cultivate an interest in other people if they try. I mean to try. I know one way in which I can please people, I can sing."

Whereupon she immediately sought Ruth and proposed music, herself going after Rich Johnson to come and sing tenor and bidding him bring a friend to sing bass. Then such music as they had that evening was certainly never heard at a party at Mr. Shipley's house before.

The music room was a little bower of a spot at the left of the parlors. It was not only the music room but the flower room; at least there were vines and plants and blooming flowers in the windows, festooning the curtains, hanging from lovely wire baskets, a profusion everywhere. Thither went Ruth, Marion, and the two young men who went in silence from very astonishment over this new invitation. In silence and embarrassment, believing in their hearts that they could not sing at all. As for Marion, she knew better. She had stood near them in Sunday school.

Ruth swept the piano clear of all sheet music and substituted the Bliss and Sankey Gospel hymns, and Marion passed a book to each, naming a page, and instantly her full, grand voice joined Ruth's music. Very faint were the tenor and bass accompaniments; but as the first verse closed and they entered upon the second, the melody had gotten possession of their hearts, and they let out their voices without knowing it, so that when the piece was ended, Marion turned with a bright face and said:

"I haven't enjoyed a song so much in years. When a splendid tenor you sing, Mr. Johnson." To herself she said: "There! I'm improving; I honestly think that. But twenty-four hours ago, I should have kept it to myself. It isn't hypocrisy, after all: it is sincerity."

Another, and another piece was tried, the music room meantime filling; for Flossy had brought in her train others of the boys. And at last, as the last verse of "Hold the Fort" rang out, Marion turned from the piano to discover that utmost silence prevailed in the rooms where chatter had been before, and every available place in and about the music room was filled with hushed listeners, while those who could not get in sat or stood outside in silence and rapt attention. Such music as that at a party they had never heard before.

"You and I are a success, I think," Marion said brightly, as she linked her hand in Ruth's arm when they left the piano.

"We are doing our duty beautifully."

"Are you complimenting yourself because you are afraid no one will perform that office?" Ruth asked, laughing.

"No, I'm doing it because I have begun to be sincere. I've made a discovery tonight. Ruth, it is you and I who are hypocritical, in refusing to say what we think about people, when it would sound really nice and would doubtless make them feel pleasanter and happier."

Meantime, Ruth had her lesson also that she had been learning. What a trial parties had always been to her! How haughtily she had stood aloof, enduring with annoyed heart and oftentimes with curling lip, sillinesses that she could not avoid, listening to conversations and joining in monosyllables when obliged to do so, that drove her to the very verge of patience, not once imagining that there was any help for her, any hope of stemming the current or in any way changing the accepted course of things.

She was learning. Several times during the evening it had been her fortune to stand near Evan Roberts and join in the conversation which he was carrying on. Each time she was amazed and thrilled to see with what consummate skill and tact he turned the current of thought toward the vital question of personal religion. Always with an easy familiarity of expression that made one feel and realize that to him it was a matter of course, and as natural to be talked about, as the sunshine or the moonlight.

Wondering over this peculiarity of his, once as they talked together she referred to it.

"I can conceive of parties being less of a trial to you than to many of us, because of the ability you have of turning the conversation to some account."

He smiled brightly. "They are not," he said. "I have often looked forward to an evening gathering with eager interest and thankfulness, because of the opportunity for meeting some there whom I could not catch elsewhere and saying a word for my Master. But, Miss Erskine, you speak of 'ability,' I simply use my tongue on that subject as on any other worthy of thought."

"But don't you think it requires a peculiar sort of tact to be able to bring in such subjects in a manner calculated to do any good?"

He shook his head, "I should say rather, it required a sincere heart and an earnest desire to interest a soul. We depend too much on tact and too little on God's Spirit. 'Open thy mouth wide, and I will fill it,' is a promise that applies to more places than a prayer meeting, I think. What we need most to overcome is the idea that there is anything wicked in talking about religion in an everyday tone, as we talk about other topics of absorbing interest."

"There are different ways of going to parties," Ruth said to herself in a musing tone as she turned from him, and she wondered if she could ever get to feel that she might even go to a party occasionally, with the glory of God in view. This started a train of thought that made her turn suddenly back to Mr. Roberts with a question.

"That doctrine wouldn't lead you to be a constant frequenter of parties, would it?"

He shook his head.

"By no means. And there are parties, many of them, which, as a Christian man, I could not attend at all. We must guard against a temptation to do evil that good may come."

28

※

A Parting Glance

DR. DENNIS and his friend, the Rev. Mr. Harrison, met again at the street corner; they stopped and shook hands, as they always did, even if they chanced to meet three times in one day.

"Meetings closed?" questioned Mr. Harrison, after the preliminary words had been spoken. "What a glorious time you have had! Such a pity that our flocks are so far apart! If we could have united with you in regular attendance, it would have been a great blessing; as it was, many a drop came to us."

"Yes," Dr. Dennis said, "we have had a great blessing; and I need not use the past tense, the work is going on yet, although the meetings do not continue. The work will continue forever, I believe; the truth is, we have had a new baptism, the members who came to us early in the fall came filled with the Spirit and have worked as no other members of mine ever did."

"You mean your Chautauqua reinforcement, don't you?"

"Indeed I do; I thank God for Chautauqua every day of my life. What a dreadful blunder I made when I limited the power of God in the way I did when we talked that matter over! Do you remember?"

"I remember," Mr. Harrison said with a peculiar laugh; "It was a wonderful meeting, but then, after all, were they not rather peculiar young ladies? It isn't every lady who, even after she is converted, lives just the sort of life that they are living."

"I know," Dr. Dennis said; "Yes, they are unusual, I think; especially one of them," was his mental addition.

"Especially one of them," murmured Mr. Harrison in his heart; and each gentleman smiled consciously, neither having the slightest idea what the other meant by the smile.

Marion Wilbur came down the street with her hands full of schoolbooks.

"Good evening," said Dr. Dennis; "How do you do this evening? Mr. Harrison, do you know this lady? She is one of my flock."

No, Mr. Harrison did not know her; and introductions followed. After she passed by, Mr. Harrison said, "I think you told me once that she had been an infidel?"

"It was a mistake," Dr. Dennis said hastily. "She had peculiar views, and I think she imagined herself at one time an unbeliever; but she is really wonderfully well grounded in the doctrines of the church; she is like an old Christian."

Many of Dr. Dennis's people were abroad; the next passerby was Eurie Mitchell; the doctor stopped her. "One minute, Miss Eurie, how is your mother tonight? Mr. Harrison, do you know Miss Mitchell, the doctor's daughter?"

Yes, Mr. Harrison had met Miss Mitchell before. In the last coming dusk, Dr. Dennis failed to see the flush of embarrassment on his friend's cheek as he acknowledged the introduction.

"She is a grand gift," Dr. Dennis said, looking after her. "Her development is wonderful; more marked of late, I think, than before. Well, as you say, they were unusual girls, but I tell you, we as pastors have reason to say, 'God bless Chautauqua.'"

"Amen," said Mr. Harrison, and Dr. Dennis thought him unusually earnest and intense, especially when he added:

"I propose we go next year and take with us as many of our respective flocks as we can beguile into it."

"Aye, that we will," Dr. Dennis answered; then the two gentlemen went on their respective ways.

It was a large city, and they were both busy ministers and lived far apart and met but seldom, except in their ministerial meetings; there was chance for each to have interests that the other knew nothing about.

Marion reached home just in time for supper; the table appointments at that home were not improving; indeed, there were those who said that the bread grew more sour every week; this week, it had added to its sourness, stickiness that was horrible to one's fingers and throat. The dried fruit that had been half stewed was sweetened with brown sugar, and the looking-over process, so necessary to dried fruit, had been wholly neglected.

But Marion ate her supper, almost entirely unconscious of these little defects; that is, she accepted them as a matter of course and looked serene over it. Things were not as they had been on that rainy evening, when it had seemed to her that she could never, no *never* eat another supper in that house; then, it seemed probable that in that house, or one like unto it, she would have to eat all the suppers that this dreary life had in store for her; but now, the days were growing fewer in which this house would be called her home.

No one knew it; at least, no one but herself and two others. She looked around on her fellow boarders with a pitying smile; that little sewing girl at her left, how *many* such suppers would she have to eat!

"She shall have a nice one every now and then, see if she doesn't," was Marion's mental conclusion, with a nod of her glad head; there were so many nice things to be done! Life was so bright.

Hadn't Gracie Dennis whispered to her this very afternoon:

"Miss Wilbur, one of these days I shall hate to come to school; I shall want to stay at home."

And she answered softly, surreptitiously kissing the glowing cheek meanwhile:

"The teacher who reigns here shall be your special friend. And you are to bring her home with you to lovely little teas that shall be waiting for you."

This matter of "teas" had gotten a strong hold on Marion. Perhaps, because in no other way had a sense of unhomelike loneliness pressed upon her, as at that time when families generally gathered together in pretty homes.

She went up, presently, to her dingy room. Just every whit as dingy now, as it had been on that rainy evening, but she gave no thought at all to it. She lighted her fire and sat down to her writing; not reports tonight. She must write a letter to Aunt Hannah; a brief letter it was, but containing a great deal. This was it:

DEAR AUNT HANNAH:

Don't you think, I am going to be married! Now, you never expected that of me, did you? Neither did I, but that is the way the matter stands. Now, the question is: May I come home to the wedding? The old farmhouse is all the home I have, you know. I hope you will let us come; I am giving you plenty of notice; we shall not want to come until after the spring term; one of us wants to be there by the seventeenth of June. I thought I ought to tell you before the spring housecleaning. Let me hear from you as soon as you can, so that I may know how to plan.

I could be married in the church, I presume, but I feel, and the other one concerned feels so too—that I would like to go back to the old farmhouse. We won't make much trouble, nor have any fuss, you know.

Dear Aunt Hannah, I am so glad the money gave you comfort. Then I am so *very* glad that you thought about that other matter of which I wrote; that is the greatest and best thing to have in the world. I think so now, when I am on the eve of other blessings; that one stands before them all. The gentleman whom I am to marry is a minister. He is very good.

Aunt Hannah, I shall want your advice about all sorts of sewing when I come home. I shall come in May, that is, if you let me come at all. I hope you will. Give my love to Uncle Reuben. My friend sends his respects to you both.

Lovingly,
MARION J. WILBUR

She had a fondness during those days for writing out that name in full.

A gentle tap at the door, being answered, admitted Flossy Shipley.

"You darling!" said Marion brightly, as she gave her eager greeting. "How nice of you to come and see me when you have so much to think of. Flossy, where is Mr. Roberts? Why don't you bring him to call on me?"

"He hasn't time to call on anybody," Flossy said with a mixture of pride and a sort of comic pettishness.

"He has so many poor families on his hands; he and I have been out all day. Marion you have no idea at all of the places where we have been! I do think there ought to be an organized system of charity in our church; something different from the haphazard way of doing things that we have. Mr. Roberts says that in New York, their church is perfectly organized to look after certain localities, and that no such thing as utter destitution can prevail in their section. Don't you think Dr. Dennis would be interested in such an effort?"

"He will be interested in anything that is good," Marion said with unusual energy, even for her.

Flossy turned her pretty head toward her and eyed her curiously.

"You like him better than you did; don't you, Marion?"

"Didn't I always like him?" Marion asked with averted face and a laugh in her voice.

"Oh, you used to think him stiff and said you felt all shut up in his presence. Don't you remember our first call at his study?"

"I think I do," Marion answered, bursting into a

merry laugh. "Ever so many things have happened since then, little Flossy!"

"Haven't there!" said innocent Flossy.

"It has been such a wonderful year! Dating from that day when it rained and you *made* me go, do you remember, Marion? Do you ever get to wondering what would have been if we had just stayed on here at home, going to our parties and getting up festivals and all that and paying no attention to the Chautauqua meetings?"

"I don't want to think about any such horrid retrospect as that!" Marion said with a shrug of her handsome shoulders and a genuine shiver.

Flossy laughed.

"But, you know, it is only something to think of, to make us more grateful. It can never be, *never*. By the way, I suppose it is early to begin to make plans for the summer, at least for those who have no occasion to talk about summer yet"—this last with a conscious laugh— "but don't you mean to go to Chautauqua next summer? Mr. Roberts and I are going; we would rather give up a journey to Europe than that. Can't we all contrive to meet there together?"

"Yes," said Marion, "we—*I* mean to go."

"Dr. Dennis is going," Flossy said, though why that had anything to do with the matter, or why it occurred to her just then, Flossy did not know. "He told Mr. Roberts that he meant to be there, and to take with him as many of his people as he could. And Eurie told me last night that his friend, Mr. Harrison of the Fourth Church was going. I don't know how Eurie heard that, through Nellis, I suppose.

"Isn't Nellis splendid nowadays? I shouldn't wonder if quite a large company went from here. I wonder if Dr. Dennis will take his daughter, Grace. I think she is just lovely, don't you?"

"Very," said Marion; and just here Flossy roused to the fact that she was doing most of the talking, and that Marion's answers were often in monosyllables.

"I daresay I am tiring you," she said, rising. "I forgot that you have to talk all day in that schoolroom, Marion. Are you sure you love to teach well enough to keep at it, year after year?"

"No," said Marion, laughing. "I know I don't; I don't mean to do it; I mean to get a situation as somebody's housekeeper."

"Do you understand housekeeping?" asked innocent little Flossy with wide open eyes. "Oh, Marion! are you sure it will be even as pleasant as school teaching?"

"I think so," Marion answered with grave face. "At least, I mean to try. It depends on whose house you get into, you know."

Flossy's sober face cleared in an instant.

"So it does," she said. "Marion, I have a nice place, but I shall not tell you a bit about it tonight. Good-bye."

"Oh, the dear blessed little goosie!" Marion said, laughing immoderately as the door closed after Flossy. "Now, I know as well as if she told me that she is going to beguile Mr. Roberts into offering me a situation in their dovecote, when they set it up. Blessed little darling!" And here, the laugh changed into a bright tear. "I know just what a sweet and happy home she would make for me. If I had only that to look forward to, if it had just opened as my escape from this boardinghouse, how very thankful I should be! How glad the dear child will be to know that my home is as nearly in view as her own."

As for Flossy, she went down the walk, saying:

"What a dismal room that is! It is too bad for our bright Marion to have to live in it, I know my plan will work. How nice of her to have put it in my head! My head must be for the purpose of carrying out nice things that somebody else proposes. Oh, dear! there are so many desolate homes here on earth!"

A cloud over the bright face for a minute, then it cleared as she said softly: "In my Father's house are many mansions; I go to prepare a place for you."

After all, that was the place for brightness. This was only a way station; never mind the discomforts, so that many were helped to the right road that the home he reached at last in peace.

She paused at the corner and looked toward Eurie's home, but shook her head resolutely, she must not go there, it was too late; though she longed to tell Eurie that Marion was going to Chautauqua and ask her if she did not think it possible for them all to meet there.

Then the inconsistent little creature sighed again, for she remembered Eurie's weary face and the long struggle with sickness, and the long struggle with ways and means to which she was looking forward. There was much in the world that she would like to brighten.

Meantime, Eurie, in her home around the corner, was arranging the pillows with tender touch about her mother's head and drawing the folds of the crimson shawl carefully about her as she said:

"Now, Mother, you begin to look like yourself: It makes a wonderful difference to get a touch of color about you."

A very tender smile preceded her answer.

"Dear child! I will be glad to get well enough so

that you may have a chance to get a touch of color about you. You are looking very pale and tired."

"Oh, me, mine is the brightest life you can imagine; there is plenty of color down in my heart so long as I can think of our Nell leading the young people's meeting, and Father to lead at the mission tomorrow; it will rest me. I have to keep 'counting my marcies.' To crown them all, here you are sitting up at this time of night with a cap and wrapper on once more, instead of that unbecoming white gown; how pleased Father will be!"

"We have many mercies," the low, feeble voice of the invalid said; "not the least among them being our daughter, Eurie; but I could wish that I saw a way for you to have less care and more rest than you will get this summer. I must be willing to be very useless, your father says, and that means hard work for you. When Ruth Erskine was in this afternoon, looking so quiet and at rest, nothing to weary her or hinder her from doing what she chose, I just coveted some of the peace of her life for you."

"There's no occasion, Mother; I am not by any means willing to exchange my life with hers; I like my own much the best. As for rest, don't you worry; there'll be a way planned for what rest I need."

Yes, and there was being a way planned, even then; though mother and daughter knew nothing of it. How queerly people go on, planning their lives, as though they had the roads opening out into the future, all under their own care!

It was at that moment that Ruth Erskine, the young lady who, according to Mrs. Mitchell, had so quiet and settled and peaceful a life that she coveted it for her daughter, stood in the great hall that was glowing with light and beauty and caught her breath with an almost convulsive sound as she rested against a chair for support; her face deathly pale, her eyes bright with a calm that she had forced upon herself, in her solemn determination to try to do just the right thing, say just the right words; her ear had caught the sound of a carriage that had drawn up before the door and the sound of a familiar voice; she knew that she was now to meet—not only her father, but her mother and sister!

Little they knew about each other even yet, with all their intimacy, those four Chautauqua girls!

But what mattered it, so long as they had given themselves over, body and soul, into the keeping of their Father in heaven, who knew not only the beginning, but the end?

THE END

Don't miss these Grace Livingston Hill Library
romance novels by Isabella Alden